HIDE AND SEEK

MAJ (RET) JEFF STRUECKER
AND
ALTON GANSKY

PUBLISHING GROUP
ASHVILLE, TENNESSEE

Printed in the United States of America

978-1-4336-7142-5

Published B&H Publishing Group
Nashville, Tennessee

Jeff Struecker is represented by Wheelhouse Literary Group
1007 Loxley Drive, Nashville, TN 37211
www.WheelhouseLiteraryGroup.com

Dewey Classification: F
Subject Heading: ADVENTURE FICTION \ MYSTERY FICTION \ MILITARY INTELLIGENCE—FICTION

1 2 3 4 5 6 7 8 • 16 15 14 13 12

Dedication from Jeff:

For Abigail,
You are beautiful, you are good, and you are brave to me.

Dedication from Alton:

To my daughter Chaundel and her husband Travis,
and to my daughter Crystal and her husband Brad,
all for bravery in the face of great difficulties. Like the men in this book, they showed grace and strength when "under fire."

ACKNOWLEDGMENTS

From Jeff:

Thanks to Christ my King and Dawn my queen for being the two great loves of my life. Thanks to Don, Ricky, Mark, and Norman for helping me make the transition. Thanks to Donna June and Jonathan for keeping me on track. And thanks to Calvary Baptist Church in Columbus, Georgia. I am honored to be one of this family of faith.

From Alton:

An author gets his or her name on the cover, not so for the hard working, skilled professionals who work behind the scenes. There would be no books without editors and publishers. My thanks to all the great people at B&H who make a difficult task possible.

MILITARY ACRONYMS/ ABBREVIATIONS

AIT—Advanced Individual Training
ICM—Improved Conventional Munitions
ECH—Enhanced Combat Helmet
ANA—Afghan National Army
SAW—Squad Automatic Weapon
CBU—Combat Battle Uniform
SERE—Survival, Evasion, Resistance, and Escape training
PTSD—Post Traumatic Stress Disorder
USACIC—United States Army Criminal Investigation Command
NVG—Night Vision Goggles
RPV—Remotely Piloted Vehicle
CQC—Close Quarters Combat
UO—Urban Operation
DA—Direct Action team
ECT—Explosive Cutting Tape
Exfil—Exfiltration (the opposite of infiltration)
DARPA—Defense Advanced Research Projects Agency

THE TEAM

Master Sergeant J. J. "Boss" Bartley, team leader.
Master Sergeant Aliki "Joker" Urale, assistant team leader.
Sergeant First Class Mike "Weps" Nagano, sniper and explosives.
Staff Sergeant Pete "Junior" Rasor, communications.
Sergeant First Class Jose "Doc" Medina, team medic.
Sergeant First Class Crispin "Hawkeye" Collins, surveillance.

PROLOGUE

MASTER SERGEANT J. J. Bartley was nervous. More than nervous; he was scared. Wet palms, short breathing, heart-pounding-like-an-airplane piston scared.

It was an unexpected feeling.

"Are you sure you're ready?" The captain was tall, trim, with a strong jaw and close-cut brown hair. His tan ran deep. When J. J. first met him he wondered if the bronzing percolated to the man's internal organs.

Of course I'm ready. I'm always ready. This is nothing. Can o' corn. Piece o' cake.

"Master Sergeant?"

I was born ready. I've endured a danger close bombing to be spared from a brutal killing by terrorists in Afghanistan. Bullets have raced by my head. I've disarmed an explosive device while it was still attached to the suicide bomber. I took a bullet in the leg and nearly bled out. I live for the smell of spent gunpowder. My hands have always been steady. I am Army trained. Of course I'm ready.

This was different. What were mortar shells exploding a few meters away compared to this? What was parachuting to foreign soil in the dead of night, leaping from a perfectly good airplane at high altitude compared to this? What was this compared to being captured and tortured in a South American country?

This was nothing. Nada. Zilch. Less than zero.

His stomach flipped.

"I'm only going to ask once more, soldier."

"I'm good to go, sir." He meant to sound more certain, more cocksure.

"Finally." J. J. avoided the gaze of the man who spoke.

J. J. closed his eyes. He didn't want to look at the others in the room. He had been staring at the monitor but the image made no sense to him.

"Outside plumbing." The Army doctor smiled.

"What?"

"It's a boy."

"YES!"

"Easy, Cowboy." Tess Rand Bartley reclined on the exam table while the doctor continued to run the ultrasound sensor over her round belly. "Would you have been disappointed if our firstborn were a girl?"

"No. Of course not. I'd be just as happy." He paused for a moment then shot his fist in the air. "Dude! A boy!"

Tess's smile widened. "Did you just call me, 'Dude'?"

"Uh oh." The doctor continued to stare at the image.

"Something wrong?" J. J.'s heart kicked up a gear.

"Inside plumbing."

"I thought you said it was boy—I mean, HE was a boy."

"I did. It appears I was right. I was hearing two heartbeats."

"Twins?" Tess turned to the monitor.

"Yep. Two for the price of one."

Tess turned her face to J. J. "What do you think of that, Stud?"

"I think I'd better sit down."

PROLOGUE 2

ALIKI URALE SHOOK HIS head. Then paused. He shook it again, his lightweight Enhanced Combat Helmet rocking on his head. He took satisfaction in being aware of that simple fact. The AK-47 round that had just bounced off his headgear left him shaken and his thinking a tad slow.

"Joker! Joker! You okay?"

Something was wrong with the voice. It poured into his mind through an earpiece connected to his radio. The voice was familiar. He knew it well. He should, Mike Nagano had been his friend since high school.

"Joker. Talk to me."

Mike didn't sound right. He was distant, muted, fuzzy. That couldn't be right. The voice came over his ear monitor. The sound couldn't be distant. He rolled to his side and tried to pull his thoughts together. The sound of automatic weapon fire hung in the air but not with the same sharp report as usual. Had the Taliban started using suppressors on their weapons? No. That wasn't it. It was the ringing in his ears that dulled the noise.

He blinked a few times. At first he saw mud, then a portion of the hillside, then several men in uniform a short distance away. Different uniforms. American military. What was the other? That took another moment to figure out. There was more green in the camo. More green in the Combat Battle Uniform. Army. Afghan Army. Afghan National Army.

Memories washed back into Aliki's brain. His team was providing support for the Afghan National Army and the 101st Airborne near Kunar not far from the Pakistani border. This was a training mission and a show of strength for resurging Taliban in the region.

He closed his eyes for a long moment, then snapped them open.

"Joker. Talk to me, man."

Aliki shook his head one more time then keyed his mike. "I'm here, Weps. I'm good."

"You sure? It looked like you took a shot to the head."

Aliki touched the right side of his helmet and found a depression. "Gotta love these new helmets, dude—"

Several rounds zipped by his head. He pressed himself to the ground. A quick glance brought the rest of his memories to the surface. They approached a village a few klicks from the border. They were told the area was safe; that the Taliban left a few weeks before. The assessment was wrong. The three-sided assault caught them by surprise. A group of armed terrorists fired on them as they approached the village. Shortly after, a barrage of bullets came from a hill a short distance to the east. Another from the northwest. The area around him was littered by soldiers from two armies.

A movement to his right caught his eye. Several men in robe-like garments raced forward, AK-47s raised. In a fluid move no man Aliki's size should be able to make, he turned his MK-17 rifle their way and let loose a hail of 7.62 millimeter rounds. Three of the men dropped without a sound. The fourth man screamed, fell, and continued to scream.

The sound of his weapon lacked the zip, the pop he expected. His ears felt full of wet cotton.

An explosion a dozen yards away brought with it another memory: an explosion a dozen meters from his position. RPG? Mortar? At the moment, it didn't matter. It knocked Aliki on his can and left his head fuzzy and his ears ringing. The bodies of soldiers surrounded the disrupted ground. Two were missing limbs; one was missing his face.

"Where are you, Weps?"

Nagano answered by firing a blistering stream of bullets from his M-249SAW. The Squad Automatic Weapon was capable of puncturing the air—and anything else—at a rate of 750 rounds per minute. Twelve bullets a second demanded respect. The muzzle flare revealed his position: an outcropping of rocks a dozen meters to Aliki's left.

"I'm coming to you." Aliki didn't wait for a response. He was on his feet a second later and sprinting down the hillside.

A hand from the ground reached for him as he sprinted by. It made Aliki think of a zombie movie and he leaped to the side with a yelp. Then he did what no soldier in his situation should:

he stopped. The hand belonged to Bryan Genet, his team leader, a short man who was tall on courage and leadership.

"Boss!"

Genet tried to speak but the blood bubbling from his throat made it impossible.

More memories flowed into his skull. He got a glimpse of his leader racing to his position after that explosion. Men were injured and Genet was just the kind of guy to run toward the problem. That was Boss, always running to the sound of gunfire when the rest of humanity was looking to run the other way. A bullet found the team leader's throat.

"Go." The word was indistinct but Aliki had no trouble understanding the order.

"Negative, Boss." He set his weapon down. Two rounds hit the moist earth next to him. "Sorry, Boss, but this is gonna hurt." Aliki slipped his fingers between Genet's chest and his body armor and clamped his big fist shut. He pushed himself up, lifting Genet to his feet, then threw him over his shoulder. Genet grunted and writhed in pain. Aliki squatted and seized his MK-17.

Gunfire. Hot. Long blasts. Muted but still recognizable. A scream of anger pounded Aliki's eardrum. The voice belonged to Nagano, who stood to provide cover fire, the SAW spewing copper-jacketed heat. Nagano swept the area in front of him and to the sides. Aliki took advantage of what was certainly his only opportunity to live a few more minutes.

He ran, moving forward, zigzagging as he went, Genet bouncing on his shoulder. The rock outcropping looked close a short time ago, now it looked a mile away. Distant popping followed the sight of bullets striking the ground in front of him. Had Nagano not been firing blindly at the hidden Taliban fighters, one of their bullets would certainly have found their mark.

Someone punched him in the ribs. Air rushed from his lungs. He was shot.

He kept running, the impact having only taken half a step off his pace. The pain dumped another quart of adrenaline into his system. He took several more strides before he realized his body armor kept the bullet from busting ribs and drilling a hole through his body. He had a new respect for Kevlar.

Aliki didn't count his steps but it felt like he was taking two kilometers to cover a handful of meters.

Something whistled by his head.

What is it with these guys and my head?

Aliki reached the outcropping as Nagano kept squeezing the trigger of the automatic weapon. He dropped to a knee and lowered Genet to the ground, doing his best to nestle the man into the rocks. A three-front attack left few places to hide.

"Are you crazy, Joker? You're a big enough target without stopping in the open."

"I couldn't leave him. We don't leave people behind. You know that."

"Yeah, I know. I'm just a little agitated at the moment." Nagano looked at his team leader. "Doesn't look good."

"Where's Doc?"

Nagano shook his head. "Dead. We're it, man. You and me. Most of the ANA guys are down. A few ran away. The one-oh-one squad went down during the first assault. This was planned, Joker. They knew we were coming and set up for us."

"Tell me Sparky got a message off."

"Yeah. Got a confirmation of inbound helos. Got confirmations of Apaches. Don't know how many."

"Where's Sparks' radio?"

"A dozen meters that way." Nagano jerked a thumb indicating east. "We can't get to it. We'll hear from the pilots when they get in range of our radios."

They carried AN/PRC-148s, the workhorse of handheld radios. "Beacon on?"

"Yep. I'd hate for them to make a mistake and think we're the bad guys." Nagano poked his head up. "They're still in position. No one advancing. I may have scared them."

"You scared me." Aliki moved behind Genet and positioned his team leader's body so the blood would drain from his mouth. The blood was frothy. "Hang in there, Boss. The cavalry is coming. Just hang in there."

Aliki looked into Nagano's eyes and saw pessimism. Nagano turned back to Genet. "You stay with us, Boss. You don't get to die. I'm not done making your life miserable."

The sound of distant gunfire punctuated his words. Maybe not distant. With his hearing he couldn't tell. As it was, he was having trouble catching what Nagano said. "I mean it, Boss. You are forbidden to die. You have two teenage daughters, and someone is going to have to terrorize their boyfriends."

"He's right, Boss. You quit now and I'll go out of my way to marry one of them. Maybe both of them."

Genet didn't respond. A moment later, the light in his eyes went out.

Aliki leaned his back against the rocks and looked skyward. Through the haze of gun smoke, floating miles overhead, he saw serene clouds moving through the Afghan sky, unbothered by the death below.

"Inbound," Nagano said.

In the distance, not far above the ground, were six black dots. Aliki rolled to his stomach then inched his way to the top of the rock outcropping, his MK-17 in hand.

A few minutes later, four AH-64D gunships came into full view, their General Electric T700-701D driving four-blade rotor systems. Moments later M230 Chain Guns belched to life, sending dirt and mud flying and Taliban insurgents running. On three occasions, the aircraft let loose Hydra 70 air-to-ground rockets. Aliki and Nagano fired at entrenched and fleeing insurgents until their ammo was spent.

Ammo didn't matter. Their assailants were no match for the Apaches, and what few remained faced fresh troops brought in on UH-60 Black Hawks.

Out of ammo and with the operation now handled by gunships and reinforcements, Aliki hunkered in the outcropping, his eyes aimed again at the clouds overhead, and wondered what to tell Genet's family.

CHAPTER 1

43.050278°N 74.469444°E
Transit Center at Manas (formerly Manas Air Base), outside Bishkek, Kyrgyzstan
June 6

THE MESS HALL WAS deserted. Master Sergeant J. J. Bartley sat alone at a long, well-worn table that had seen thousands of airmen, soldiers, and Marines pause from their work long enough to pound down some grub before returning to their duties. On the table rested a chipped plastic coffee cup and two file folders. The expansive room seemed twice the size J. J. remembered the last time he passed through the air base. Of course the room was full of hungry servicemen then, many headed to Afghanistan. That was Manas's primary role over the last decade: the jumping-off spot for troops headed to hostile country.

As an Army Ranger he did two tours of duty in Afghanistan before being hand-selected by Sergeant Major Eric Moyer to be part of a unique spec ops team. He made several other missions into the country as part of that squad, including one he was sure would be his last moment on earth. As it turned out, a pair of F-18s came to the rescue of the six-man unit as they fought off overwhelming numbers of Taliban fighters advancing on their position. The jet jockeys saved their lives by dropping a pair of ICM bombs on their location. The Improved Conventional Munition bombs exploded fifteen feet above their heads, leaving the ground littered with dead Taliban and a ringing in J. J.'s ears that took a week to go away.

That seemed a lifetime ago. Since then, as the sniper and explosives expert for his team, he traveled to a dozen different places on the planet, none of which he was allowed to name, and carried out missions he was forbidden to speak about.

"Stare all you want, Boss, but that coffee ain't going to do any tricks."

J. J. didn't have to look up to know that Sergeant First Class Jose "Doc" Medina was approaching. He raised his gaze anyway and returned the medic's smile. Jose was a solid man with a keen mind, quick humor, and an admirable steadiness. If the sky were to rip in half and a million alien ships from another dimension appeared ready to take over the world, J. J. was sure Jose would look up and say, "Well, look at that. A man doesn't see that every-day." J. J. liked the man for another reason. In addition to his being a superior soldier, he also saved J. J.'s life after a gun battle. He owed the man several pizzas for that.

"Hey, Doc, where you been?"

"They have a great rec hall here. I was shooting pool with the Air Force guys." He pulled out a chair and sat.

"All in the name of inter-service fun, no doubt." J. J. lifted his cup. The coffee was cold.

"Of course. You know I believe we should respect all branches of the military, even the inferior, less skilled ones."

"How much?"

"Huh?"

"You heard me."

Jose shrugged. "Maybe a couple of twenties."

"Total?"

"Each." Jose pretended to look guilty.

"How many airmen did you fleece?"

"Oh, who keeps track of such things? I was just killing time."

J. J. narrowed his eyes.

"Okay, just four. My conscience was beginning to bother me."

"Lucky for them." He put the cup down. "Seen Pete and Crispin?"

"Not since Crispin gave his little demonstration. He did a good job. I was impressed, and I've seen his tech kung-fu in the field. All those itty-bitty surveillance drones were a hit. Left the local tech boys drooling."

"Yeah, I was there, but I haven't seen them since."

"Do you need them? I'll go round 'em up."

"Nah. Just as long as they're front and center when the new guys arrive."

"Ah, that's it."

J. J. cocked his head. "What's it?"

"You look down, Boss, like you've lost your favorite girlfriend."

"'My favorite girlfriend.' You know I'm married. Tess won't let me have girlfriends."

Jose slumped in his chair. "Wives are funny that way. My wife won't let me date either." He paused to let the quip die before establishing a more somber tone. "I miss them too."

"I didn't say anything about missing anyone."

"I was listening to your face."

"Sometimes you confuse me, Doc."

Jose chuckled. "You know what they say about Hispanics: we're inscrutable."

"I thought that referred to Asians in old movies."

"Eh, Asians, Hispanics, whatever." Another pause. "You're thinking about Boss and Shaq."

"They're home safe and sound. I'm not worried about them." Images of the team's former leader and second-in-command strobed in his mind. Last he saw them, they looked well and happy. He could hardly tell both were severely wounded and the latter lost an eye. Both retired shortly after the mission in eastern Siberia and took jobs with a civilian security firm.

"I didn't say you were worried about them. I think you're worried because they're not here. You went from team member to boss in short order. There's gotta be some psychological whiplash in that."

"Psychological whiplash? They teach you that at Fort Sam Houston?"

"Nope. Medic training taught me many things but not much psychology. Life, on the other hand, has taught me a ton."

"Okay, Doc. What's eating me?"

Jose sat up and leaned forward on the table. "Nothing bad, Boss. You're just being human."

"I don't think I'll ever get used to being called Boss. Every time someone calls me that, I think of Moyer."

"You'll get the hang of it." Jose paused. "Can we talk like a couple of old buddies?"

"That's what we are, Jose."

"Well, at least in here. Anyone else walks in this room and I'll go back to being formal."

The corner of J. J.'s mouth inched up. "You have a formal side?"

"I'm nothing if not a model of Army decorum." He inched closer to the table as if he were about to whisper a secret. His volume remained the same. "Okay, here's how I see it. We are creatures of training. We enlist and start at the lowest rank. Time in service and experience lead to promotions. We have a good idea how that's going to progress. You've just been pushed up the ladder faster than expected. The view is different up there."

"True."

"So now you've been selected to take over for a man we admire and respect. He's one in a million. He's got it all: brains, courage, loyalty, and a soldier's sixth sense. He left under tough circumstances. Nearly lost his daughter to kidnappers trying to sway him in his mission. Took a beating. Nearly died. To hear him tell it, he did die and came back. His cover was blown so his usefulness as field operative was gone and that's all he ever wanted to do."

"He is a great man. Taught me more about soldiering than basic, AIT, and Ranger training combined." A wave of sadness ran over J. J. "I can't be Eric Moyer, Doc. In my mind, he will always be Boss."

"But he's not, J. J. He *was* team leader. Now you're the man. No one is asking you to be Eric Moyer. The Army—the team—wants you to be you."

"Is that enough?"

Jose straightened and stared into J. J.'s eyes. "It is in my book."

"It's not that I'm afraid—"

"You'd better be afraid. I don't trust a man who says he's not afraid. Such men are either liars or lunatics."

J. J. raised an eyebrow. "Really? And which am I?"

"You're neither. I've seen you afraid and you've never been braver. You can do this, J. J. I got your six. You know that. Pete danced a jig when he heard of your promotion. At least I think it was a jig. The man has no rhythm."

J. J. laughed. "You got that right. First time I saw him bust a move I thought he was being electrocuted."

Jose chuckled, then the grin evaporated. "Seriously, J. J., I'm proud to follow you into battle. Don't doubt yourself and don't doubt us. Besides, if you screw up, Moyer will kick your butt then turn on me for not straightening you out."

"There's a terrifying thought." J. J. gazed into the black fluid in his cup. More than self-doubt was eating at him but he had endured all the pep talk he could. Jose seemed to sense it.

"You happy with the new guys?" The medic motioned to the personnel jackets.

"Yeah, as much as I can be. It's hard to judge a man's character from notes on evaluation forms. Both are experienced and decorated. Seen lots of action, mostly in the last half of Iraq and in the wind down of Afghanistan. Both Rangers. One comes in at the same rank as me: Master Sergeant. He's got six months on me as well."

"Doesn't matter, J. J.; you're team leader. He'll know that."

"He'll also know that I was frocked. I have the extra stripe but not the official promotion and pay."

"It's just a matter of time, J. J. You know once there's some head room, you'll get the full promotion and maybe more. It's all a numbers game. There are scores of soldiers working at a higher rank than the Army is allowed to give them. Functionally, you're the man, and I'll fight with any man who disagrees."

"You're a pal, but you may want to hold on to the boast for awhile."

"Why?"

"You'll see."

The door to the mess hall opened and a skinny airman stepped into the dim space, saw them, then walked to the table. "Master Sergeant Bartley, I've been asked to tell you the transport plane you've been waiting for has touched down. It's pulling to the tarmac now."

J. J. glanced at the rank insignia on the man's upper sleeve: one stripe and an Air Force star in a circle. "Thank you, Airman. I would like to meet the plane. Can you get me there?"

"I was told to have a vehicle waiting."

J. J. stood, lifted the cold coffee to his lips, and drank. He grimaced. "Where did the Air Force learn to make coffee?"

The young airman remained straight-faced: "From the Navy."

"Figures." He set the cup down. "Gather the team, Doc."

CHAPTER 2

THE BLONDER PUB SAT back from a tree-lined Ibrainmova Avenue and a short walk from a parking lot in need of maintenance. The place was a local Bishkek hangout but new owners were making an effort to attract a higher class of patrons, as high as one could get in an unsettled, impoverished nation.

Amelia Lennon, dressed in a plain woman's business suit, left her silver Russian-made Lada Priora sedan in the parking lot, the heels of her spectator pumps tapping against the hard surface. A cool wind from the east—a Chinese wind—blew over the area, sending the flowers and bushes in the newly landscaped planters into a gentle waltz.

The parking lot was nearly deserted, just a handful of cars, most old and battered by a life spent on degrading roads. Kyrgyzstan was a country on the ropes. It had, for a time, shown promise but without the old Soviet system to bolster its economy, the country grew weaker by the month. Throw in government corruption, rebellion, riots, and ethnic strife, and Kyrgyzstan was a powder keg one match away from conflagration.

The wind ruffled Amelia's shoulder-length, chestnut hair. She was unassuming in appearance: not catwalk beautiful, but not overly plain. She had enough East Europe qualities to pass as a local but not stand out on any U.S. street.

Amelia glanced back at the parking lot. One car stood out: a sporty red BYD sedan that looked very similar to one of the more expensive Mercedes-Benz. The Chinese automaker, like many Chinese automakers, was accused of stealing designs from American and European countries. General Motors sued Chery, another Chinese manufacturer back in the early 2000s. Fiat, Toyota, and others made the same complaint. For China, piracy was not limited to movies and music. *At least they steal from the best.*

It wasn't the copycat car that bothered Amelia, it was who owned the vehicle. The car was a gift to Jildiz Oskonbaeva, the woman she came to meet. China gave the car to Jildiz and ones like it to other Kyrgyzstan leaders. They made no secret of that. What they did keep under their hat were the gifts they gave to those seeking to upset the sitting government. Those gifts were not well known, but they were known to Amelia. It was part of her job as an Army Foreign Affairs Officer, and she had a pretty good information pipeline.

The pub/restaurant was repainted recently, replacing the dark, nearly black theme with something almost as obnoxious: lavender paint with blue trim. Someone somewhere convinced the owners this was a cool way to go. Firing squads were created for such people.

The wide, arched wood doors remained the same. So far. The windows were also arched. As Amelia entered the eatery she had a passing sense she was being swallowed by a disco.

She walked through the lobby, closing the door behind her. The smell of cooking meat assaulted her nose. The aroma was strong with seasoning. The room was empty. She had been to the pub several times over the last year and it was always full of noisy patrons and cigarette smoke. The silence was stunning even though she expected it. This meeting was to be private, just two women from different cultures seeking a common good.

Jildiz Oskonbaeva sat in the middle of the room, surrounded by empty tables, a glass of red beer in front of her. At five foot five, she was two inches shorter than Amelia. She wore her black hair short and parted on the right. The first time Amelia met Jildiz she was impressed with the intelligent look in her eyes, an intelligence revealed in the conversation that followed. At times the daughter of the Kyrgyzstan president could be aggressive, pushy, and even obnoxious. Amelia liked that even though much of it was bluster learned in Western law school. Behind the confidence and assertiveness, Amelia sensed Jildiz was frail. She didn't know how. The woman always appeared healthy. Maybe it was the pressures of her job. As chief negotiator for her father's government, she had been called upon to deal with very difficult situations. Manas Air Base was one of them. *No, not Manas Air Base, it is still the Transit Center at the Manas International Airport.* Call it what you will, it was still home to the Ninth Air Force garrison and the jumping-off point for flights into Afghanistan.

At least for now.

Jildiz stood as Amelia approached and smoothed her black jacket. She wore a white blouse, black slacks, and black loafers. "It is good to see you, Jildiz. You look wonderful." She kissed the lawyer on the cheek.

"But not as good as you, Amelia. I would kill for long hair like that." Jildiz returned the kiss.

"What, this old stuff? I've had it all my life."

They exchanged a chuckle and sat. Jildiz waved at a waiter who stood near the entrance to the kitchen. As the dark, middle-aged man approached, Jildiz asked, "Beer? You know they brew it right here."

"I do know that and I don't mind if I do."

Jildiz addressed the waiter. "One more beer, please, and you can bring the food when it is ready. Thank you." She faced Amelia again. "I took the liberty of ordering some food for us."

"Wonderful." Amelia forced her face to ignore her impulse to grimace. *Please, no horse meat.*

"Besh barmak."

Oh yuck. "I haven't had that for some time." Amelia avoided making eye contact.

"Not to worry, my friend. No horse meat and no goat's head. I thought we would keep this casual. I know you Americans can be sensitive to such things so I asked the dish be prepared with beef."

"You are a gracious hostess. I didn't know I was being so transparent."

Jildiz leaned closer as if there were others in the room listening. "Your face went pale." She leaned back. "But I understand."

"Is it all right if I use a fork? I know the dish means 'five-fingers' but I tend to be a little messy when I eat with my hands." In this country food was a reminder of the people's nomadic heritage. While the country was well grounded in the twenty-first century it still clung to its past. Normally a good thing, such historical memory is what fueled the tension between Kyrgyz and Uzbeks.

"Eat in whatever manner makes you most comfortable."

"Thank you." The conversation lagged as Amelia wondered when to broach the subject.

As soon as the waiter brought Amelia a glass of beer and left, Jildiz took the lead. "There's been another offer."

"From the Chinese?"

"Yes. And the Russians have upped their offer too. There is a chance, since both want the same thing, they might combine their efforts."

Amelia sipped her beer as if they were talking about weather. "May I ask how much?"

"In dollars? The Chinese have offered the U.S. equivalent of $10 billion and the Russians, $2 billion. Their economy is still shaky."

"The Chinese seem to be doing okay."

Jildiz shrugged. "Everyone owes them money. They own over $1 trillion of your Treasury bonds and Japan owns nearly that much. Of course, your country owes money to many other countries."

"That is true but, if I may say, a little off the topic, Jildiz. We have provided aid to your country several times and continue to pay a fair rate of rent for our presence in the transit center at Manas."

"Yes, but it is a fair trade. You need a departure point for troops moving in and out of Afghanistan. Even though there has been a reduction of troops in that country, America still needs a Central Asia airport. We have Russia to our north with just Kazakhstan in between and we share a border with China on the east. How do I put this delicately, Amelia? Both countries are uncomfortable with your air base and are willing to pay to have you evicted."

"Sometimes those who appear to have our best interest at heart have secret motives." Amelia turned her glass on the table. "I don't need to tell you that your country separated yourself from Russia in 1991."

"You are correct. You do not need to tell me that. The Russian government has done many things to help us in our difficult times. I am not so naive as to overlook their agenda, but then again, my friend, your country has an agenda too. You need a base in our region because you fear China, because you fear a Russian relapse, because you fear growing tensions with Pakistan, because you fear a Taliban resurgence in Afghanistan. Shall I go on?"

"No need, Jildiz. My country has been open about such matters with you. Everything you have said is true. We do have such concerns. China has become aggressive economically, technologically, and even militarily." Keeping track of stresses between the U.S. Army and Central Asian countries was part of her job. As such she was privy to information she could not discuss with people shouldering less than one star on the uniform and the right security clearance. She knew of China's action to down a U.S. military satellite. It went bad for China and very nearly went bad for the United States.

She sipped her drink to buy a moment of thought. "I believe your country needs us here to keep a balance in the region. There are new stresses between the Russians and the Chinese. Having an American air base between them can be useful."

"Perhaps, but my country's biggest need is money." The words seemed to sadden her. "I dislike being so crass. We are not a greedy people. Kyrgyz and Uzbeks are a proud people used to making their own way through difficult times. Our history in the region dates 2,200 years, longer than Christianity. This is a difficult land. We have survived much but the world has changed. To remain a free republic we need outside help and we're getting that from Russia and China. Russia is a trade partner and accounts for 44 percent of our trade; China is 15 percent of our trade. That means 60 percent of our trade involves just two countries. You may not like them, but they have helped us."

The waiter brought the noodle and meat dish to the table but Amelia's appetite was gone—even if the meat was beef and not horse.

After the waiter left, Amelia resumed the conversation. "Jildiz, are you saying your father's government is wanting more than the $60 million we pay each year in rent for use of the airport at Manas?"

She looked sad. Amelia met with Jildiz several times after the topic of the air base closure first came up. Most of those were formal discussions, a couple were casual. Amelia had begun thinking of Jildiz as a friend, although she doubted they'd ever go shopping together.

It took a moment for Jildiz to answer. "I spoke with our president—my father—again this morning. He tells me the cabinet and the prime minister are pushing to accept the offer from the Chinese government. The $60 million your country pays is very much appreciated, but what is that compared to the billions the Chinese are offering?"

Amelia hated calling the annual payment "rent." The money was demanded and the United States came very close to being evicted from the facility. Only money and a change to the name of the facility made it possible to stay the next few years.

Jildiz dished out the noodles and meat concoction. Amelia watched. This was going the wrong way. Kyrgyzstan was in trouble, more this last year than ever before. For years they suffered under a corrupt government until a rebellion brought an end to the administration. Riots in April of 2010 demonstrated how bad things had become. An interim government was able to settle the situation but most observers considered the country a powder keg ready to explode into civil war. Meklis Oskonbaeva, a former soccer player turned attorney turned politician, became the first president after the interim government. He was popular from his exploits on the soccer field decades before and now in his manner of governing. Even so, winning 76 percent of the vote didn't guarantee peace in the government or in the land. He was a man leading his followers through a flood of gasoline with a lit match in his hand.

"Jildiz, surely you and your father know the air base is a sign of American and Kyrgyzstan cooperation and our determination to end terrorism in the world. By allowing us a base to move troops into and out of Afghanistan, countless lives have been saved. Your government—your people—are heroes. Sending us packing will say to the world you've given up on your commitment."

Jildiz froze for a second then raised one finger. "Careful, Ms. Lennon. I will not tolerate attempts to intimidate me or play with my emotions. Ending our agreement on Manas says no such thing. Your country is winding down the war more and more every day. Soon, you'll be gone. You will have no need for the base except to irritate the Russians and the Chinese."

Amelia felt her face warm. She made a tactical mistake. "I worded that poorly, Jildiz. The world owes your country a debt of gratitude."

"Gratitude won't fix our economy or raise our people out of poverty." She studied her food. Apparently she, too, had lost her appetite. "My father will be meeting with his key leaders and the prime minister. Prime Minister Sariev Dootkasy has made it clear he wants you off our airport. He believes the American presence is a destabilizing force. My father has not committed to that action, but . . ."

"But he's leaning that direction."

Jildiz shook her head. "He feels the pressure but he plans to argue your case."

"That's wonderful news."

"Don't be misled, Amelia. It's not all about the base. The distance between him and the prime minister has grown. Dootkasy is driving a wedge between my father and his government. Manas is a sharp wedge."

"I appreciate you being honest with me about this." She took a bite of the meal. Besh barmak was definitely better with beef than horse.

"I didn't want you to be surprised. My father will push for an extension of the agreement but he may fail." She sipped her beer. "And to be candid, I think he's making a mistake."

"I wish I could change your mind, Jildiz. I know the people at the U.S. Embassy have been working with our Department of Defense and with our president. While there is a chance we might get more money, it won't come near to what the Chinese have offered."

"The Chinese have also indicated an interest in buying our treasury notes. That money will go a long way in helping us build a more vital infrastructure, roads, and job creation. I know this is unwanted news, but you have had a base in our country since 2001. No one expected you would need it for so long." She picked up her glass of beer and stared at it but never brought it to her mouth. "We are at a breaking point. Civil war is just around the corner. Our unemployment is crippling. Our military wanes for lack of funding."

"But your father still thinks keeping us at the base is a good idea?"

"For the moment. If it means losing his power and influence, if it means giving up his position, I think he'll change his mind."

"But it hasn't come to that, Jildiz."

The lawyer put her glass down. "It's closer than you seem willing to believe." She sighed. "There is a bond between us, Amelia. Perhaps that is why your government has placed you in the lead for these negotiations. Bond or no bond, I must advise my father based on what is best for our country and for him. I am sorry, but you should prepare your people for a change."

Jildiz rose. "I'm afraid I've lost my appetite. I should go." She pulled a few bills from her purse and laid them on the table. Amelia let the woman walk from the room before she rose and exited the restaurant. She was facing an impossible situation but the optimist in her led her to believe the status quo would remain.

Amelia left the eatery emptier than when she arrived.

CHAPTER 3

J. J. STOOD AT the edge of the tarmac as the C-17 Globemaster taxied to the far end of the small Manas International Airport. The rear ramp lowered and soldiers, many weighed down by weariness, descended, their kit bags slung over shoulders. Some were completing their third or fourth tours of duty. Most had home to look forward to. Two didn't.

Placing his hands behind his back, J. J. rocked on his heels and waited. Most soldiers were eager to leave the transport behind. J. J. had flown on many types of aircraft, few were comfortable. Twice he flew on business jets and even once on *TP-01*, the Mexican equivalent of *Air Force One*. That spoiled him.

Soldiers streamed by and J. J. scanned every face, interested in their expressions. Some smiled. Others walked with heads down. In his world there were only two types of soldiers: wounded and those about to be wounded. Many of those injuries were invisible, shielded behind scalp and skull. Some saw things they would never forget; some did things they would never share.

J. J. saluted a pair of officers as they walked by. The men he looked for should be easy to find. One was five foot eleven, a Japanese-American; the other was a Samoan and a mountain of a man. He waited another few moments before two men appeared at the top of the ramp and started their descent to the tarmac. Watching them, J. J. could only think "Mutt and Jeff."

The two exchanged a laugh and the big man slapped the smaller on the back, forcing him to take an extra step. They moved like two men who knew and respected each other. They spied him and changed their course. J. J. held his ground, letting the men come to him. It went against his nature. He was outgoing, outspoken, a kidder, and quick to make friends. But that was before he became "Boss." Now he felt the weighty mantle of leadership. He might have to order the two men walking his way to take action certain to leave them dead. He had no problem hearing and obeying those orders, but giving them was something very different. He was also insecure that one of the men carried the same rank and more seniority. The Army "frocked" him, giving him a higher rank and authority, but somehow it didn't seem the same.

"You must be our welcoming party," the Samoan said.

J. J. grinned. "I'm afraid it's just a party of one for now." He held out his hand. "J. J. Bartley, team leader."

The Samoan cocked his head an inch as if he hadn't heard correctly, then took the offered hand. "Aliki Urale. A pleasure."

J. J. turned to the Japanese-American. "Mike Nagano. Thanks for inviting us to the lodge."

For a moment J. J. was stunned not to hear an Asian accent, then reminded himself again: the man was a third-generation American, born and reared in San Francisco. "You'll have to thank Colonel Mac for that. He did the selecting, but judging by your jackets, he made good choices. How was the flight?"

"Dreamy, but the stewardess was really ugly," Aliki said.

Nagano shook his head. "Dude, that was no stewardess, that was the flight mechanic." He spoke loudly and only after Aliki turned his way.

"That explains the five o'clock shadow."

"Okay, gentlemen, now you're just grossing me out. Let's get back into military country." He motioned to a Humvee waiting a short distance away.

The driver pulled from the tarmac and slowly moved along the road by the staging area where the Air Force parked a few billion dollars of aircraft. Kyrgyzstan and Russian commercial aircraft were kept in a separate area.

A few minutes later they were at Manas Air Base. Officially, the site bore the name of international airport but that was for PR reasons. Everyone on base used the older title. The old-timers sometimes called it Ganci Air Base, a name meant to honor New York Fire Chief Peter J. Ganci who died on September 11, 2001. Unfortunately, the U.S. Air Force had an "instruction" on the books forbiding the naming of any out-of-country air base after an American citizen.

"We'll be meeting in the admin building." J. J. gave them the room number. "You guys need to hit the latrine or grab a bite?"

Nagano answered. "I could use a few minutes."

"Very good. Let's meet in thirty."

"Will do," Nagano said. Aliki didn't respond.

The conference room was small, able to seat only ten people, fifteen if they really liked each other. A conference table that looked like it saw action in WWII dominated the middle of the room. Padded folding chairs circled the piece of furniture. J. J. found the team waiting for him when he stepped through the door. They were laughing when he entered.

"Hey, Boss," Pete Rasor said. "I see you got our newbies."

"They're not newbies, Pete. They have as much field time as we do. . . . Hey, what do you mean you *see* I got the newbies."

Pete looked at the table. "Um, nothing, Boss. Just, um, a figure of speech. Yeah, that's it, a figure of speech."

"You know you blush when you lie, don't you." J. J. stepped to the head of the table. "Come clean." Everyone looked at Crispin Collins, the junior member of the team and the surveillance man. "Don't tell me."

"I'm sorry, Boss, but some jet jockey bet me I couldn't follow a man without being noticed." A small control with a tiny video screen rested on the table.

"He recorded it too," Pete said.

"Hey, shut up. I'm in deep here."

Pete shrugged. "I told you not to do it."

Crispin's face drained. "No you didn't. You jumped on the bet."

Pete shrugged. "I think you misunderstood me."

"You said you'd back me up if I got caught."

"There's your problem. You tend to believe me when I say such things."

"Spill it," J. J. said. "That's an order."

"And I had such a promising career." Crispin reached for the controller and switched it on. "Get the window, Pete."

"Excuse me?"

"You're the one who gave me up, the least you can do is open the window."

Pete grumbled but did as asked as Crispin worked the controls. A few moments later a tiny helicopter zipped into the room and settled on the table. It was black, flat, and had four tiny fan-like propellers in the corners. Crispin used a nano-helicopter while on mission in eastern Siberia a few months before. That one he had dubbed *Voyager*. Being more technically inclined than creative, the surveillance man christened this device *Voyager II,* and it was one of his show-and-tell items during his demonstration.

J. J. rubbed his eyes. "Did you record?"

"Will I be in more trouble if I say yes?"

"Answer the question, Crispin, or you'll be riding on the wing when we fly home."

"Okay, Boss. Anything you say." He paused long enough to gulp. "Yes."

"Let's see it."

Crispin pointed to a flat-screen television mounted to the wall near the head of the table. "Give me a second and I can set it up so it shows on the big monitor. I mean, if that would be a good thing."

"Can you get ESPN?" Jose asked.

"That would take more work but I could try—"

"Back to the subject, Crispin." J. J. tried to sound firm but struggled to keep a grin from erupting on his face.

Several minutes passed as Crispin tried to get his controller to share its stored video. The team made the work more difficult with constant harassment. J. J. almost felt guilty for the man. Almost.

Just as he finished, Nagano and Aliki walked in. All eyes went to them then settled on Aliki. They were used to having a big man on the team. Former assistant team leader Rich "Shaq" Harbison made football linemen look puny. Aliki was no smaller and maybe a dozen pounds heavier.

"Have a seat, gentlemen. You're just in time for a little entertainment."

"Ooh, I love a good movie," Aliki said and took a chair at the end of the table. "What, no popcorn?"

Nagano settled in near the open window. J. J. saw him eye the four-inch square device on the table. "Remote control toy?"

"You'll see," J. J. said. He directed his attention to Crispin. "I'm growing old here."

"Yes, Boss. I mean, no Boss, you're not getting older. What I mean is . . ."

Pete roared with laughter. The two became friends on the last mission. Both were computer junkies. J. J. tried to follow one of their conversations once but could only hear, "Geek, geek, geek," and "Nerd, nerd, nerd."

"Let me make introductions while our former team member tries to redeem himself." J. J. made sure there was enough humor in his tone so Crispin wouldn't faint.

"Former?" said Crispin. "I am so misunderstood."

"Okay guys, listen up. Joining our team are Sergeant First Class Mike Nagano and Master Sergeant Aliki Urale. Both have extensive field experience and served on a number of spec ops missions in Afghanistan and Iraq and a few other places we won't talk about here. Mike goes by 'Weps' in the field; Aliki's nick is 'Joker.'"

Crispin perked up. "Jack Nicholson or Heath Ledger." He looked at Aliki.

"What?"

"I mean Nicholson was a great Joker but Heath Ledger was brilliant and he was so ugly in that movie . . . not that you're ugly. I'm not saying that. I just mean . . ."

"Hey Crispin," J. J. said, "at this point a smart man would shut up."

Mike answered for Aliki. "He didn't get the nick from the movie. He's called Joker because he likes bad jokes."

"Really?" Pete said. "Like what?"

"Don't ask," Mike began.

Aliki rose to the occasion: "A man walks into a bar. Thunk. Ouch." He leaned back in the chair.

The team stared at him for a few minutes. Jose was the first to speak. "Yep, that's a bad joke alright. Can we send him back, Boss?"

"We put up with Shaq's musicals, we can tolerate a few punny jokes."

"Don't bet on it," Mike said. "I've heard them all and haven't laughed yet."

"I think I'll just keep going," J. J. said. "You've met Crispin Collins. He's our surveillance guy. We call him 'Hawkeye,' when we're being nice."

"We call him other things too," Pete said.

"And the comment belongs to Pete "Junior" Rasor, communications. Last, and sometimes least, is Jose 'Doc' Medina. When he's not patching us up in the field, he's home with his wife trying to build his own basketball team."

"How many kids?" Mike asked.

"Four." Jose seemed proud.

"Colonel Mac selected Aliki and Mike to bring our team back up to full strength. Mike will be filling my old position as weapons and explosives; Aliki will be second in command. Clear?"

"Clear." The response came in unison.

"Got it," Crispin said. "Ready when you are, Boss."

"This should be good." J. J. moved to the back of the room. "Roll it."

"It's all digital. Nothing really rolls—"

"Crispin, don't make me shoot you."

"Okay, Boss."

The flat screen lit up and a moment later a blurry image of something gray appeared.

"That's the roof of this building." Crispin sounded oddly pleased.

A few seconds later the indistinct image seemed to fall away and clarify. Sure enough, it was a roof. The little device hovered a dozen feet above the structure and moved over the air base. Buildings passed beneath, cars, people walking.

"Tell me this isn't going by the enlisted women's barracks." J. J. put as much threat in his tone as the situation would allow.

"No, Boss. I'd never do that, even if Pete offered me money to do so."

"Funny," Pete said.

"Just what am I seeing?" Mike asked.

J. J. kept his eyes on the image. "Hawkeye is an expert in nano drones. We used a couple on our last mission. To hear him tell it, his skill saved the mission."

"No one can deny it," Crispin said.

J. J. ignored Crispin and continued. "Micro aircraft like the one on the table is being used in the field more and more. Part of our team's directive is to test new DARPA and private contractor toys in the field. I kinda hate to admit it, but it is pretty cool."

Something on the image looked familiar. From an estimated forty-foot altitude, J. J. watched himself and the driver from earlier enter a Humvee and drive away. *Voyager II* followed overhead.

"Tell the truth, Boss. You didn't even know I was there, did you?"

"I can't say I did. Didn't see or hear a thing."

Crispin smiled. "And this is broad daylight. You see, the body of the craft doesn't reflect light. No glint to catch someone's attention. The camera rocks. I can even zoom in or switch to wide angle. Pretty sweet."

"Except you were spying on me."

"Um . . . well yeah, technically, but in my defense I was making a demonstration video. I have one more seminar to lead for the incoming spec ops team. When Jose told us you were headed to pick up the new guys and that we were to meet in the conference room, well, it was too much to resist. It will be a great teaching tool."

The device followed the vehicle as it moved along access roads and past fabric-covered Quonset-hut-style structures and long tent-buildings, each colored desert-dirt brown. They passed through a parking area. People moved from place to place, some in uniform, some in civilian clothing.

Voyager II kept pace with the car and began to climb slowly. "The key is not to make quick movements. People notice sudden changes but not slow ones." Crispin slipped into lecture mode. "The device is less that six inches square. At an altitude of fifty or sixty feet, it becomes almost invisible. If you're looking for it, you can see it, but you'd have to know it was there, and with the new, quieter motor it is almost impossible to hear." He pointed at the screen when the Humvee reached the tarmac and J. J. exited. "I took it up to about one hundred feet here. So there would be no way for you to hear it."

"And if he did?" Mike asked.

"He would have trouble locating it. You ever heard a private plane go overhead on a clear day? They're noisy and you can recognize the sound right off the bat, but they're still difficult to locate. It can be done of course, but you have to make an effort. This baby is really tough to find."

The video continued and the team watched a steady stream of soldiers depart the C-17. When Nagano and Aliki arrived, the video showed J. J. shaking their hands. The camera zoomed in, tightening the shot.

"Hey, I look good from this angle," Aliki said. "That cinches it. I'm impressive no matter what angle you use to look at me."

"We'll have to work on your weak self-esteem," J. J. said.

"Pretty impressive, isn't it?" Crispin said like a father who just watched his son hit a home run in a Little League game.

"Yep," J. J. said, "but I do have a question. Do you suppose it's wise for one of my team members to fly a military drone—no matter how small—over the sovereign soil of a foreign country? Without permission?"

Crispin looked stunned. "I-I . . ."

"You know the Air Force doesn't own the airfield, they lease it."

Crispin ran a hand through his hair and tried to speak, but the words never came.

"Boss," Pete said. "I egged him on and I'm senior to him. I'm responsible."

"Probably." J. J. moved back to the front of the room. "Kill the video, Crispin. I assume you have a delete button somewhere."

"Yes, Boss. You want me to erase—of course you do, otherwise you wouldn't be asking. I'll take care of it right now."

"See that you do." J. J. straightened. "That was pretty impressive." Crispin smiled and his shoulders lowered in relief. "Okay, men, listen up. I'm going to spend the rest of the day bringing our new team members up to speed on the team. Crispin has another presentation to make in the morning, then we are going to run some drills with three new spec ops teams Colonel Mac is sending over. That will last three days, then we're headed back stateside. So enjoy your evening—" The door to the conference room opened. "Group ten-shun!"

Colonel Danny Weidman, base commander, entered the room accompanied by an Air Force captain. Chairs slid as the team came to attention.

"As you were," Colonel Weidman snapped. He looked at J. J. "Master Sergeant, I need you and your team in the main conference room."

"Sir?"

"Colonel Mac wants to talk to you."

"Yes, sir."

"You got five minutes." He walked from the room so quickly that J. J. expected to sense a vacuum.

"That can't be good," Jose said.

"He looked pretty tense," Pete added.

J. J. looked at his watch. "It's 1600 here, that means it's 0200 in South Carolina. At least he'll have had a few hours of beauty sleep."

"Think that'll help?" Crispin asked.

"No." J. J. took a deep breath and looked at Nagano and Aliki. "Welcome to Manas."

CHAPTER 4

AMELIA DID NOT INTEND to follow Jildiz and was somewhat surprised to find herself only a few blocks behind her as she drove through the heart of the city. No doubt Jildiz was headed to the seven-story structure called the White House on Chuy Avenue. It was the seat of government and at times the focus of rioters. In April of 2010, the building was looted and government papers were strewn across the lawn, plaza, and street. Things had settled since then but, like a pressure cooker with a sealed vent, it was only a matter of time before things blew up again. The intelligence agencies had been issuing warnings for months.

She kept a respectful distance from Jildiz, not wanting to appear like a diplomatic equivalent of a stalker. Still, she had to travel the same road through the city before reaching Mira Avenue and heading south to the U.S. Embassy a few miles away. She wasn't looking forward to that meeting.

A black column of smoke caught Amelia's attention. Then she saw another. Her first thought was a small structure fire, but the rising smoke appeared to be separated by several blocks. She grew unsettled.

Ahead, Jildiz made a turn to the north. That was to be expected if she were headed to Chuy Avenue from the side street they were on. Her disquiet grew and her muscles tensed. Something was wrong. What, she didn't know. She was trained to trust her instincts and she saw no reason to stop now.

A white panel van pulled from the curb and made a sharp turn onto the street. No country was exempt from stupid drivers.

Amelia slowed as she passed through the intersection and looked up the street Jildiz just entered. She saw a mob at one end. She also saw the van slam into the back of Jildiz's car. Her speed carried Amelia through the intersection but not before she saw several men exit the van. At least one was armed.

Amelia pulled to the side then cranked the steering wheel hard the other direction, the wheels of the sedan screaming at being asked to move so quickly over decaying asphalt.

She snapped the wheel straight and slammed the accelerator to the floor. By the time she made the turn she saw Jildiz in the clutches of two men, both armed, and a third man with a handgun. Amelia wished for time to think, but having none, she hit the gas again and aimed the front of the vehicle at the group. Two of the men, both big and rough looking, held Jildiz between them. One was grinning like he had just won the lottery. The smile disappeared when the roar of the engine became impossible to ignore. He and his pals did what Amelia hoped: they tried to save themselves and, in doing so, released the president's daughter, each leaping to the side. One man was too slow and scrambled to the wrong side.

Amelia felt a sickening thud.

Jildiz stood stunned and shaken as Amelia hit the brakes and banked hard to one side, missing Jildiz by inches. "In! Get in!"

Jildiz blinked, then awareness flashed into her eyes as she scampered for the passenger door.

"Back seat. Now!"

Jildiz complied. The moment she was in, Amelia dropped the car into reverse. "Down. Lay down. Cover your head." She glanced in the driver's side mirror. The man with the handgun pushed to his feet and began to raise the weapon.

The man Amelia hit was screaming, but she didn't look at him. Thinking was a luxury of time. Instinct was all that mattered. She pushed her door open and floored the accelerator. The door caught the man as he squeezed off a shot that missed Amelia by an inch and shattered the windshield. Cracks spread from end to end and top to bottom, the safety glass held in place by the embedded plastic laminate sheet.

She snapped her head around and sighted the man taking fresh aim.

The car picked up speed.

The door caught him just as he pulled the trigger. Amelia's mind tried to make sense of the sounds: the gun's explosive report, the impact of the metal car door on human flesh, the dropped watermelon sound of the assailant's head hitting the street, and the noise of her front tire rolling over the human speed bump.

"Down. Stay down."

The car picked up speed as it backed away from the panel truck and Jildiz's car. *Two down. That leaves one. Or are there more?* Amelia was in no mood to hang around and find out. To hesitate might be to die.

She entered the intersection and spun the wheel, jerking the car around so it faced the street she traveled a short time before.

Sounds of rapid gunfire and bullets hitting the car's metal hide and windows blended into a terrifying, ear-pounding fusillade of fear. Something stung the side of her arm and hand. Again she rammed the accelerator down. The car tires spun then the car lurched. Steam poured from the radiator. She glanced up the street and saw the one man still standing, running their direction. He held a submachine gun and it was spilling a stream of bullets.

Something warm dripped into her left eye.

The engine stammered but kept turning. Ear-piercing noise poured from beneath the hood and the steering wheel pulled hard to the left. Another sound. A small explosion and a rattling. At least one tire was flat. Amelia hoped it was just one tire. Another pop and the vehicle leaned to the left.

"He's shot our tires and engine. I won't be able to get far."

As if uttering the words aloud brought the prophecy to pass, the engine sputtered, rattled, and died.

And there was more to worry about. When Amelia first looked down the street where the abduction had occurred, she saw distant fires and a mob of people. She hadn't had time to gauge the size of the group but her sense was that it was large. The city had seen thousands turn out in riots and protests.

The driver's side door was still open, frozen in position by the force of striking the big man with the handgun. Amelia popped her seat belt and rolled out of the car, her eyes directed down the street. She was having trouble seeing. Something sticky made the vision in her left eye blurry.

"Out. Let's go!" She pulled open the rear door. Jildiz lay on the floor boards, jammed between the rear seat and the front. "Come on, Jildiz."

"It's not safe."

"It's not safe in the car."

Jildiz hesitated. Amelia did not. She reached in the back seat area and grabbed Jildiz by the collar of her coat and pulled with as much strength as she could muster. The small woman came out easily.

"Stay on this side of me. Let's go." Amelia kept Jildiz on her left, positioning her own body between her charge and the killer. They were two strides closer to the sidewalk when she heard the sound of bullets hitting the car then the road behind them. A glance to her left showed the machine gun man hobbling their way. He had been injured, maybe when he dove out of the way of her speeding car. That was the good news; the bad was twofold: he still had an automatic weapon and was talking on a handheld radio. *Great. He's calling for reinforcements.*

"In here." She pushed open a glass door that led into one of the small businesses lining the side street. A second later she realized they were in a small, neighborhood-style restaurant. "Keep going."

Patrons looked up from their meals. Several were families and Amelia immediately felt concerned for the children. "Run. Hide!" She didn't know if she spoke English, Russian, or Kyrgyz and had no time to repeat the message. She pushed Jildiz forward, again interposing her body between the dignitary and the pursuer. "To the kitchen."

A terrible thought occurred to Amelia: the very people she was worried about could be the ones to point the direction of their flight. "Go, go, go."

They pushed through a pair of double doors and stumbled into the kitchen. Jildiz tripped over a rubber mat near a pair of large metal sinks. "Get up." Amelia barked the order as she helped Jildiz to her feet. She heard a loud voice from the dining side of the restaurant. He was closing the distance. Exiting the car took too long. "Forward. To the back door. Run. Run."

Amelia's heart felt like the fist of a wild man trying to break out of her chest. Her mind raced only able to think of a few things at a time.

Then she saw it. The back door. And next to it, another door, larger and metal. "Do as I say. No questions."

"Yes. Okay." Jildiz's words were soft and tumbled out between gasps.

Just as they reached the rear exit, Amelia slowed, pulled back on Jildiz's coat as if she were a race horse. She pulled Jildiz, then changed her mind. The large metal door was familiar to her. She had started her working career slaving away in a fast-food joint. She knew a walk-in freezer when she saw one. She pulled the door open until it touched the back wall, found a knife on a prep table just behind a head of cabbage, seized it, and moved to the lone cook who stood behind an old stove and grill. The man blinked in puzzlement until Amelia, hunkered down behind the grill, put the business end of the knife to the inside of the man's thigh. "Speak and I cut an artery." She said it both in Russian and English. A young worker standing to the side saw what was happening and stiffened, stupefied. His expression showed his confusion. Amelia raised a finger to her lips. To the young man's credit, he nodded, saving his boss an unneeded surgery.

The gunman exploded into the kitchen. Crouched behind the cook and the stove, Amelia couldn't see the attacker but assumed he still had his weapon. Jildez was on her hands and knees a foot or two away from Amelia.

"Where?" The man demanded.

Amelia pushed the point of the knife a fraction of an inch deeper into the man's leg. The cook said nothing, Amelia was able to see the man's feet as he moved to the freezer.

Wait for it. Wait.

When she saw his boot-clad feet reach the freezer's threshold, Amelia charged.

She lowered a shoulder and plowed into the gunman with all the strength she could muster. She heard a furious scream then realized it was her own.

The man staggered a step then tripped over the wood-pallet flooring of the freezer. He landed facedown but rolled to his back immediately, gun in hand. A kitchen knife versus an automatic weapon was a battle Amelia didn't want. She stepped to the side as a burst of gunfire tore up the wall behind her. Seizing the freezer door, she slammed it shut. On the wall, hanging from a hook, was a Yale lock with a long shackle like a bicycle lock. She retrieved it and closed the lock.

She turned to face the cook. He was gone. So was the young worker.

Amelia opened the rear door. "Let's move."

CHAPTER 5

COLONEL WEIDMAN WAS A lanky man with a nearly bald head that reflected the light from the overhead fluorescents. J. J. met him when he and what remained of his team first arrived at Manas. The base commander was polite, even jovial. Now he looked as if his breakfast was rusty nails with sour milk. The red-haired captain standing next to him looked to be countless-hours-in-the-gym thick. J. J. wondered if he was compensating for his height.

The room was twice the size of the one they just left and much better furnished. J. J.'s first impression was that of a home theater. A large, flat-panel screen was mounted to the far wall and three rows of eight theater seats faced it. To the side of the monitor was a simple wood podium with the emblem of the Ninth Air Force garrison mounted to the upright, its white-winged yellow circle with a red nine staring back at them.

"Have a seat, gentlemen." The team spread out, settling into the padded chairs. An Air Force sergeant sat at a control center. Weidman looked at him. "Dismissed."

The man rose without a word and left. The captain took the man's seat and placed his fingers on a computer keyboard. "Ready, sir."

J. J. wondered if the colonel would introduce the other officer.

"Let's get started, men."

Apparently not.

A knot formed in J. J.'s stomach. Being yanked from one meeting to attend an unscheduled one couldn't be good. "I take it this isn't a surprise birthday party, Colonel." J. J. kept his voice even and respectful.

"No, Master Sergeant, it is not." Weidman clasped his hands behind his back. "What you're about to see was broadcast thirty minutes ago. One of our intel groups recorded it and forwarded it to my desk. It's short and to the point. After that Colonel Mac will join us by video link." He paused one second. "Captain."

"Yes, sir."

The screen glowed, flickered for a moment, then began to play. The knot in J. J.'s belly doubled in size. A woman with skin two shades too pale and dark hair hanging to her jaw appeared. She looked into a camera in typical foreign correspondent fashion made popular by CNN and FOX News. She stood in the middle of a wide street. Two- and three-story buildings bracketed her. Perhaps it was a camera setting gone wrong, but the sun seemed a tad too dim. The woman looked nervous, glanced over her shoulder several times, and shifted her eyes to look beyond the camera at events only she could see.

She touched her ear and cocked her head one inch to the right. She straightened and held a microphone close to her lips. "Kyrgyzstan has been a country on the edge for years." Nervousness gave her voice an unwanted vibrato. She had an Eastern European accident. "In 2010, it saw riots and protests leaving many dead and thousands injured. Later that year a near civil war erupted, displacing hundreds of thousands of citizens who were forced to flee for their lives. At the roots of tension is a cocktail of distrust, accusation of government corruption, an uncontrollable rate of inflation, unemployed near twenty percent, and the growing global financial crisis that began in 2008 and which, despite efforts of many governments, continues to grow worse with no hope in sight. The situation has become grave."

The camera captured a growing mob some distance behind her. Black smoke rose in a dozen narrow columns. J. J. assumed they were burning vehicles and tires. A small sedan pulled through an intersection as if nothing were going on.

"The United Nations recently called this country a tinderbox and it appears they were right. A short time ago, crowds began filling the streets of downtown Bishkek, chanting in Kyrgyz: 'Out with America. Death to America.' The United States has had a presence in this country since the earliest days of the Afghan conflict. At the heart of the problem is the Manas Transit Center, formerly known as Manas Air Base. The facility, a short distance north of the capital city of Bishkek where I now stand, has been a source of hatred."

The sound of distant gunfire invaded her microphone, and the woman ducked. Then, realizing the shots were not nearby, continued. J. J. couldn't decide if she was brave or just crazy. He saw embedded journalists at the frontline of battle and knew of several who were wounded or killed.

"While it appears there are many reasons for the unrest, hatred of America seems to be the flame to the fuel. Eight percent of the population is Muslim, and several religious leaders have called for followers to protest the presence of infidels in their country. That, however, may not be the primary problem. Tensions between the Uzbeks, which make up only 14 percent of the population, and the majority Kyrgyzstani have grown rapidly over the last year. Whatever the cause—"

A red sedan came to the intersection behind the reporter and made a right turn, headed straight for the approaching mob. Brake lights came on, then the back-up lights blazed. The driver realized he or she was headed into the open maw of trouble. The sporty car began to back up and the mob sprinted forward.

A white panel van rounded the corner from the opposite direction and rammed the back of the sedan. Three armed men poured from the inside of the van and approached the car. J. J. recognized an AK-108 and what looked like a Serbian-made Zastava M92 submachine gun. The third man carried some kind of handgun but was too distant and indistinct for J. J. to identify. They pulled a short-haired woman from the red car.

"Crowds have gathered in several parts of the city. Some demonstrate peacefully, but there have been reports of violence and looting."

"Keep your eyes fixed on the action behind the reporter," Weidman said.

A silver sedan shot through the intersection and out of view, only to reappear a moment later, smoke billowing from spinning tires. The sound of the engine and screeching tires made its way to the microphone and the reporter. She turned.

The silver sedan charged forward at the three men and the woman held at gunpoint.

The car plunged toward the men and the woman. They scattered, but one assailant was too slow. He flew up and back, his AK-108 flying several feet beyond where his body landed. The woman scampered to the side then, after only a moment's hesitation, bolted for the silver sedan. A moment later she was in the back seat, then disappeared. She must have ducked to the floorboards, J. J. decided.

The driver pulled forward, which at first made no sense, but then J. J. realized why. The man with the submachine gun had stepped forward and raised his weapon. He squeezed the trigger for a moment before leaping to the side to avoid being run over.

"He's got nowhere to go," Pete said.

"She," Weidman said.

"She? You're kidding, right?" Crispin said, then quickly added, "Sir."

He didn't answer. The colonel kept his eye fixed on the video.

The sedan's brake lights came on and, as with the first car, so did its back-up lights.

The thug with the handgun was on his feet and aiming at the car as it raced backward. The driver's side door swung open and the car accelerated at stunning speed. The open door caught the gunman as he squeezed off a shot, knocking him to the ground and dragging him along the asphalt until they reached the intersection. The driver yanked the car around. The front wheels drove over the assailant. The man with the submachine gun was up and firing at the car.

The car door dangled as the sedan pulled away with a lurch, veering first right then left.

"She was wounded," J. J. guessed.

"We think so," the colonel said.

The gunman let go another burst as the car pulled away. The reporter glanced at the camera and said, "Run!"

Red fluid and gray spongy material splattered the camera lens. Hardened to violence as J. J. was, he turned his head.

"I did not need to see that." Pete sounded stunned.

The video ended and Weidman stepped to the center of the room. "What you saw happened less than half an hour ago. Here's what you don't know. The woman in the red car, the one they tried to abduct, is Jildiz Oskonbaeva, the daughter of the Kyrgyzstani government."

"So she's safe, right?" Pete asked. "I mean, we saw her rescued, and, man, what a rescue. I mean—"

"Let the colonel talk, Pete." J. J. said.

"Yes, Boss."

"I'm sorry to say, no. I sent up a helicopter to sweep the area. The car made it only a few blocks. The tires were shot out, as were the rear and front windows."

"Sir? You sent up a helo?"

"Yes, but we were called off by Sariev Dootkasy, the country's prime minister. He speaks for the government. He said flyovers by U.S. aircraft would make the protests worse."

"Protests? Looks more like a riot." Mike Nagano sounded angry.

"That's what it is, Sergeant," Weidman said. "We know that but politicians the world over use a different language than we mere humans." He paused. "The helo crew was able to confirm the make, model, and license number. The car belongs to Captain Amelia Lennon. She's our Foreign Affairs Officer. Lives in-country, travels under civilian passport. She was working with the embassy and the local government on renegotiating our base's right to remain in-country. Sadly, we believe both are dead but we can't verify it."

The knot in J. J.'s stomach became a brick.

Weidman turned to his aide. "Captain, bring Colonel MacGregor in."

The video monitor activated again, this time with a familiar image: a middle-aged man with Army-short hair, a tanned face, and chiseled features. He had intelligent eyes that J. J. was sure could see through steel. As the spec ops commander in the recently built Concrete Palace at Fort Jackson, he oversaw most Army spec ops efforts. He was a legend who refused praise and preferred action over talk.

A small red light appeared below the monitor: a video camera J. J. hadn't noticed when he first entered the room. No doubt Colonel Mac could see them.

"They're all yours, Colonel," Weidman said.

"Thanks, Danny." Mac leaned over the table in the situation room and deep into the camera lens as if trying to push his will through the device and halfway around the world. "I see your new team members have arrived, J. J."

"Yes, sir. All present and accounted for."

"You've been brought up to speed?"

"We've seen the news video, sir, and have been told a few things about Captain Lennon."

He nodded. "I'm going to do what I'd rather not. I'm sending you on mission. You leave as soon as you kit up." He raised his head, settling his vision on something behind J. J. "Sergeants Urale and Nagano, I assume you brought your kit and weapons case."

"Yes, sir." The men answered in unison.

"Okay, it's time for the straight skinny. Master Sergeant Bartley is under orders to test your continued fitness for spec ops duty. You can't lose a whole team and not be changed. You've been cleared by medical in Afghanistan. That's all just peachy, but I need to know if you're fit for boots on the ground work. J. J. won't have time to test you. I'm about to ask a lot of you. Before I do, I need to know from you two if you're good to go. Are you?"

Aliki stood. "Good to go, Colonel."

Nagano joined him. "Same here, Colonel. Speak it and we'll do it."

"Good to hear, gentlemen. As you were." Mac's eyes shifted. "J. J., I need to hear from you. Can you lead a team with two members you haven't tested yet?"

"Affirmative, Colonel." J. J. wondered if he just lied.

Mac straightened. "We have several problems, gentlemen. The locals have told us to remain on base and to not interfere with what's going on. Riots have been breaking out in several cities including Talas, Osh, Jalal-Ahad, Tokmak. Intel has sent an alert to Colonel Weidman and the State Department that there may be an assault made on Manas by radicals. That means all soldiers on the base are required to protect our assets. That leaves you as our only Direct Action team. You still with me?"

"Yes, sir. With you all the way."

"Good. Your mission is simple to say but may be a bigger challenge than it sounds at first. Your job is to go in covertly, find the body of Captain Lennon, retrieve it, and bring it back to the base. Understood?"

"Understood, sir. What about the president's daughter."

Mac seemed to soften. "You are not to recover her body. That will be the job of the local military." He paused. "It's a diplomatic decision, gentlemen, one that sticks in my craw big time."

"Are we certain that Captain Lennon is dead?" Jose asked.

"High probability, Doc. If not, then your job will be a thousand times more difficult."

"Why is that, Colonel?" J. J. didn't like the tone.

"Captain Lennon is SERE Level C trained."

Survival, Evasion, Resistance, and Escape training. Only the Army had high-risk training, something J. J. knew well. He still had nightmares about the twenty-one days of training.

"Understood, Colonel."

"You will make entrance into the city, find the car she was in, if possible retrieve the body, then make a safe exit back to the base. Be good, be fast, be safe. Understood?"

A chorus of "Hooah!" filled the space.

Mac seemed proud.

And worried.

CHAPTER 6

"WH-WHAT JUST HAPPENED?" JILDIZ insisted they stop and rest for a moment. Amelia argued against it but she could tell the woman was exhausted by fear and the unexpected exertion. She held a hand to her chest, fist clenched.

"I'm not sure. The only thing I know was that those men were trying to snatch you. Have you ever seen them before?"

They were hiding next to a dumpster. A cat strolled by seemingly perturbed by unwanted humans in his domain.

"No. They hurt me." She rubbed her arms then brought her fist back to her chest. She looked into Amelia's face. "You're hurt. You're bleeding."

Amelia wiped at her eye. She used her right hand. Odd, since she was left-handed. That's when she noticed the deep gash on her hand. It continued to ooze blood. A wound recognized hurts worse than one not noticed. The open gash began to burn as did the one over her left eyebrow. "Just a graze, I think." It felt worse than that.

"I'm so sorry. I didn't know . . ."

"There's nothing to be sorry about, Jildiz. You're not the first powerful person to be a kidnapper's target."

"I'm not that important."

"You're the daughter of the president. You should have security around you all the time. I can't believe your father lets you travel alone."

"That's my idea. I don't like having security around me."

"This might change your mind. Do you have your cell phone?"

"No. I had it on the seat in the car."

Amelia pulled hers from a pocket and tried to place a call to the embassy. Nothing. There was no signal. "Cell system is down. That means things are worse than they seem."

"Is that possible?"

"Yes. Very possible." Amelia glanced up and down the alley in which they had taken refuge. She estimated they had run a mile ducking in and out of alleys. Overhead, smoke began to darken the sky. The smell of burning buildings and the pungent smell of tire smoke assaulted her nose.

"Do you think they've let him out of the freezer yet?" She cringed when she spoke.

"Not if they're smart. They should wait for the police." The wail of sirens clawed through the thickening air.

Jildiz straightened. "The police might be slow in coming. They have other things to deal with."

"Riots?"

The lawyer nodded. "Yes. In 2010 it took all the police and firefighters and a good number of soldiers to restore peace." She took a deep breath.

"Are you okay?" A sudden panic washed over Amelia. She had been so intent on escape and her own injuries she hadn't checked Jildiz for wounds.

"I'm okay. Asthma. Exertion sometimes brings on an attack." She conjured up a smile. "It's why I gave up being a downhill skier and became a lawyer. An asthma attack in court is always good for a postponement."

"I guess so. Do you use an inhaler?"

"Yes, it is in my purse, which—"

"Which is still in your car. I should have guessed."

Jildiz shifted uncomfortably. "Sorry. No one sent the memo about the kidnapping. I could have been better prepared."

"I didn't know. I'm sorry." Amelia studied Jildiz, fearful she would stop breathing.

Another grin. "I am smart. I am persistent. I am also vain. Sucking on a rescue inhaler makes me feel less attractive."

"Nonsense. It's all the rage these days." Amelia patted her on the shoulder. "Jildiz . . ."

"I know. We can't stay here. We have to keep moving."

"Can you do that?"

"Do I have a choice?"

Amelia pursed her lips. "No. If Machine Gun Mike was calling for backup then more of his kind may be crawling out from under the rocks." She stood. "We're miles from the nearest hospital. Maybe we can find a landline and get you out of here."

"And you, too."

"Sounds good to me."

They stood. "Okay, our priority is to find a safe place with a phone." In her haste to lead Jildiz to safety, Amelia struck a course without much thought. Instinct told her to put as much distance between her and the spot where the attempted abduction took place, a decision that landed them in a rundown part of town, the first victims of the recent depression. Most of the buildings in this section of town were empty.

Certain that no danger was close, she turned to Jildiz and looked deep into her eyes. "You need to listen to me. I'm going to get us out of this and get you back to safety, but to do that you need to do everything I say. You need to do it without question or debate. Clear?"

"Yes."

"I also need you to be honest with me. No false bravery. If your asthma gets worse I need to know. Complete honesty. Got it?"

"Got it. The smoke's not helping."

"I was afraid of that."

"Amelia, complete honesty goes both directions. You're not just a diplomat with the U.S. Embassy, are you?"

Amelia hesitated. Technically her role was not secret, but she preferred to be thought of as a civilian. "Not strictly speaking."

"What are you? I mean, the way you handled the situation and the thing you did with the knife . . . Are you CIA?"

"No, Jildiz, I'm not. Not the CIA or any other group like that. I'm not a spy."

"Then what?"

More hesitancy. "It doesn't matter, Jildiz."

"Military?"

Amelia didn't want to waste time arguing. Since she was breaking no laws or orders, she yielded. "I used to be in the Army. Actually, I'm still in the Army but I work as a civilian. I specialize in foreign affairs. Technically, I'm an Army captain, but these days my battlefield is a conference table. I just get to keep my retirement this way."

"Retirement? Really, retirement?"

"Let's keep moving."

"I've never seen a diplomat kill two men with a car and knock a thug to the ground."

"We don't know the two men are dead."

Jildiz hiked an eyebrow. She seemed to be breathing easier. "We don't?"

"Not officially. Let's go."

As they started down the alley the sound of angry mobs and police sirens clashed in the thickening air.

MEKLIS OSKONBAEVA WOULD LIKE to have taken time to remember simpler, less stressful days, but he was too busy. When he awoke this morning he knew he would be facing difficult decisions. Such was the nature of his job as president of a country on the edge of self-immolation. By breakfast he had been briefed about rising tensions within his own government and the growing frustrations of his people. By his third cup of tea he had a sense things weren't right.

When were they? He'd been president for three of his five-year term and a day hadn't gone by he hadn't wished he'd traveled to the United States or England to teach history when he had the opportunity. But no. He was infected with a virus that made him feel he owed the country of his birth some help. A lot of help. It was the way of his father who taught him men who believed the world owed them a living couldn't be trusted, but a man who believed he owed the world something could.

His daughter called earlier in the day to say she would be meeting with American representative Amelia Lennon. Lennon wasn't the decision maker and he wondered why Jildiz would take the time. Still, the woman was bright and seemed to care about Kyrgyzstan and its people. Of course, she might just be a good actress. She did have one advantage: unlike many ambassadors, including the one operating at the U.S. Embassy on Prospect Mira Street, hers was not a position bought with political contributions. The U.S. Diplomatic Corps was composed of highly trained and dedicated people. That couldn't be said for the ambassador. Maybe Jildiz saw more in the woman than she did in the man who spoke for the world's most powerful country. Maybe.

The news of the riots came at lunch. First it was a call from the mayor of Osh and the mayor of Talas, both troubled cities. There were riots and ethnic conflicts there before. Like sparks from an unattended campfire, the blaze spread to Bishkek. Its quick spread made Meklis suspicious. Suspicion came with the job. The number of people he could trust diminished weekly.

Local news broadcasted the carnage on the television stations and it appeared as if the entire country had lost its mind.

"We have news that several police officers have been injured, some seriously." The report came from Boris Gubuz, his minister of internal security. "That's in Bishkek. Talas has four confirmed deaths, three police officers, one firefighter. Osh reports about twenty injuries. The hospital emergency rooms are filling up."

Boris was a good man. Trustworthy, but his age and health limited his days. At seventy-two, he still projected confidence and intelligence flashed in his eyes. It occurred to Meklis he hadn't seen the man smile in the last two years. Boris was never a drunk, but he was well acquainted with vodka, both domestic and that produced in his family's homeland of Russia.

Meklis rubbed his chin, striking the perfect blend of dismay, shock, concern, and courage. "Ethnic?"

"Too early to tell, Mr. President, but I suspect some of that is going on. So far the protests have been aimed at government buildings. Osh has seen the worst outbreak. Talas is not far behind."

"My officers have been able to keep the crowds from growing too large but they are overwhelmed." Emil Abirov served as chief of police for Bishkek. Normally he would not be in Meklis's panel of advisers but the situation demanded it. His officers would be the first point of contact with the mobs. They were the first line of defense. "On two occasions we've used tear gas. Our goal is to keep the groups under two hundred people in one place. After the last outbreak of violence we undertook a study on mob management and control."

"How effective has it been so far?" Sariev Dootkasy's words were low but pointed.

"Not as well as we hoped, Mr. Prime Minister. In the first hour it seemed to go well, but then unexpected results came about."

"Such as?" Dootkasy pressed.

Abirov cleared his throat and leaned his elbows on the wide conference table. "The principle is this: Large groups—say groups of a thousand or more—become a danger to themselves as well as innocents nearby. A group psyche develops."

"Mass hysteria?" Meklis asked.

"Not exactly, Mr. President, but the principle is the same. It begins with chanting and marching. Then someone starts shouting insults about the government. Others join in. Inevitably a counter-group forms to protest the protests. More insults. Someone throws a punch; another throws a rock; then come bricks and bottles. In ethnically mixed countries such as ours, a protest against the government becomes a racially or religiously charged one."

"Our greatest fear," Meklis said.

The police chief nodded. "One can't help but think of Rwanda or Serbia. The list is long."

Prime Minister Dootkasy pushed Abirov to continue. "So by keeping the mobs small you hope to remove the psychological aspect?"

"That was our hope."

"Is it working?"

"No, Mr. Prime Minister, it is not. It has helped some but as the numbers grow the ability of my officers to divide the group declines. And now we're seeing too many groups. I do not have enough officers to make the system work, not with a crowd so intent on violence."

"But we've only seen a small number of injuries," Meklis said.

"I believe that is about to increase." Abirov sighed. "The smaller groups—let's call them cells—simply round a city block and meet up with another group. It's like swatting at hornets. Knock one down and another comes at you."

"How many do you estimate are in the streets?" Meklis shifted in his seat.

"When I came in to the meeting, we were estimating three thousand." The chief picked up his cell phone and activated it. He stared at it for a moment. "I was going to ask for an update from my leaders in the field . . . I don't have a signal."

As if orchestrated, the half dozen men around the table looked at their phones. No one had a signal. Meklis tapped the intercom button on the conference room phone and called for one of his assistants. "Find out if our cellular system is down."

"Yes, sir." The aide was a fresh-faced young man who looked like he should still be in university.

Meklis looked at the landline phone. Something that felt like a small creature gnawed at his stomach. He picked up the receiver and punched a button for an outside line. Nothing. "Phones are out."

Seated to Meklis's left sat General Nurbeck Saparaliev. "Excuse me for a moment, Mr. President, Mr. Prime Minister." He rose and moved to the conference room door and exited. Less than a minute later he returned. "Basic radio communications are intact, including those dependent on repeaters. Television and radio are still working. The outage seems confined to the cell system and landlines."

"Internet?" Dootkasy asked.

"Also intact. Interesting." Saparaliev returned to his seat.

"How so, General?" Meklis already had a suspicion.

"This may be more than a series of antigovernment protests. I can't be sure yet, but this might be planned. It would be one thing to lose a cell tower, but to lose several sounds more like a—"

"Rebellion." Meklis pinched the bridge of his nose.

"I don't follow." Dilara Novakosa, the government press officer broke her silence.

Meklis motioned to Saparaliev. "General, if you would."

Saparaliev turned to the middle-aged woman, a former journalism professor. "Riots are seldom planned. Protests, yes, and those can evolve into something worse. Rebellion begins with planning. Knocking out phones, landlines, and cell, hinders the ability of the military and police some; the government a great deal. Police and military have field radios and are immune to outside influence except by highly technical jamming. Jamming can be traced and neutralized."

"So why knock out the phones if the police and military can still communicate?"

"To frustrate the populace. Imagine being injured and not able to call for help. Civil leaders communicate primarily with phone. This won't end communications, but I have to ask why protesters would do such a thing."

"But they couldn't close down the Internet?" she asked.

"Or didn't want to," Meklis said. "Think about Arab Summer, the protests in Lybia, Egypt, Syria, and other places. The protesters used the Internet to coordinate much of their actions."

"I still don't understand." Dilara looked puzzled. "They might have the Internet, but they can't use their cell phones to broadcast video."

"Maybe their leaders don't want that. They don't want the world to know." The general made a face as if his words had a bad taste.

"Why would they care about that?" Chief Abirov looked pale as if he already knew the answer.

"We can't know for certain, but they may have something worse in mind. Something they don't want the world to see."

All the faces turned to Meklis, and he once again wished he had chased the path of the academic. He was the leader and it was time for him to lead.

"I'm assuming that much of this has to do with the extension of the contract for the airfield at Manas."

"I still think that is a bad idea, Mr. President."

"And I am leaning in your direction, Mr. Prime Minister." Dootkasy's comment annoyed Meklis. He returned his attention to the others. "I have forbidden the United States from flying anything over our soil except the troop transport planes. Seeing U.S. military aircraft in our skies may incite more riots. General, you are to take over crowd control. Work with the police. I also want a contingent of police and military at our government building. I want the police in uniform and visible. I want the military nearby and ready to act but not visible. I don't want this to become a Lybia or Syria situation in which the military kills its own citizens." He paused and stared at General Saparaliev. "In Egypt, much of the military sided with the protesters. Will I have that problem?"

"No, Mr. President. That was a very different situation. Our troops are loyal to the government and its leaders."

"Good." Meklis gazed at Dilara. "I want you and your people to prepare a release to be distributed on our Web sites. I also want to prepare an address to the public."

"Yes, sir."

"Mr. President," the general said, "may I suggest contacting the U.S. Air Force at Manas and the U.S. Embassy to be on alert. If my fears are warranted and this gets even more out of control, they could be in some danger."

"The air base is north of the city," Meklis said.

"Yes, sir, but it's not that far. People drive there everyday to use the international airport."

Meklis nodded. "I'll make contact. With phones down, I'll send couriers. I also want increased security for key government officials and their families." He thought of his wife. He thought of Jildiz.

CHAPTER 7

IT TOOK ONLY A few minutes for J. J. and the others to kit up. He glanced around the ready room. No one spoke, each man was focused on his gear. It was the way with warriors before battle. Talk was cheap and it was big when not on the front line, but minutes before a mission boastful chatter gave way to private thoughts; thoughts of home, of family, of comrades wounded or killed in previous action.

J. J. was scared. He felt fear every time he was called to do what only a handful of men would or could do. At first his fear bothered him but over time he learned to embrace it. Fear never made him turn his back on the action; never hesitate to walk into the line of fire. It did, however, make him sharper and smarter. If he wasn't terrified he would begin to worry. His former team leader once told him he preferred to lead frightened men because he knew they were sane. "Men without fear are not brave, they're nuts."

If that was true, then J. J. was the sanest man on the planet.

While the apprehension was not new, there was a new flavor to it. Images flashed in his mind. In his early spec ops days he thought of his Army chaplain brother and his parents, maybe the girl he was dating at the time. After he married, he thought mostly of Tess. Now a movie of children not yet born playing on the white sands of some beach flickered on the screen of his mind.

And it brought the deepest ache he ever felt and fanned the flames of anxiety until they were white hot.

"You okay, Boss?"

J. J. looked up at Jose. "Me? Yeah. Sure. Why?"

"You been staring at your shoelaces like you expect them to tie and untie themselves."

"I'm a fan of shoelaces."

Jose crossed his arms. "Who isn't?"

J. J. straightened and turned to his team. "Okay, ladies, fall out." Jose turned to join the team as they left the room. "Not you, Doc. Hang a sec, will ya?"

"Sure thing, Boss."

A few moments later only J. J. and Jose remained. J. J. cleared his throat and broke eye contact. "Doc, you got, what, three dozen kids?"

"Not quite that many . . . yet. Just four. Or is it five? I'm not good with numbers.

"How do you do it?"

Jose narrowed his eyes. "You're asking me how to have kids? I would think you and Tess had that figured out by now. You said she was expecting twins . . . Oh. I get it."

"Good. I was starting to worry about you."

"You're looking for advice from me, Boss?"

"Yeah." He looked into Jose's eyes and saw understanding.

"Having kids changes a man, soldiers especially. You want the pat answer or the truth?"

"I want it straight."

"Okay, I have no idea how I do it. I just do. When I was a kid, my dad used to tell me to eat what was on my plate. I'm a little thick-headed but I finally realized he wasn't talking about Mom's cooking. He was teaching me to deal with what's in front of me. It's the only thing I can change. That's what I do. I deal with what's on my plate at the moment."

"So you don't worry about your kids growing up fatherless?"

"Don't be stupid, Boss. I worry about it all the time."

"You're confusing me."

Jose nodded. "Welcome to my world."

CHAPTER 8

FOR J. J. BARTLEY the most difficult hours of a mission were those immediately before a mission began. That was true from the beginning. No matter how well prepared he felt, he never felt ready. He used to use the prep time to double- and triple-check his gear, or review mission objects. He would be told what his role would be and he'd do it without question. That was then, a time that seemed decades ago but was only a few months in the past. Now the job of mission prep fell on his shoulders, so he studied the street maps of Bishkek, trying to commit to memory the area around the abduction attempt. He saw streets very much like those at home; a business and retail section, and several narrow alleys behind buildings.

Colonel Weidman stepped into the ready room with photos in his hand. "This just came in. President Oskonbaeva won't allow us to overfly the area, but I was able to get these." He waved the photos. "Pull it in, men."

The team gathered around a table in the room. "We might not be able to send an aircraft over the city but we can use a space-borne asset. A bird was redirected over the area and took shots for us."

J. J. looked at the satellite images. "So these are fresh?"

"Ten minutes tops, Master Sergeant." Weidman pointed at one of the photos. "This is the area we are concerned about. As you can see, fires have been started at key intersections, most likely to bring traffic to a halt in the city." He jabbed a finger at ten fires, some from a pile of something J. J. assumed were tires and a couple were from burning cars.

J. J. pointed at the image of a white van, a dark sedan, and two men lying in the street. The detail of the image was amazing and showed a resolution twice what was available just a few years ago. Had the angle been different, J. J. could have read the license plate on the sedan. Several people gathered around the bodies, but they looked untouched, as did the automatic weapon laying near the body of the man Lennon hit with her car. He couldn't find the handgun the other man was carrying. It was likely someone stole it, or the resolution, good as it was, couldn't distinguish it from the dark asphalt. It was sharp enough, however, to show the man's bent and broken body. Lennon did some real damage to the attacker. Good for her.

"We have a problem." The colonel put another picture on top. "This is Captain Lennon's car. She left it in the middle of the street, doors open."

"Why would she abandon her vehicle?" Aliki asked.

"Because it wouldn't go any more," Nagano said. "Machine Gun Guy was firing when she pulled it away. A stray bullet killed the reporter. My guess is he got a few rounds into the car. Tires maybe. Engine perhaps."

"Good news is two doors are open and there are no bodies in the street." J. J. searched the photo for signs of a female corpse or two.

"When it hit the fan, I had our intel guys monitor the police, fire, Kyrgyzstan military frequency. As you can imagine, the airwaves are burning up with transmissions. Some patrons in a restaurant complained about a gunman running through the place. That restaurant is right here." He pointed at the street in front of a building a few strides from the car in the middle of the street.

"Did they respond?" Jose asked.

"No. The cops have their hands full with the riots. If I didn't know better, I'd say the two are related."

J. J. looked at the base commander. "Do you know better, sir?"

"No, I don't. I'm a tad paranoid, an attribute that has served me well." He straightened but still looked like a man who had several bags of cement on his shoulders. "So here's what we have: an Army-trained officer on the run from at least one gunman. He may have called for backup. With her is the president's daughter. There are riots in the city that are getting worse and, I am told by my advisers, will get worse when the sun goes down. We are forbidden by U.S. law and by the locals to intervene in any way. So what are we about to do? Intervene, at least until we get our soldier back."

"We will find her, sir," J. J. said.

"Are you being confident or cocky?"

J. J. shrugged. "Both."

Weidman nodded. "Okay, a couple more things: one, the cell system in the country is down as are the landlines. The intel guys think that may be more ominous than it sounds. Your communication will be like that in the field. All radio." He looked at Pete. "You're the communications guy, you got the gear to do that?"

"Yes, sir, and more. We have CONNIE."

Weidman blinked and waited for an explanation. Pete pulled an electronic tablet from his gear. "Look's like an iPad or one of those other tablet gizmos."

"That's what it looks like, sir, but it's a good deal more than that." Pete looked like a proud father. "Is the colonel familiar with the way the Navy communicates with submarines?"

"Faster and funnier, Pete," J. J. said. "Don't waste the colonel's time. You new guys need to hear this."

"Modern submarines seldom surface except to retrieve communications. Even then they just send up an antenna. Their base sends a transmission in condensed digital packets, in bursts. It takes only seconds and the sub can then be on its way undetected. This is a field version of the technology. It's new but we had great success with it not long ago. We can receive written orders, maps, images, and even video. It comes to us by satellite feed."

"I imagine it's faster than carrier pigeon."

"But not nearly as tasty." Aliki tried to look serious. He looked at the others. "What?"

"Hence, 'Joker.'" Nagano shook his head. "I've been putting up with this for a lot of years."

Weidman pulled the conversation back to target. "I have two vehicles for you. You'll be leaving during daylight, but you can't be seen running around in full gear. Your CBUs have no insignias, but your weapons are clearly American as are your accents, so if you're compromised, we won't be fooling anyone. We'll deny ever knowing you but no one is going to believe us. Understood."

J. J. answered for the team. "Yes, sir. Five by five."

"I wish we could wait until nightfall, but too much is at stake."

"Understood, sir. We'll be ready in ten."

"You have five." Colonel Weidman walked from the room.

"Okay, gentlemen, I'm going to have to say this quick and I'm only going to say it once. I expected a couple of months of drills and practice before our team was mission ready. Well, that's not going to happen." J. J. looked at Aliki and Nagano. "Everything I've heard about you is good, but I need to hear it from you. This team had to deal with Post Traumatic Stress Disorder problems once and it almost got us killed. You guys lost a lot of men a few weeks ago. Are you still able to function in the field?"

"Sure, Boss," Nagano said. "The medics cleared us for duty and our psych evals are clear."

"I know what the paper says, Mike. I need you to look me in the eye and tell me straight: You good to go?"

"Golden," Aliki said. "Good to go."

"Mike?"

Nagano stared into J. J.'s eyes. "You can count on me, Boss."

J. J. searched their faces, eyes, demeanor for any tells indicating a problem.

"Anything I need to know about before we hit the streets?"

"No, Boss," Aliki and Nagano said in stereo.

"Excellent." J. J. looked at the others. "Gear ready?"

"Ready." They spoke in unison.

"Okay, Aliki is the second on this mission, just like Shaq was before. Clear?"

"Clear."

"We'll be moving out in two civilian vehicles. Vans." He looked at Pete. "Junior, you'll be with me. Doc, you too—and you'll be driving. Junior, you got maps on CONNIE?"

"Yes, Boss."

J. J. knew a mission had begun when proper names gave way to nicks. "Joker, you lead the second team. That's you, Hawkeye, and Weps. Don't break Hawkeye. He's young and fragile."

"I'm not that young. Wait. Or fragile."

They laughed and J. J. had no doubts Crispin was trying to lessen the tension. "Doc, introduce the new guys to the tradition."

Jose moved closer to the table, removed his wallet, something he would soon, like the others, lock away, and removed a photo of his wife Lucy, seven-year-old Maria, eight-year-old Matteo, ten-year-old Jose Jr., and two-year-old Tito. He set it on the flat surface. Pete retrieved a photo of his wife and set it next to Jose's family photo. Unmarried Crispin set a picture of his father on the table. J. J. looked at Aliki, who seemed stunned. He withdrew his wallet and withdrew a family photo that looked like it represented three generations. Mike was ready when his turn came. His photo showed a petite Japanese-featured woman. "My fiancée." He spoke softly.

Finally, J. J. set his picture on the pile of photos. It was black-and-gray-and-white, indistinct.

"That's your wife, Boss?" Aliki's brow furrowed. "Man, you married badly."

"It's a sonogram of my unborn twins."

"Oh." Aliki grinned. "I can see the resemblance."

J. J. didn't respond. He placed a hand on the photos. Jose followed, as did Pete and Crispin. A moment later, Mike's hand joined the others. Aliki put his big paw out. It shook. J. J. took a deep breath. "For them, and for those like them, we do this."

The team repeated the words. "For them, and for those like them, we do this."

A few moments of silence passed. J. J. prayed silently, then said, "Let's rock, gentlemen."

J. J. Bartley led his men from the room and wondered what awaited them.

CHAPTER 9

OUTSIDE THE ADMIN BUILDING awaited two ordinary-looking vehicles: one a Russian-made delivery-style van, the other a Chinese-made van. Both looked as if they rolled off the assembly line a mere two decades before. The Russian GAZ was painted—repainted, J. J. assumed—a charcoal gray and bore injuries of years of use. The red Chinese JAC Motors looked less damaged but no one would take it for anything other than a well-worn van looking for a place to park and die.

"Choose your vehicle, Joker." J. J. stood, doing his best not to look stunned.

"Do I have to?" He shook his head. "I have a reputation to maintain."

"It's like choosing between which disease you want," Nagano said.

"Is that supposed to be funny?" Jose stood next to the new guy.

"There's nothing funny about those things." He turned to Aliki. "Choose the red one."

"Why?"

"Because it's red? Because it's Chinese? I don't know. Red and Chinese seem to go together."

"That's your logic?" Jose said.

"It's all I got."

Aliki shrugged. "One bag of garbage is like any other. We'll take the red one. Weps, you got the wheel. Come on, Rookie, you're in the back with me."

Crispin looked offended. "I'm not a rookie. I did tours in Afghanistan and have one spec op under my belt."

"Of course you do, Rookie. I mean no offense. How can I make it up to you?"

"Stop calling me Rookie."

Aliki slapped Crispin on the shoulder. "Will do, Rookie."

"Mount up, men. We have a couple of damsels to find." J. J. started for the gray delivery truck. "Take the wheel, Doc."

"Roger that."

Once in the vehicles, J. J. led them through a radio check. Once satisfied, he uttered one word: "Talley-ho!"

Jose spent the time during the radio check to get acquainted with the vehicle. "At least they drive on the right side of the road." He dropped the car into gear and started for the front gate. By plan, Aliki's team would leave five minutes later.

The sun touched the horizon.

THE SOUND OF BISHKEK grew louder and more ominous. Sirens wailed unceasingly. Shouts once distant were closer now. Amelia was hearing more gunfire. She had no idea the kinds of weapons being used. The closest reports sounded like handguns and a few like automatic weapons. She was certain one weapon out here was a Russian-made machine gun. That one had been aimed at her and she had no reason to believe the attacker called it a night.

Something in her gut told here there was more going on than she knew. She didn't like the feeling.

"You still with me, Jildiz?"

"Where else would I go." The woman's words were weak and robed with raspy breathing. Her pace had fallen off. *What a team. One wounded woman leading another woman who can barely breathe.*

"Here." The word was soft but Amelia got the idea that Jildiz was attempting to be forceful but lacked the air to do so.

Amelia stopped and peered through the darkening alley. Jildiz pointed at a rear door. A small, utilitarian sign was attached to the wood surface with screws. *Apetka* was painted on the sign in Cyrillic. The equivalent word in Kyrgyz was below it.

Taking Jildiz by the arm, she led her charge to a spot next to a large metal trash container. "Stay here while I scope things out." She didn't wait for an answer.

Amelia inched to the door. It was solid and showed years of wear. Who painted back doors anyway? A small window with bars was to the right of the door. She moved to it but didn't look in.

First, she listened for voices but heard none. She moved her head closer to the window, then peeked in. What sunlight remained poured through the front windows and the rear window she stood by. She saw shelves and guessed she was looking into the back area of the store where the pharmacist did his prescription work. The place looked empty.

She returned to the door and tried the knob. Locked. Of course. Bars on the window and a locked door. Why had she expected it to be easy? She studied the door and remembered a line from one of her Army instructors during SERE training: "Most locks just give the illusion of security."

She returned to Jildiz. The lawyer labored to draw a breath. She needed help and help now. "I'm going to have to break in but it's going to take a few minutes, if I'm able to do it at all. I expect you to hang in there. Okay?"

Jildiz nodded. Apparently talking was becoming more difficult. Amelia's mind raced trying to form a plan she could implement quickly. The door swung in, which meant she had no access to the hinges. The lock was a dead bolt and while it looked old, it appeared sturdy. She glanced down the alley and saw another store—a hardware store.

"Bingo."

"What?"

"Stay put."

Amelia moved through the twilight to the store two doors down and across the alley. It had a pair of rear access doors, no doubt to allow for deliveries of materials and larger power tools. It, too, had a rear window. She surveyed the place as she did at the pharmacy. Empty. No doubt store owners felt closing down for the day to be safer than trying to carry on business as usual.

The lock on the door looked as formidable as the one on the pharmacy but there were no bars on the window. Like alleys everywhere, trash bins and containers lined the sides. Amelia went Dumpster diving and found a segment of metal electrical conduit, a hallow tube used to shield wiring. Retrieving the three-foot pipe, she returned to the window. She glanced up and down the alley, then added to the noise in the air by driving one end of conduit through the glass pane then using it to clear the shards from the window frame.

Pulling herself through the small window was difficult, her hips barely clearing the narrow opening. On the other side of the window was a wood workbench covered with catalogs only a hardware store owner would find interesting.

She pulled herself through scattering catalogs, order forms, and three-ring binders to the side and onto the floor. Quickly as she could, she finished her breaking-and-entering by finding her footing and pausing to listen for sounds of employees drawn to the clatter she just made. No one came.

Amelia allowed herself a moment to pause. Her wound burned in protest to what she just asked it to do. The wound on her forehead began to bleed again and she had to push the blood from her eye.

"Keep going, girl. You can lick your wounds later."

The dimming daylight made it difficult to see but she wasted no time moving up and down the aisles looking for a tool to use for her next B&E. Scores of ideas ran through her head but she dismissed them all. A power tool required electricity or compressed air. That meant moving a long extension cord or an air compressor. Other ideas floated by before she fell back on a bit of wisdom she learned from her medical doctor father: "Start with the simple then move to the complex if needed."

Two minutes later, Amelia unlocked the delivery door and emerged into the alley with a ten-pound, yellow-handled sledgehammer.

J. J.'S MIND SWIRLED as the old panel truck bounced down streets on metal-fatigued springs and shocks five years past their usefulness. The team once traveled through part of eastern Siberia by large panel truck painted to look like a FedEx vehicle. The back was equipped with seats. Uncomfortable seats, but seats nonetheless. This contraption had seats too: metal folding chairs with a backrest screwed to one of the narrow uprights supporting the sheet metal sides. J. J. never thought he would, but he missed the Siberian FedEx truck.

"The Air Force spared no price in fixing us up with these digs." Pete studied the tablet device they nicknamed CONNIE. A GPS map was on the screen. A green dot indicated their location; a blue dot Aliki's team. A red dot marked the street where the attempted abduction took place.

"Just remember, it isn't the kind of vehicle that makes it military, it's who's in it."

"So you're enjoying the ride, Boss."

"Not in the least."

"Uh oh," Pete said. "Just got a burst transmission."

"Let's hear it." J. J. leaned closer, spreading his feet to keep from sliding off the chair.

"It's from Colonel Weidman. The riots have spread. Intel tells him the phone system was sabotaged. Same for the cell towers."

"So this is more rebellion than riot."

"I guess."

"That's not good. Riots are headless beasts; rebellions come with planning." J. J. felt his gut twist.

"The colonel must have some computer jockey pulling things together. He's sent a map showing where the crowds are and the fires."

"Hand it over." J. J. took CONNIE.

"There's more than one map. Slide your finger to the left, you'll see the 'then-and-now' map."

J. J. did. "They're still near our area of operation but the numbers seem to be further north of the street."

"But they're moving that way, Boss. We may have company when we get there. Weidman says the numbers are growing. There are more fires. It's like the city has gone mad."

J. J. frowned. "Maybe the whole country." He wanted to tell Jose to step on it, but he was trying to avoid attention. Could that be done in a city filled with rioters? They charted a course around the edge of town to avoid the growing crowds in the downtown streets. This was taking longer than he wanted.

A pop-up announcement appeared above the map image. J. J. tapped it. As with all transmissions, he had to enter a code to retrieve the message. Unlike most handheld computers where one password gave access to all e-mail, CONNIE required the code be given every time it was activated or a new message arrived, thereby limiting the amount of information a hostile could glean from the device should it fall in the wrong hands.

J. J. tapped in the password. "Not good."

Pete raised an eyebrow. "Two words I hate to hear."

"Crowds seem to be moving closer to the base. Weidman says it's slow but wants us up to speed in case we have to figure a new way into the base or have to hang out for awhile."

"Or retreat to the safe confines of Afghanistan."

J. J. chuckled at the sarcasm. The war had been winding down but Afghanistan could not be considered safe. "That'd be a far drive, Junior. There's a whole 'nother country between here and there."

"A long drive could be nice."

The van rocked and bounced as one of its tires found a pothole.

"Sorry." Jose veered to the side again to avoid something only he could see.

"You were saying?" It was J. J.'s turn to raise an eyebrow.

"Me? Nothing, Boss. I didn't say anything about a long drive." Pete turned his gaze to the floor.

"Something eating you?" J. J. handed CONNIE back.

"Not really. I'm good."

"But . . ."

Pete brushed something off his boot. "I've been thinking about the new guys. I hate going on mission with men I haven't trained with. With Moyer and Rich, we knew what to expect: Moyer would be grumpy all the time and Rich would threaten our lives. It was like being home. When things turned bad, however, you knew they were there for you. Know what I mean?"

J. J. nodded. "Yep. I know. They were the best—are the best. Aliki and Nagano have good records and a ton of experience."

"I'm not questioning that. It's just, well, before we were a well-meshed set of gears. Sure we had to replace team members before but just one at a time. To have a third of our unit new . . . Forget it, Boss. I'm just thinking out loud."

"I hear ya, Pete. I've wondered the same thing, but we have no other choice. This is the way it has to be done. Both men have the same training we do. Both are Rangers. They'll pick up your quirks soon enough."

"My quirks?"

"Sorry, I meant to say *our* quirks."

"Sure ya did, Boss. Sure ya did."

"Get on the radio and bring the rest of the team up to speed about the riots."

"Will do."

"Doc?" J. J. turned to the opening between the front seats and the cargo area. "Kick this pig."

The van sped up.

THE STAMP ON THE side of the sledgehammer read 4.5 k: four and a half kilograms. Ten pounds. That didn't sound like much to Amelia, but the tool felt three times that weight. She checked the alley several times, fearful the man with the machine gun and no regard for life might have been able to trail them here. She saw nothing but more smoke in the sky. She saw something even more frightening: Jildiz leaning against the Dumpster, her chin resting on her chest. Amelia moved to her side.

"Jildiz. You still with me? Come on, girl. Stay with me."

"I'm . . . here. Just trying to breathe." Her voice was weak. She pointed up. "Smoke."

The smoke was acrid, a blend of burning buildings, cars, oil, and tires. It burned Amelia's eyes. An idea popped into her brain. "Sit still."

"As if I could . . . do anything . . . else."

Amelia sprinted back to the hardware store, chastising herself for not thinking of this sooner. Once again, she moved through the empty aisles and found the box she was looking for: a safety mask, the kind used by painters to keep fumes out of their lungs. She sprinted from the hardware store and back to Jildiz. She ripped open the box and removed the mask, helping Jildiz don the contraption.

Jildiz looked up. Amelia could tell she was smiling by the wrinkles around her eyes. "How do I look? Is it me?"

The words came with great effort. The mask would keep airborne particulates out but didn't provide oxygen or the medication Jildiz needed. Those things were inside the pharmacy.

"It's you, girl. Brings out the color in your eyes."

Jildiz nodded slowly. Amelia couldn't waste another moment. She rose, picked up the sledgehammer, and stepped to the backdoor of the pharmacy. She took one more minute to study the exit. It was a standard-sized wood door with a typical doorknob and a dead bolt. *Look for the weakest link. Wood.* The door was wood, not a metal safety door. The jambs were wood also. The wood would give before the locks.

She hefted the sledgehammer, making sure to hold it near the end of the handle to increase the force of the blow; set her eyes on the dead bolt; and swung for all her might. It made a much louder noise than she expected. She took no time to worry about that. The whole city was making noise, what was one more bang? Of course, a gun-wielding hood was searching for them—maybe several—and any noise they made might prove counterproductive.

What choice did she have?

She swung again, then again, until she pounded the lock through the splintering wood door. Then she took aim at the doorknob. It gave in after just one swing. Pushing the door open, Amelia entered the pharmacy verifying it was as empty as she thought. It was.

A minute later she had Jildiz on her feet and moving inside the shop. She had to support her as she shuffled her feet. Even through the mask she could hear Jildiz wheezing.

Inside, behind the pharmacist counter, she saw a chair and lowered Jildiz into it. The woman sat and swayed as if she were about to face-plant onto the polished nicotine-yellow linoleum-covered floor. Amelia placed a steadying hand on her, then started a search for a rescue inhaler. She found a white box with the phrase "bronchodilator" printed in English on the label. She recognized the name of the pharmaceutical company. It was American. Another label in Kyrgyz had been pasted over the instructions.

"Bronchodilator . . . broncho . . . Bronchial? Dilator." Amelia thought for another second, then continued to mumble. "Dilates the bronchial tubes? Sounds right." She ripped open the box and removed an L-shaped device. It looked like something she saw as a kid in elementary school. *Amy Littleton had asthma. This looks like what she used to carry.* The box contained a small, metal container. Amelia spun and fast-stepped to Jildiz.

"I think I have something." She helped Jildiz remove the mask, then showed her the inhaler.

"Yes." Jildiz took the device and the metal vial in shaky hands. Amelia helped her insert the medicine into the inhaler. Jildiz stuck the business end of the inhaler in her mouth and activated it, inhaling deeply. She did it again, then waited. Her breathing eased some but she was still in distress.

"Is there something else I can get?"

Jildiz responded with an upraised hand and shook her head. A moment later she extended one finger, indicating she needed a moment. She took the medicine twice more for a total of four.

"Can you take too much? Is it dangerous?"

"W-wait." Jildiz closed her eyes and drew in a lung full of air, letting it out slowly. It came and went easily. Her ashen skin turned pink.

Amelia plopped down on the floor, sitting with her knees up, and concentrated on her own breathing. "This is more fun than two women should be allowed."

"I know I'm enjoying myself." Jildiz's words were stronger. "Did you find more of these?"

"Yes. Several boxes and some other stuff I didn't understand. I think they have a shelf full of stuff for breathing problems."

"Oxygen tank?"

Amelia lifted her head. "Of course. I should have thought of that. I'll go look." It took only a moment for her to find a portable oxygen tank that fit in what reminded Amelia of a large purse. She carried it to Jildiz, opened the case, and removed a long, clear tube attached to adult-size nasal cannulas. Within moments, she helped Jildiz don the breathing apparatus, inserting the short nasal tubes. She cranked the oxygen valve and the sound of flowing air rose like soft music.

Jildiz closed her eyes and let the precious gas do its work. As the minutes passed, Amelia watched the color return to the woman's face. When she was certain Jildiz was strong enough to leave unattended, she went to the back door and closed it the best she could. She had pounded the dead bolt through the door. It would take a craftsman to fix the door so it would seat properly. She then found delivery boxes waiting to be unpacked. She piled them against the door to hold it in place. The boxes were not heavy and any one persistent enough could get in but not without being heard.

She searched the back of the store and found a ceramic tea set. She set the pot and cups on the boxes. If someone forced their way in, the teacups would fall to the floor with a crash. Not the best alarm, but it would have to do. She stepped to a phone behind the counter and picked up the receiver. Dead.

When she returned, she found Jildiz sitting upright and breathing easy, but still with a wheeze. "Still no phone." She pulled her cell phone from her pocket. No bars. She didn't like the implications. She moved back to Jildiz and sat on the floor next to her. "How are you feeling?"

"Much better. I'll be okay. I've had worse episodes."

"Really?"

Jildiz made eye contact. "Maybe not. I had a few scary events when I was a child. I was hospitalized twice, but not for long." She looked away. "I carry a rescue inhaler—the one I left in the car—but haven't needed it for a long time. I hoped I was over it all. I guess the smoke and stress set it off."

"Stress? What stress?" Amelia tried to look puzzled.

"I'm allergic to guns, especially those aimed at me."

"Oh, that little thing."

Jildiz fell silent for a moment. "I haven't said thank you."

"There hasn't been much time with all the running and hiding and all."

"And the shooting. Don't forget the shooting."

"True." She patted Jildiz's knee. "Any idea who those guys are—the one's who tried to nab you?"

"No. I want to believe I was just the wrong person in the wrong spot at the wrong time."

Amelia could hear the fear in her voice and she couldn't blame the woman. Amelia was Army trained and better equipped emotionally and mentally to deal with fear, yet her stomach continued to flutter like a flag in a hurricane. She was working on instinct and adrenaline, the latter of which was waning, leaving her hands shaking and filling her with profound fatigue. "I want to believe that too, but we both know that's not the case. They targeted your car and were heavily armed. I have a strong suspicion that they knew the path you would be taking."

"That means they knew where I was and how I would travel back to the capitol building."

"That's exactly what it would mean. How could they know that, Jildiz?"

She shook her head and the color that had returned to her face drained. "I have no idea. It's too much to believe. Not many people knew I was going to meet with you."

"But someone did."

"Yes. My father and a few of his advisers."

"We can rule out your father . . . can't we?"

"Of course. I don't like the implication."

Amelia fixed her gaze on Jildiz. "I meant no insult, I'm just processing information."

Silence hung between them. Amelia let her mind race. Ghosts haunted her thoughts; specters of terrible possibilities. "Jildiz, if I'm going to be any help to you—to us—I need to ask a few questions."

"I'm not afraid of questions."

Amelia smiled. "I doubt much frightens you."

"The guns."

"Well, those frighten everyone. Especially if they're pointed at you." She hesitated. "First question, why did you go to the restaurant without security?"

"People watch my coming and going. When I travel with security, it is easy to recognize me. I wanted to meet with you in private."

"Forgive me, but that's a little weak."

"It is the truth."

Amelia studied her for a moment. "Is it the whole truth?"

Jildiz looked away. "No."

Amelia waited but no other information was offered.

"Jildiz, listen to me." She paused, waiting for Jildiz's attention. "Jildiz, look at me." Finally, the president's daughter did. "A short time ago we were women on the opposite sides of a debate, but that has changed. Now, we're a pair of women fighting to stay alive in some pretty dire circumstances. Someone, most likely several someones now, are looking for us. We can't call for help and this part of the city is turning to anarchy. There's a little but loud voice in the back of my head screaming things are going to get worse. I'm inclined to agree. So for now, we need to put aside the issue that's brought us together and focus on survival. Agreed?"

"Was it your people? Did the Americans stage my abduction?" The hard look on Jildiz's face told Amelia she wasn't kidding.

"No, Jildiz, it wasn't us. Remember, I ran over two men to save you. It's a bad career move to run over fellow citizens."

"Perhaps they kept you out of the loop."

"There is no reason for us to kidnap you. What would we gain? We wouldn't use a person as a bargaining chip to keep the air base open. Think, Jildiz, you're not the final decision maker. Like me, you represent your government but others are going to decide what happens."

"Are you CIA?"

"What? No. I told you that."

"Many in the government and the opposition party think you are. Why would an American civilian choose to live and work in this troubled country?"

"It's what I do. I'm not part of the Diplomatic Corps. I represent the military in general and the Army in particular. You know that. I've been very up-front."

"FAO."

"That's right, Foreign Affairs Officer, but not CIA. That fact was included in material we provided you before our negotiations began. I have nothing to do with any intelligence agency."

"I'm sorry. I don't mean to accuse. I am just trying to make sense of things."

"You have a right to be suspicious. I agree that something bad is going on."

"What do we do now?" Jildiz's voice was stronger now. Almost normal. Her breathing was regular and respiration came easily.

Amelia feared the question, mostly because she had very few answers and only one made sense. "I'm leaving."

Amelia stood.

CHAPTER 10

"WHAT?" JILDIZ STOOD, WAVERED a moment, then found her balance. "You're leaving me?"

"Not for long. I'll be back."

"You can't leave. I don't know what to do. What if he finds me here alone."

Amelia wanted to correct her, changing "he" to "they" because she was sure the guy called in reinforcements. Amelia placed her hands on Jildiz's shoulders. "Listen carefully. I am not abandoning you but I need to do something."

"What? What could be so important you'd leave me to the wolves?"

"There may be people looking for us—"

"That's what I just said."

"No, I mean good guys. My people. But they're going to have trouble finding us. The city is too big."

"How do you know they're looking for you?"

Amelia took a deep breath. "I don't know, Jildiz, but my status as an American FAO means they'll come for me if they know something has happened. I don't know if they have that figured out but at some point they will. Maybe by then, things will have settled down, but we can't depend on that. My cell phone isn't working so I doubt they can track me by GPS. This means I have to go old school."

"'Old school.' What does school have to do with it?"

"It's an American expression. It means I have to do things without technology. It's something the military taught me." She didn't feel the need to describe SERE training. "I need you to trust me."

"But if you go out there, they might find you. They might kill you."

"That's not going to happen . . ." She couldn't complete the lie. "Yes. That's true, but they could find us here as well. If they have any training they know we'll seek shelter and that we'll probably stay away from the riots where we can't tell the good guys from the bad guys. They will have to assume we're on foot and estimate how far we could have traveled. If they come down the alley, they'll see the broken window in the hardware store and the busted door into this place. They'll figure it out. Being proactive is better than being reactive." She lowered her hands. "I need you to trust me."

"I'll go with you. I'm feeling better. I have the inhaler—"

"No, Jildiz, I can move faster by myself. I will be back. I promise."

Tears brimmed Jildiz's eyes and Amelia could almost smell the fear. "O-okay."

"There's a couple of things I'm going to do first and I need you to pay attention. Will you do that?"

"Yes."

There were no sobs, but the tears ran freely.

Amelia tried to fight off the sense of guilt. She lost the battle.

JILDIZ DID EXACTLY AS Amelia ordered: she locked the front door of the pharmacy the moment after Amelia crossed the threshold into the freshly dark street, a street made darker by the funerary shroud of smoke hanging over the city. The mere sniff of it made her chest tighten and she was sure another bout of asthma was on its way. To her relief the tightening in her chest eased, at least the tightening caused by the disorder. Fear continued to tighten around her thorax like a constricting straitjacket. She moved back to the chair behind the counter. Seated, she could see the glass front of the store and enough of the rear storage area to know if anyone came in the back.

She sat and listened. She heard distant sirens, pops, and cracks as the old building settled in the cooling evening. With every unfamiliar sound her heart skipped several beats.

Steady yourself. She wished she could be as strong as Amelia. The woman amazed her. Of course she knew Amelia's background. In many ways, Kyrgyzstan was a backward country compared to those in the West. It wasn't that her people were dimmer than the others. It was a national poverty, a fragile economy, high unemployment, limited goods to export, corruption in government, crime in the streets, the Russian Mafia, and its Chinese equivalent that kept them several long strides behind other countries. Her father was committed to changing that. So was she. If that was still possible; if her country could endure yet another round of riots and anarchy.

Amelia was what Jildiz wanted to be, needed to be: firm, committed, and courageous. At the moment, she felt none of those things. She was a mouse hiding behind a counter in an ever-darkening store. Amelia's fear was apparent on her face but not in her actions. She entered a fray most people would have fled. Using just her automobile she battled three men with weapons, killing two of them and rescuing her. Jildiz doubted she would have thought to do what Amelia did for her.

If she were a jaded person, she might assume Amelia did all that to make Jildiz beholden to her, but at her most paranoid—a quality she possessed in large measure—she couldn't bring herself to believe another woman would do all she did just to score . . . what did Americans call it? Brownie points. Yes, brownie points. If she and Amelia lived, she would have to ask what the origin of that phrase was.

Before Amelia left, she helped Jildiz select several medications to help with her asthma, should another respiratory crisis arise. They even found self-injecting adrenaline pens. She also gathered snacks from the public side of the counter. Nothing healthy but it would keep her going if Amelia took longer to get back than she estimated.

"You know what this makes you, don't you," Amelia said when she situated the materials around Jildiz's "nest."

"I am afraid to ask."

"You and I are now official looters. Do you think your father can change the law for us?"

"I'm sure the extenuating circumstances will help. I will make sure the shops get paid for the damages."

"Good. Also, I broke a nail so I'll be billing for a full manicure."

Jildiz said, "I'll go with you."

"Outstanding, I could go for a girls' night out." Amelia sounded too serious to be believed. She disappeared into the storage area and then returned. "In a larger pharmacy we might have found something more useful. The large pharmacies in the United States carry a little bit of everything. I've seen cameras and pocketknives. I'm more interested in the latter, but no such luck here. So . . ." She held up a ten-centimeter-long metal case. It was narrow and took only a moment for Jildiz to recognize it.

"A box cutter."

"I'd prefer to leave with a 9mm Glock handgun, but the place seems to be fresh out."

The tool had a silver metal slide. Amelia thumbed it up, extending a long, silver-gray blade.

"I couldn't."

"First, yes you could—can—and let's pray you don't have to, but if you do, I want you prepared."

"Amelia—" Jildiz looked away. A moment later she felt a soft but strong hand cup her chin and lift.

"Look at me, Jildiz. You've seen riots in your country before. You're an educated woman who follows world events. I know you saw the riots in Greece in 2011, and in Egypt, and a dozen other countries. You know how violent things can get. Normally smart people go stupid quick and do things they never dreamed they would. It happens over and over again all around the world. You have to be prepared to defend yourself."

"I hate violence."

"I'm not crazy about it either, but I know there are people who want to hurt others. It seems they're roving the streets now. Add to that the fact someone tried to kidnap you. Well, we have to assume they're searching for you right now. When I come back, I don't want to find you missing or dead. Clear?"

"Yes, but—"

"Nope. No buts. You listen and you take to heart what I say. I don't have time to repeat all of this. Okay?"

Jildiz nodded. In the darkening shop, she ran the scenarios Amelia gave her through her head.

AMELIA REMINDED HERSELF FOR the twentieth time that what she was doing was crazy, bizarre, against common sense. Had she just herself to protect, she would have done things differently, but Jildiz was blood kin to the president of the country. *When I get out of this, I'm going to resign my commission, move to Hawaii, and paint seashells for tourists.* "Or something," she whispered.

The night seemed warmer than it should. Kyrgyzstan was a mountainous country with more than its fair share of snow in the winter. There should still be a cool breeze rolling off the peaks. Perhaps she felt warm from exertion. Or maybe it was the blanket of smoke overhead. Or maybe it was her imagination. It didn't matter. What did matter was retracing her steps back to the car and avoiding human contact while she did.

Part of her wanted to seek help from others, but she didn't know who to trust. Besides, the sane people left the area for safer digs. That left only the insane, the furious, and mixed in with them, an unknown number of bad guys.

Without Jildiz, Amelia made good time. She reached the restaurant faster than she thought possible. The place was closed and locked up. In a just world, she would believe that machine gun man had been arrested. Maybe he had, but she saw him shouting into a radio. Other goons had to be around.

She came to the back of the eatery and paused, looking and listening for sounds of danger. Not hearing any, she moved casually to the street, like a lost tourist. Her car, lifeless as a brick, was still in the street. Several of the buildings on the street had fresh graffiti in various colors. Some called for the overthrow of the government, a few demanded Uzbeks leave the country, and she saw several stylized *A*'s in a circle—the universal symbol of the anarchist movement. The street was littered with garbage. A breeze shoved bits of paper down the asphalt lane. "Lovely."

She pulled a marker from her coat pocket, something she snagged from the stationery aisle of the pharmacy. After checking the street again to make certain she was alone, Amelia moved to the car. The bullet holes made it look like the carcass of some large animal shot by hunters. Leaning over the hood she drew a circle with the black marker on the silver surface. The action forced her to see her wounded hand. By gunshot standards it wasn't much, but it hurt like the bullet took a finger off.

She kept at it. In the circle she drew an *X*. At the top of that she wrote a *2*; at the right side she penned *1*; and at the bottom an *M*. She stepped back and looked at the cryptic symbol. The *X* indicated she had been here, the *2* that there were two people evading capture, the *M* meant they were on the move. She then added a plus symbol with arrow heads on one end of the horizontal bars and one on the vertical. At the other end of the vertical she drew a small circle, at the end of the horizontal she penned a dark dot. If any civilian or local militia saw the symbol they might guess that it was pointing the direction they had run and follow the arrows. Those in the know would focus on the solid dot and go in the direction opposite that indicated by the arrows. Now she hoped someone had been sent for them.

She returned to the alley behind the restaurant and turned right—into the three young men. One seized her by the arm.

"Look, we caught a frightened rabbit."

She judged the men to be in their early twenties. The one who held her arm wore dirty work clothes. She assumed construction. He was six foot two and at least 180 pounds. His two friends looked a year or two older and wore similar clothing. The man holding her arm pushed her back to one of the walls lining the alley. His breath smelled of cheap booze and bad gums. His friends laughed.

"What's your name, girl?"

He spoke Russian. For some reason, lewd behavior seemed worse in Russian.

She didn't answer so he took a handful of hair and pulled her close. "I think she likes me, boys. What do you think?"

They agreed.

CHAPTER 11

AMELIA'S MIND RACED, HER heart tried to punch its way out of her chest. She thought of her father. He was a protective man and when she reached junior high school age and boys started showing an interest in her, he became concerned. A gentleman by nature, he, for the first time, displayed a side she had not seen.

If you ever find yourself in trouble, you need to fight.

She had never heard her physician father use the word. He was always soft spoken, kind, never harsh. A small man, she never heard him raise his voice to her or her mother. The memory poured into her brain. His voice rose from the back of her head. "There is no such thing as a fair fight. Anything outside a boxing ring is uncontrolled and there are no rules. An attacker follows no rules; neither should you."

She was too stunned to respond. He took a breath as if the conversation were causing him pain. "The best fight is a quick one. They begin it; you end it. To do that, you have to let loose the fury in you."

"The fury?"

"There is a small gland on top of the kidney. It's called the adrenal gland. Have you studied this in school yet?"

"No."

"When a person is frightened or angry the gland floods your system with epinephrine—adrenaline. It makes you stronger, more aware, and increases your heart rate. Some people call it the 'fight or flight' factor."

"Um, okay."

"When you need it, it will be there. You have to let it loose and do what needs to be done."

"What needs to be done, Dad?"

"Whatever it takes to get you out of the situation. Hurt the other person enough and they will leave you alone."

"Is this like some kinda karate thing?" The conversation made her uncomfortable.

"No, although that might be a good idea." He led her to the middle of the living room. "I'm going to show you a few things. I won't hurt you."

"Dad, really, this isn't necessary."

"It is for my peace of mind."

The lesson was nothing like what she learned in the Army, but it did get her out of a couple of scrapes in high school. She had to press for an answer but he finally relented and told her of the one time he needed to become the very thing he hated. They were living in San Diego at the time as he finished up his internship at one of the Scripps hospitals.

"A carjacking attempt." His gaze went distant. "You were just two at the time and in your car seat in the back of our sedan. Your mom was in the back with you. We stopped at a red light . . ."

She could tell the memory burned him from the inside out. They moved to the dining room table and she placed her small hand on his.

"I was tired. I had just come off a thirty-six-hour shift and all I wanted to do was get home and go to bed. If I hadn't been so tired, I might have seen the man approaching. I didn't."

"What happened?"

To her surprise, he teared up. "A man with a gun pulled open my door, put the barrel . . . put the barrel to my head and told me to get out. I . . . you were in the back . . . your mom screamed. I put the car in park and did what I was told. The image of him driving away with you and Mom." His hand began to shake. "I couldn't let that happen." He rubbed his eyes. "I still have nightmares."

"What did you do?"

"A lot of it is a blur. I do my best not to remember."

"If you don't want to talk about it—"

"You have a right to know and it will drive my point home." Deep inhalation. "He pushed me back and held the gun on me. Then he turned his attention to the car and leaned in. I think he was making sure I had left the keys in the ignition. Truth is, I don't know what he was thinking. All I know was, he leaned into the car. I could see you in the back and your mother . . . oh, the fear on her face. Something in me gave way."

"The adrenaline?"

"That was certainly there. I thought my heart was going to combust."

"You hit him?"

"I kicked the car door closed—on his head. He screamed, swore, and pulled back. He still had the gun. The guy was twice my size. I didn't think for a moment that I could wrestle the thing from him. I wouldn't know what do with it if I could. The pain made him close his eyes for a moment. I knew I had to finish this as quickly as possible."

"The best fight is a fast one."

"Right. His eyes were closed but that would only last a second then he'd shoot me without thinking. I had no doubt about that. His eyes opened and he lowered his gun hand from his head. I punched him. In the neck. On the carotid artery. I hit him as hard as I could. I got lucky. It did exactly what I hoped it would. It sent a pulse of blood to his head. He swayed and I saw his eyes roll up. That's when I grabbed the front of his shirt and pulled him away from the car and pushed him to the street. I'm ashamed to tell you what else went through my head but I ignored all that. You and Mom were my priority. I got back in the car and sped away."

"How did you know to do that? I mean, how did you know to punch him there?"

"What? You don't think your old man knows a few things?"

She remembered grinning. "No."

"You're right. You know as part of their training, doctors rotate through the various departments of the hospital. When I was working the emergency room someone brought a man in who had suffered a blow to the neck just like that. It caused a stroke."

"Is that what happened to the attacker?"

He shrugged. "I don't know. Don't want to know. Knowing won't remove the trauma." He leaned to his side and kissed her on the top of the head. "Remember what I said and let's pray you never have to use it."

It was the first time Amelia understood that, at times, violence was a necessary evil.

"PLEASE . . . please . . ." Amelia pleaded. "Don't hurt me. I'll do whatever you want. Just tell me. Please don't hurt me."

"I like a woman who cooperates," the large attacker said. His two companions laughed. "So who wants to go first?"

"Just one thing." This time there was no pleading in her voice. She had only needed the man to relax for a moment. Her father's simple lessons would not help her much in this situation but the philosophy behind did. Army training would do the rest.

As the man returned his gaze to her she drove the marker pen into his temple. The marker cap was too large and dull to pierce the skin but she delivered it with enough force to cause the skull, thinner at that point than any other place on the head, to release a satisfying crack.

He released her to seize his head. She pushed him back with just enough strength to make him backpedal three steps. She took a long step forward, raised a foot, and drove the heel of her black and white pump into the area just above his knee cap. She heard a snap. The big man screamed and reached for his leg. Before his hands had traveled half the necessary distance, Amelia threw a punch: a long, sweeping punch that carried all her weight. Her fist hit the side of the man's neck just over the carotid artery. He collapsed like an empty bag.

A hand took her shoulder, but rather than resist she moved with it, turning to face one of the other men. Fury covered his face. Amelia erased it, shoving the marker into the man's eye. His screams rolled down the alley, joining the loud groans and swearing of his big friend writhing on the alley's asphalt.

She spun to face the third man, every muscle taut, every neuron firing, her fury in high gear.

The man ran.

Amelia turned to the first attacker. "That's for Dad," she said in English.

ANYONE LOOKING AT THE living room of J. J. and Dr. Tess Rand Bartley might be easily misled. On the wide coffee table, an object twice as old as her twenty-plus years, was an odd mixture of magazines: *Foreign Policy, U.S. News and World Report, Time, Military Times, The Economist,* and *New Mommy.* There were also issues of *American Cyclist, Sports Illustrated,* and *Guns of the World.* There was a well-worn Stephen Bly Western, and a thick tome titled *The Cold War: Reagan the Early Years.* Joining the clutter was a Christian devotional book by Pastor Adam Bridger. Some might assume the news and foreign policy publications belonged to J. J. but they'd be wrong. Those were her interests, that and the *New Mommy* mag.

The apartment in Columbia, South Carolina, was close enough to Fort Jackson to suit J. J.'s needs but a nine-hour drive from her work at the War College in Carlisle Barracks, Pennsylvania. J. J. was often gone and so was she. They valued the time they had together. Fortunately, Tess only traveled to the War College a few times a month to teach a seminar or two.

She walked into the living room with a bowl of Special K in one hand, a cup of decaf coffee in the other. Having the apartment to herself allowed her to be as casual as she wished and she wished to be very casual. She set the coffee down and used the free hand to move the magazines.

She had been at Carlisle Barracks all week doing research, making the most of J. J.'s absence. Today would be different. She had a full schedule of nothing to do. She might read, or she might not; she might go to a tear-jerker movie, or perhaps not; she might nap or eat a chili dog. Having a day with no structure or plans was like a Christmas present.

She scooped a fresh load of cereal into her mouth and the phone rang. She glanced at the clock. Not quite eight o'clock. She snapped up the wireless phone. "Hewwo." Milk dripped down her chin.

"Tess?"

She swallowed. "Yes. Sorry. I was eating."

"Something healthy I hope."

Tess looked at the cereal and the coffee. "Kinda healthy."

"Kinda? Do I need to come over there and give you pregnancy lessons?"

"Too late, I'm already pregnant."

"You know what I mean."

"I do. I'm living within the guidelines the doctor gave me." She glanced at the coffee again. She had cut way back. J. J. accused her of drinking coffee like a sailor. "Mostly."

Lucy sighed. "Mostly?" Lucy Medina, a normally bubbly woman, was subdued. Having four children could do that. Tess heard two of her children squealing in the background.

"Are you okay, Lucy? You sound a little off. Kids got you down?"

"Have you seen the news?"

"No. It's my first real day off this month. I was avoiding the news." She knew where Lucy was going and reached for the remote control to turn on the fifty-inch television, a set much too large for the room but still not large enough for J. J. He wanted a television he could live in. She pushed the power button and set the cereal down. "What's up?"

"I saw it on CNN. There are riots in Kalickstan."

"Kyrgyzstan, Lucy."

"Isn't that where . . ." Lucy went into stealth mode. "Isn't that where the boys are meeting."

Tess translated the phrase in her head as she switched to the news station: *Isn't that where our husbands are and are they in danger?* She watched for a moment, sipping her coffee. "I'm not seeing . . . hang on. Here it is."

The image of rampaging crowds, fires, and battles with police filled the screen. It looked like every other televised riot except it seemed to involve more of the city, at least according to the news report.

Tess chewed her lip. "Can you get a sitter?"

"Sure. My mother is staying with us while Jose travels."

"Let's meet at Bernie's Beans. I could use some more coffee."

"Decaf, right."

"Yes, decaf."

Tess hated decaf.

BERNIE'S BEANS WAS AN independent coffeehouse owned by a former Ranger who was injured in Iraq, an injury that took his left arm. He had adjusted to the artificial arm enough to be able to whip up fancy coffee drinks faster than any other place in town. The place differed from most coffeehouses in that it had several areas where small groups could gather and chat, usually soldiers or soldiers' wives. Bernie understood the need for a place where conversations that few could understand could take place.

"You're glowing," Lucy said as she walked to an alcove table in the back. Several cushioned chairs dominated the space.

"I think I'm just shiny." Tess rose and gave Lucy a kiss on her brown cheek. How a woman with four high-octane children could look so lovely this early was beyond her.

"Nonsense. Pregnancy suits you. And twins. Wow, what a blessing."

"I don't feel blessed in the early morning. I feel like throwing up."

Lucy laughed. "I've spent my share of time staring down the toilet."

"Tell me it ends."

She sat and waved a hand dismissively. "Sure. Any day now."

"Really?"

"No."

Bernie approached. Tess had ordered an herbal tea for herself and a mocha for Lucy before she arrived. "Ladies, good to see you again." Bernie held one cup in the pinchers of his artificial arm and the mocha in the other hand. "Can I get anyone a muffin? I've got some fresh blueberry."

"Me, pick me," Tess said. "I'm hungry—again. Let's have two of those." She looked at Lucy. "You want one?"

"Just one apiece, Bernie. She's kidding about eating two."

"I am?"

"Yes, you are." Lucy sounded firm.

Tess sighed. The moment after Bernie brought the muffins on a plate, Tess shifted to face Lucy better. "Okay, what's on your mind?"

"You saw the video of the riots, right."

"I did but I don't think that affects our guys. They're there on a training mission and to meet the two new team members. They're coming home in a couple of days."

Lucy didn't looked convinced. "Jose told me there was tension in the country about the air base being there."

"He's right. It's common knowledge. It's not a new problem, Lucy. The debate about the U.S. base has been going on for years. We pay to be there. And by 'we' I mean the United States."

"But what if they send them into the riots?"

"I don't think that will happen." She sipped her tea. Good but not as satisfying as strong coffee. Pregnancy changed her tastes. She wanted almost everything she couldn't have: fish (mercury poisoning), soft cheeses, caffeine, and alcohol. The last one wasn't a problem. She had never been a drinker.

"How can you be sure?" Lucy pulled a bit of the muffin from the top.

"Sure? Well, I can't be sure, but I can tell you it is highly unlikely. Sending soldiers into Kyrgyzstan soil would be a problem. The riots are a problem for the Kyrgyzstan government. They have no reason to go in. No mandate. At some point, the United States may have to move out of the airport but that won't happen quickly.

"Could the rioters, you know, attack the base?"

"That would be an insane decision. Who in their right mind would attack an Air Force base filled with soldiers and Marines? I really don't think there's anything to worry about."

"Tess . . . I don't know how to ask this."

"Let me guess: You wonder if I'm telling you the truth. Right?"

Lucy looked into her cup. "It's not that. I mean, I wouldn't put it that way."

A twinge of guilt pinched Tess. She hadn't meant to sound accusatory. She patted Lucy's hand. She understood the emotion, the hurricane of fear raging in every wife of a special operations member. The questions came unbidden to mind and could never be silenced no matter how hard a person tried: Will he come home alive and whole, or come home in a flag-draped box? Would all his limbs be intact? Would the stress and the sights wound his mind? Would he return home with a brain full of post-traumatic stress?

Tess knew the fears and since her relationship with J. J. began, knew them to the depths of her soul. J. J. had been captured, tortured, and wounded in a gun battle. When she closed her eyes she could see the healed leg wound, looking very much like a crater on the moon. It healed but Tess knew her husband could return home with more just like it. J. J. blazed through rehab so he could rejoin the team. She never said so, but a part of her wished he had been unable to do so. The rest of her knew J. J. found his meaning in life doing just what he was doing. The Army was his dream job.

And the stress. The team was almost compromised by a team member suffering PTSD. Things worked out and Jerry Zinsser overcame the disorder but it cost him his position on the team and in the Army. Now he spent his days working for USACIC—United States Army Criminal Investigation Command. He remained a family friend.

"Lucy, you've been a special ops wife a lot longer than I have. You know there is more they can't tell us than they can. I'm in the same boat."

"I just thought . . . Never mind. It's wrong of me to ask."

"No, it's not. You have a right to know. So do I. That doesn't change anything. We are kept in the dark." Tess paused. "Look, I know I'm married to the team leader but that doesn't buy me any more information. Stacy Moyer never knew what her husband was doing when he was team leader."

"But you do have an inside track. I mean, you consult, right?"

Ah, so that was it. Tess leaned back. "True, I am a civilian consultant to several departments in the Army, but only if a mission touches on an area of my expertise, which is fairly limited." Tess was an expert on suicide bombers in general and the growing number of women and children being used as walking bombs. She consulted with Colonel Mac, head of the spec ops division to which the team belonged. She lent an intellectual hand to help the team track down a group kidnapping families and forcing women to sacrifice themselves as bombers to save the lives of their loved ones. She was also called in to advise on a mission to recover a downed U.S. spy satellite.

Tess continued. "Lucy, I can tell you I haven't been called in on this. I don't think they're on mission. J. J. told me they were doing training in Manas and picking up their new team members, nothing more."

"But the riots—"

"Are a problem for the local government, not the United States. It would not be in the Americans' interest to send armed men into the streets of Bishkek or any other Kyrgyzstani city. I know enough to know the United States wants to keep the base they have and won't do anything to endanger that."

"Nothing?" Lucy looked up as if hungering for one more bit of assurance.

"It would have to be something especially unique." She paused before saying, "Feel better?"

"Yes. I think so."

"I'm glad I could be of help."

Lucy grinned. "It wasn't you. It was the muffin."

CHAPTER 12

SARIEV DOOTKASY STOOD AT his office window and gazed to the heart of the city. He allowed himself a moment to feel like the king of his domain, although few kings would want what he was seeing. The seven-story, neoclassical, "modern-Stalinist," mid-rise office building represented an era when Kyrgyzstan was a valuable part of the Soviet Union. Dootkasy was young back in 1991 when his country declared independence from the former USSR on August 31, 1991. It, like the other fourteen members of the Soviet state, started toward the new millennium with the demise of the communist state. It should have been a glorious time.

It wasn't.

The single-party system of the old USSR was a hard taskmaster, one that kept a mud-laden boot on the neck of its many member countries. Freed, the once Kirghiz Autonomous Soviet Socialist Republic looked to a bright future, but quickly learned that golden glow over history's horizon was a mirage. Corruption remained. Poverty grew. Unemployment escalated. The economy was like an inverted pyramid resting on its point and waiting for a puff of air to send it toppling.

Such hardships rose and fell like a road through the valleys and mountains making up the country. More than once the people took up arms. The Tulip Revolution broke out in 2005. On March 24, 2005, those protests reached Bishkek, and tens of thousands of protesters congregated in front of the stately White House. Violence was unavoidable. Progovernment defenders clashed with antigovernment rioters. Police beat a number of youthful demonstrators near the front of the crowd in an effort to defend the government building and to make a lesson for the others to see.

The others did see but instead of dispersing, the crowd drew closer. Soon a number of protesters swept past and over the security teams. It took a mounted cavalry to disperse the crowd. It gave time enough for President Askar Akayev and his family to escape by helicopter and fly to neighboring Kazakhstan. From there, he flew to Moscow.

The thought of those days filled Dootkasy with a sense of pride. He knew the unseen leaders of the protests. He was one of them.

Promises were made; peace was restored—for a mere five years. The year 2010 brought more unrest, much of it centered on this building. That year the number of protesters was enough to crowd around the White House and fill Ala-Too Square a short distance away where there once stood a statue of Stalin, a spot now occupied by a statue dubbed "Freedom": *Erkindik.*

"Freedom" might occupy a significant place in Ala-Too Square but in 2010 it didn't occupy the hearts and minds of the citizens of Bishkek and other cities in the country. Dootkasy recalled it well. He was a member of the ruling minority party in the parliament and had left for the day. He left because he knew what was coming, as well he should. He planned much of it.

The police and government security stood their ground using tear gas and rubber bullets to keep the crowds away from the building but that changed when a pair of trucks rammed the front gate. Nonlethal weapons went out the window. Nearly fifty protesters were killed. Protesters overran the building, scattering government papers to the wind and setting fire to part of the building.

Hatred for the government and deteriorating economy turned to bigotry with Uzbeks and Kyrgzi clashing in the southern part of the country. Fires were set among the minority Uzbeks. Over a 100 people were killed, thousands wounded, and 75,000 people were displaced.

Dootkasy studied the city from his window, his attention fixed on the number of fires burning in the streets. Kyrgyzstan was a barrel of gunpowder and there were many people with various goals holding matches.

Things worked his way. It was his match setting things blazing again.

"Mr. Prime Minister?"

Dootkasy turned from the window to see his chief of staff Apas Isanov. "Yes, Apas, what is it?"

Apas closed the door to the large, well-appointed office. "The lights are off."

"You have always been observant, my friend." Dootkasy closed the curtains to the window. "It is not wise in such a situation as ours to stand at a well-lit window. You may turn on the lights now."

The aide did. "The people love you, sir." He carried something in his hand.

"At a distance a silhouetted figure like mine might be confused with that of someone else, say, a gunman perhaps. Besides, in any large protests there are two sides: those against something, and those who support the very thing the others hate." Thanks to the paranoia of the Soviet-era leaders, all the windows in the building were bulletproof, but Dootkasy didn't get to this level of power by being undercautious. Paranoia could be a useful ally. "You bring news?"

"Yes, sir. I—"

"The situation in the streets?"

"As expected, sir. Police are keeping the crowds at a distance for now. The military has shown itself but has not engaged the citizens. They're leaving that to the police. Security for the building is in place. Sir—"

"The complex?" Dootkasy knew what few did. A complex of tunnels and rooms existed beneath the White House—again, thanks to the Soviet need to be prepared for attack. The tunnels led to Ala-Too Square. One of several escape routes out of the building. All were improved since the 2010 revolution.

"It is as it should be: safe and secure should it be needed." Apas waited a moment before saying, "There is something you should see." He held up a thumb drive.

"What is it?"

"Best for you to see it for yourself, Mr. Prime Minister. There's been a stumble in your . . . in *the* plans." He moved to Dootkasy's desk and activated the prime minister's laptop, a computer used only by him. Apas put some distance between himself and the device, giving his boss the necessary privacy to enter his password, which he did.

Apas was one of the few men Dootkasy trusted. In the alchemy of loyalty, Apas had just the right amount of dedication, idealism, trust, and fear. Early in his life, Dootkasy learned there were many types of men in the world but two interested him most: those with money and power, and those who found fulfillment helping the first group achieve their goals. They were willing sacrificial lambs who preferred to stand in the shade of great men rather than strive for greatness themselves.

"Shall I, sir?"

Dootkasy nodded and moved to the side so Apas could insert the thumb drive in the laptop. "I've had the file encrypted." He tapped the keys, stood erect, and turned to pull the desk chair close.

Dootkasy sat and turned his attention to the screen. A woman reporter appeared on the screen. She spoke English and looked into the camera. Young, pretty, lively eyes, hair parted down the middle. In some ways, she reminded him of his first love. As he listened his eyes danced around the screen, taking in the rising columns of smoke a short distance away and the crowd of protesters a block or two away.

He then saw a familiar red car. Saw a white van. Watched an abduction attempt. At first he felt nothing, but when the silver sedan returned after speeding through the intersection, a stab of anxiety pierced his gut. When he saw the car plow into one of the gunmen and send another to the ground, his apprehension grew. When the target of the abduction jumped in the second car and the driver ran over a second gunman, Dootkasy stood. A third gunman, one with a machine gun, fired on the fleeing vehicle. One of the rounds hit the reporter in the head.

Dootkasy turned away, not from the gore but from the realization that there was now a big hole in his plan. "This was recorded in daylight. Why has it taken so long for me to learn of it?"

"The reporter, as you can see, Mr. Prime Minister, is a foreigner. The video was not broadcast over our television stations. The reporter and her cameraman were doing a live report through a satellite uplink. It was broadcast in the United States. It's only a matter of time before it makes it here."

Dootkasy put his hands behind his back, squeezing them until he felt pain. "Where is she now? Where is Jildiz?"

"On the run, Mr. Prime Minister. The third man—the one with the machine gun—attempted to chase them. He caught up with them but someone overpowered him."

Dootkasy turned. "Overpowered him? Jildiz overpowered an armed man?"

"No, sir. The person with her. Another woman. We think they're hiding in the central city."

"I want her found."

"Yes, sir. I assumed that and gave instruction. Nasirdin had already called in reinforcements."

"You've spoken with him?"

"Yes, sir. I wanted to bring you a full report."

"It's dark outside. This should have been brought to my attention sooner."

"Yes, sir. I made that clear. You were, however, meeting with the president and advisers when the event happened. Still, Nasirdin should have made contact sooner. I can only assume he was pursuing the target."

"Who is this woman who overcame a trained operative?"

"He didn't know, sir. She, um . . . They fled into a restaurant and into the kitchen. She somehow managed to trap him in a large freezer. I'm afraid I don't have many details about that part of the story."

"This is awkward. Very awkward." Dootkasy paced the room. "Finding her in the dark could be a problem, especially if she has help."

"Yes, sir. We know they're on foot."

Dootkasy thought for a moment. Scenarios streaked through his mind. "Another woman risked her life to help Jildiz?" He returned to the window as if he could see through the drawn curtains. "You don't suppose . . ."

CHAPTER 13

NASIRDIN TANAYEV WAS FURIOUS, as much with himself as with anyone. Things should have gone smoothly, easily. They didn't at all because of that woman. Who was she? Why did she have to get involved?

Nasirdin walked another deserted alley, straining to see in the dim light provided by the occasional streetlight. Darkness helped conceal his movements but it also concealed those of his prey. He had other men working the streets but the search was difficult. The stores in the area were closed, unpopulated. The women could be anywhere. His biggest fear was they made it to another vehicle, stole it, or were picked up by some person wanting to help two women in distress. If that was the case, looking for them was a waste of time.

He had another problem. The woman driver killed two of his men. That was bad, but worse was this: one was his brother.

At some point, the police would retrieve the bodies and identify them. Then they would look for family. They would come to him and questions would flow like water.

Of course, he could plead ignorance and say he stayed home to avoid the riots. His brother must have been killed by some crazy rioter driving to or from the riots. That would have worked. No doubt several would die in the riots. They did before. Yes, that would have worked had it not been for that reporter. Of all places to choose to report from, why did she have to choose that street at that time. He knew part of the answer, that's where some of the action was and reporters weren't reporters if they didn't have something to show. Bad luck. All along the way. Bad luck.

His brother lay dead because of that interfering woman, and Nasirdin had to leave his body in the street. He would find her. He would make her pay. He was the leader of one of Bishkek's largest criminal elements; he had a reputation to protect. She would pay painfully and slowly. He would see to that.

Nasirdin knew his time was running out. He transferred the Zastava M92 to his left hand, giving him a few moments to exercise his right.

"Where are you?"

He rounded a corner and saw a bit of graffiti. He took several steps past it then stopped. He had seen one like it a short distance back: a circle with an *X* in it and a number *2* written to one side. There were other marks that made no sense to him.

Could it be?

AS THEY NEARED AMELIA Lennon's disabled car, J. J. split the two-vehicle convoy, bringing Aliki's team in from the east and his men in from the west. J. J. would never say it aloud, but he was getting jumpy. They passed several large mobs of protesters. They seemed to be spreading through the city. In a few cases, they saw looting. What he didn't see were local police. Most likely they were pulled back to protect the government building. He didn't know if he should be grateful for that or not. Both vehicles stopped five meters from the vehicle. Down the side streets, J. J. caught a glimpse of a crowd.

"Stay put, gentlemen. I'm going for a little walk."

"I'll go with you, Boss." Jose reached for the door handle.

"Nope. You stay here. I don't need the company."

"But, Boss."

"Think about it, Doc. A bunch of guys all dressed in black standing around a shot-up sedan might get noticed. Let's stay invisible as long as we can." He radioed Aliki and passed the order on. The moment Aliki acknowledged the order, J. J. removed his gear and body armor, leaving behind his weapon and sidearm. His goal was to look as much like a curious pedestrian as he could.

"Keep an eye on me, Doc."

"Count on it, Boss."

J. J. shuffled past Pete in the back of the truck and exited the back doors.

The air outside was worse than inside the closed environment of the panel truck. The night seemed warmer than it should and it smelled of burning destruction. J. J. sauntered to the silver sedan, seeing bullet holes in the truck and a busted window. The front of the car had several punctures and two of the tires were flat. It was a wonder she got it this far.

He peeked through the shattered driver's side window. The dim streetlights let him see enough but not as much as he would like. He saw a spot on the seat and several on the steering wheel. He touched them. Damp.

Blood. Not much.

He looked at the ground searching for a blood trail, but didn't find one. *Light injury.* A deep or more vicious wound would have bled more and would have been impossible to not leave a trail if she were on the run, which she surely must have been.

"*Chto ty delaesh.*" The voice was large and sounded lubricated with liquor.

J. J. turned to see five men in their late twenties or early thirties standing nearby. He should have heard them. Why hadn't he? Because they didn't want to be heard. He glanced to the side and saw an open door to a nearby business. The door looked as if someone kicked it in. Just his luck, he walked by a store being looted.

A thick, well-muscled man said something else. It sounded Russian and J. J. could only recognize a word that sounded similar to "automobile."

J. J. shrugged and smiled. He didn't want to speak. He didn't know Russian or Kyrgyz. The man didn't seem to enjoy the smile. He stepped forward and drove a fist to J. J.'s jaw, knocking him back a step. The car kept him from falling. The evening darkness dimmed two more shades. The other men laughed. It was easy to be brave when it was five-to-one. J. J. spit out a glob of blood, which landed on the attacker's shoe. There was some satisfaction in that.

The man uttered angry words which J. J. took to be some kind of cursing. The powerfully built man pulled a fist back and let it fly, but this time J. J. saw it coming. He moved a half-step to the side, raised an arm to block the punch. Then delivered a punch of his own to the man's midsection which felt unexpectedly soft.

As the attacker doubled over from the blow, J. J. grabbed the back of the man's collar and drove him face-first into the car. The vehicle rocked from the impact. J. J. pulled back and up, kicking the man in the tendon just above the heel. The sudden motion and pain sent him to the pavement.

J. J. spun to face the others. Two of them had knives drawn but they were frozen in place, rooted to the ground by automatic weapons pressed to the backs of their skulls. Each soldier wore a black balaclava face mask/hood, black helmet, and wraparound goggles.

The sound of two knifes hitting the ground filled the air.

No one spoke. The barrels of the automatic weapons were placed with enough force to knock the men's heads forward.

J. J. made eye contact with Aliki and nodded to the man on the pavement. He lowered his weapon but Jose took his place one second later. Aliki towered over the man for a moment, letting his size speak for him. The man whimpered. Aliki shot a hand down and seized the man's shirt, lifting him to his feet. The man hobbled on one leg. Aliki pushed his face close to the attacker. J. J. thought he heard Aliki growl. The Samoan pushed the man back and he fell into his friend's arms. He pointed down the street. The gang got the idea. Whatever booty they had planned to take from the store they left behind, the leader hanging on to two of his pals so he could remain upright.

"You know what guys, you look kinda scary."

"That's the point, Boss. You okay?" Doc started forward but J. J. waved him off. "My wife hits harder." He moved his jaw and it sent flashes of pain into his head. "Thanks, guys."

Aliki shrugged. "Eh, we were in the neighborhood."

"Hey, Boss, did you see this?" Nagano was pointing at the hood.

"Not yet, Weps. I was kinda interrupted." J. J. moved to the front of the car.

Nagano pulled a small flashlight from his vest and shone it on the hood. "I know this."

"It's a SERE technique," Aliki said. "She's leaving us a message."

"Agreed. I read that there are two people on the move and this is the arrow that indicates the direction."

"It points behind the building, Boss." Pete had joined them. "I remember the maps showing a bunch of alleys in this section of town.

"There's another one here on the glass," Crispin said.

"Okay, our girl is playing according to her training. Now let's do our jobs. Let's see if we can get the vehicles through the alleys. If not, then we go in on foot. Mount up."

AMELIA WAITED TEN METERS from the front of the pharmacy for a full fifteen minutes. Was she followed? Was Machine Gun Mike—as she began to think of him—nearby? Or one of his men? She didn't want to lead them to Jildiz so she waited, listened, and scanned the street. She considered going to the alley behind the building, but that would require Jildiz to move boxes to clear the way for her entry. She wanted Jildiz to expend as little energy as possible. The woman might need the strength later.

Hearing only distant noises, sirens, and shouts, Amelia made for the storefront. She reached the door and finding it securely locked gave her a sense of relief. Peering inside, she saw little more than darkness. Another good thing. She tapped on the glass, first with two knocks, then five, then three. A shadow moved through the store, with slow determined steps. Amelia wanted the door opened now, but she also wanted Jildiz to be careful.

She tried to calm her breathing and slow her heart, but they did not obey. Calm would not come. Adrenaline ruled the day. The urge to shout, "It's me, Jildiz," was almost impossible to resist. She bit her lip.

A head peeked around one of the long counters near the entrance. Amelia could barely make out Jildiz's features. The woman's head swiveled and Amelia assumed she was scanning the street. *Good girl.*

Jildiz moved to the door and twisted the handle on the dead bolt. She still carried the box cutter with the blade extended.

Amelia poured into the room like water. Jildiz had the door closed before Amelia made three steps. Amelia moved to the pharmacist's desk at the back of the store and collapsed on the floor near the chair she set up for Jildiz.

"Amelia? Amelia! Are you hurt? What happened?"

Amelia rolled on her back and raised a hand. The hand shook, something that embarrassed her even though it was merely the result of the strain she had just endured. She gulped air like a fish on land. "I need a sec. Just . . . I took the long way home."

"What can I do for you?"

"Tell me you're all right, and give me a moment to regain my composure."

"I'm fine. Everything here is fine. I'm worried about you. I was afraid you wouldn't come back."

"I'm here. I won't leave you alone, Jildiz. We girls have to stick together."

Jildiz took her hand and gave it squeeze. Her grip felt good, strong. She was recovering. A few moment's later, Amelia sat up and took several deep breaths.

"Something happened, didn't it?"

"I got into a little tussle. No big thing."

"Not with the machine gun man?"

"No. I didn't see him or any of his cronies. Just some men trying to take advantage of a simple, innocent girl like me."

"You were attacked?"

"Initially. I returned the favor. All that matters is I got away and back here. I'm okay. Really. They didn't harm me in any way."

"But they meant to. Did you achieve what you set out to do?"

Amelia nodded. "I hope it works." She told Jildiz what she did. "Of course, I'm assuming the base will send someone after me. They may not. The politics with your country has grown very complicated."

"Complicated. Yes, that is a good word for it. Won't other people follow your markings?"

"They're designed to be misleading. It's like a code. You have to have the key."

"Now what?"

"Now we stay alert. I've been thinking about stealing a car and driving you to your White House but my guess is we would have trouble getting through the protesters. Worse, if we get too close to the White House, the security might take us out. I'd hate to see us killed by the good guys."

"I'd hate to see us killed by anyone."

Amelia smiled. "Humor under pressure. A good sign." She crossed her legs. Jildiz did the same. "I still think getting a car is a good thing. We could drive south, out of the city to one of the villages until we can make contact with your father. He must be missing you by now."

"Mother will be worried."

"Yeah, that's what mothers do. Do you know anyone in this part of town?"

"No. I don't have many friends. It's one of the problems of being the daughter of the president, especially in this country. Most of my friends and extended family are in Osh. That's a long way from here."

"And if I remember my Kyrgyzstan history, a place just as volatile as Bishkek. I wouldn't doubt they have some protests going on there."

"If we leave the area and your people send a team for you, won't we be running from help?"

"Yes, but that's how it works, Jildiz. Survive first, evade next, resist when possible, escape if captured. If things settle down, then we might be able to wait here. Perhaps the owners will open up again."

"Not if the protests continue. In 2010, the rebellion closed many businesses."

"Okay, for the moment then, we rest."

The sound of falling teacups came from the back door.

CHAPTER 14

"I'LL SAY ONE THING for the guy, he can take a punch." Aliki turned his vehicle north beginning a spiral search pattern for their missing FAO.

"You got that right, Joker." Nagano moved to the front seat. "A shot like that would have floored Binky here."

Crispin rolled his eyes. He sat near the opening between the driver/passenger area and the cargo area of the van. The vehicle rocked and swayed, and he was glad he didn't suffer from motion sickness. "Binky? Really? Binky?"

Crispin hated being the new guy. Technically, he wasn't the new guy on the team any longer. When he first heard about incoming replacements he felt a moment of exhilaration. Someone else would be the target of the verbal pokes and jabs. Then he learned that both men outranked and had more years of experience. Technically, Aliki outranked J. J. When all was said and done, Crispin, while longer on the team, was still the runt of the litter. That meant he would be the target of choice for a long time.

Nagano turned. "What? Binky is a fine name. Goes back to the days of kings in England."

"You're lying to me, aren't you, Weps?"

"Aye, laddie." The faux Irish accent coming from an Asian face made the situation more surreal. Nagano cranked his head around and continued searching the streets and back alleys. "See, Joker, the kid ain't half as dumb as everyone says."

"What?" The big man leaned a little closer to Nagano and tilted his head.

"I said, you drive beautifully."

"I do everything beautifully." The assistant team leader addressed Crispin: "Tell me about Boss, kid. I ain't had time to get to know him. Is he a good leader?"

"Yes. I've been on one major mission with him and a few outings."

Aliki looked at Nagano, to which Mike replied, "He said yes, but not as good as you."

"Suck up."

The van rattled, the engine hummed, but Crispin was sure he spoke loud enough to be heard. After all, Nagano heard him. An unsettled thought percolated in Crispin.

They slowed as they reached another intersection, and turned east. J. J.'s team would make the opposite turn the next street up. Together they would create a grid search pattern. J. J. made it clear it was unlikely they would see Amelia and the president's daughter. The FAO was too smart and too well trained for that. Perhaps if they were in Humvees instead of an old van and panel truck, things would be different. At least they would be recognizable. Being recognizable would not be a good thing in this situation. While not as experienced as the others on the team, Crispin was an experienced soldier and one of the brightest—even if that was his own assessment.

The problem as he saw it was this: People who didn't want to be seen were searching for people who didn't want to be seen. To make things worse, all they had to go on were cryptic symbols left on the hood of a car. That's what they were searching for now: more symbols. All they had to do was find symbols written in black marker and do it at night.

That last fact is what prompted J. J. to stay on the main streets first. Streetlights made the search for markings a degree or two easier.

"So you've seen Boss in battle?" Aliki spoke loudly, keeping his gaze scanning the road and buildings to his left. Nagano's eyes traced the buildings to the right. With no windows in the cargo department, Crispin could only stare out the windshield.

"Yes."

"He any good?"

Crispin didn't like the questions, especially on mission. "He proved himself to me, although that wasn't the issue. I was busy proving myself to our team leader."

"Eric Moyer?"

"That's right. A good man. A better soldier."

Aliki nodded. "I've heard of him. Got a good rep. Who was the second?"

Crispin had a feeling the man was testing him; that he already knew the answers. "Rich Harbison. Big bruiser like you."

"What happened to him?"

"Lost an eye on the last mission. Very nearly lost his life. Same for Moyer. Things fell to J. J. after that."

"What mission was that?"

"The last one we did. You'll have to talk to Boss if you want more details. Are you testing me?"

Aliki tipped his head.

Crispin raised his voice. "I said, are you testing me?"

"I heard you." He shrugged. "Maybe."

Crispin decided to be bolder than he felt. "Here's what I can tell you, Joker. Boss is a great guy. Smart and dedicated. A tad religious but never pushy. He knows what he's doing. He was our sniper and explosives man. The guy's hand never shakes. It's spooky."

"Religious?"

"Yeah, he's a Christian."

Nagano turned. "A Bible thumper?"

"I wouldn't call him that, but I've seen him reading the Bible many times. He was the heart of our team. You know, Moyer was the backbone; Harbison was the muscle. J. J. was the heart. His brother is an Army chaplain."

The conversation died.

"What?"

"Nothing." Aliki continued, swiveling his head.

"If you're wondering if his faith keeps him from pulling the trigger when he needs to, I can put your mind to rest. He's not one of those guys who lives to put bad guys in the crosshairs but he does his job." He paused. "Without hesitation."

"How far now?" Nagano asked.

"We've gone five miles north. I don't think she would have run this far. Most likely she and the other chick are hunkered down."

A voice crackled over the radio. "Move to pattern two." Crispin recognized J. J.'s voice. "Roger that."

The message went into the ears of every team member, so Crispin felt no urge to tell Aliki what he already knew. The big man turned the wheel and entered the first alley he saw.

The alleys were narrower than the streets but wide enough for easy passage. Trash cans, Dumpsters, and empty cardboard boxes lined the wall of the empty businesses. Crispin pitied the trash truck driver who had to negotiate the area.

NASIRDIN FOUND RASUL DJAPAROV talking to a small group of men. Rasul was in his twenties, narrow from head to foot, with coal-colored hair atop a sadistic mind. He served in the army but was discharged against his will. Too many of the other soldiers feared him. It was in the army that Nasirdin first made his acquaintance and the man did not frighten him. Of course, Nasirdin never felt fear, even when, as a child, his drunken father beat him with a wood dowel. Emotion, he learned very early, was counterproductive. It was best not to feel fear, or love. Day by day, he learned to strip away those unnecessary things.

Nasirdin slowed his trot as he approached, sizing up the situation. Rasul held a handgun at his side. He smiled as if sharing a joke with the men. Nasirdin made eye contact with his man. Rasul motioned him to come over.

"My friends, this is the comrade I spoke to you about. He is a man of the people. You can trust him."

Nasirdin noticed Rasul used no names. He nodded at the men, all of whom noticed the machine gun in his hand. Nasirdin grinned. "It is a violent night, my friends. A man must be careful." They nodded.

"We were just discussing that. These patriots have a strange story to tell. Please, tell us again what happened."

One man stood on one leg, leaning against one of his cohorts. "We were attacked by men with guns."

"This night?"

"Yes," the man said. "One of them attacked me. He beat me for no reason."

"Tell me of these men. How many?"

"At least ten or twelve."

That didn't sound right. "Please, accuracy is very important to me this night. I can tell you are all brave men, solid stock. It is my honor to know you, but I need facts. Did they number ten or twelve?"

"No," one of the other men said. "I saw only five or six."

"It must be six," another said. "There are five of us and they pointed guns at each of our heads. Of course, there was the one that attacked you."

"Yes, yes, of course," the injured man said. "As you can see, I've taken a blow to the head. My math has left me." He chuckled but it sounded insincere.

"How were the men dressed?"

"Black. Black uniforms and they had masks on their faces. Well, except the one we caught by the car."

"What car?"

"A few blocks down. There is a car with flat tires and bullet holes sitting in the street. The man without the mask was looking inside."

Nasirdin exchanged glances with Rasul. "The silver sedan I saw down the road and a few blocks south of here?"

"Yes, it was silver." The injured man shifted his weight on his one good foot.

Nasirdin studied the hobbled man. "What did he do to you, friend?"

"We were just offering our help when he turned on me. As you can see from my face, he came at me hard. He also broke something in my foot."

"We should get some medical care for you." Nasirdin was certain the alcohol he smelled on the man's breath was all that was keeping him from screaming like a school girl. "But first, tell me about the uniforms. You say they were black. Where they all dressed the same?"

"Yes."

"Black military uniforms."

"Oh yes, definitely military. They had vests on and helmets. At least the ones with guns did."

"But no markings?"

"No markings. Did anyone see markings?"

They shook their heads and said no.

"The guns then, what about them?"

"Military guns," Injured Man said. "The automatic kind."

Nasirdin rested a hand on the man's shoulder. "Tell me, did they speak?"

"No. Not a word. Well, one growled like a dog."

"Anglo? Asian? Slovic?"

"We only saw the one man's face but he was as white as any of us here."

"I see. May I ask what you were doing when you saw these men?"

A long pause greeted the question. "We were just going out for drinks."

"You know there are riots going on, correct?"

The man looked away.

Rasul spoke. "I believe they found a liquor store with a broken window. I believe they were making certain no one was stealing an honest storekeeper's wares."

"Yes. That's exactly what we were doing."

Nasirdin forced the corners of his mouth up. "I believe you. Excuse me for a moment." He stepped to the other side of the street, changed the channel on his radio, and made a call. A few moments later, he returned.

"Are we in trouble?" one of the men asked.

"No, of course not. You were doing what any good citizen would do, but I must ask one last favor."

ON THE PROMISE OF payment, the men led Nasirdin and Rasul back to the car. Nasirdin didn't need guides. He knew exactly where the car was. He needed something else. They moved slower than Nasirdin wanted but the wounded man set the pace.

"There, there it is."

"Very good. Show me where you were when the men attacked you." Nasirdin watched as they stepped close to the vehicle. They turned as if they were posing for a picture.

It was then, Nasirdin thumbed off the safety, leveled the weapon, and pulled the trigger. The men didn't have time to scream. Nasirdin wanted to conserve ammunition so he did a single sweep of the barrel, bullets striking the men in the chest. He looked at Rasul who seemed unconcerned about the massacre. "Make sure they're dead."

Rasul stepped forward, his MP-446 handgun in hand, and put a 9mm round in each of their heads, then walked back to Nasirdin as if he had done nothing more than pull a few weeds from a neglected garden.

"Burn the bodies and the car. Make sure they're unrecognizable. I want it to look like the gas tank exploded. Can you do that?"

"I can. Where are you going?"

"To a pharmacy store."

AMELIA KEPT JILDIZ MOVING as fast as she could. There had been no time to grab the respirator mask she took from the hardware store. A half mile down the road, she saw Jildiz reach for her inhaler. She couldn't blame the woman. Her own lungs burned from the stench of smoke.

The sound of distant, but not distant enough, gunfire rolled through the polluted air.

CHAPTER 15

SARIEV DOOTKASY LET THE chief administrative assistant announce his presence. The middle-aged, dowdy woman hesitated only a moment. Dootkasy had not called ahead. The phones were out, but the intercom system wasn't dependent on an outside line. His unexpected appearance surprised her.

"I know President Oskonbaeva is very busy, but I need to see him immediately."

"Yes, Mr. Prime Minister, but he is occupied with a meeting right now. The riots have—"

"I am well aware of the riots." He kept his voice calm when what he wanted to do was slap the toady. "This pertains to that and a . . . personal matter."

She hesitated a moment then reached for the button on the business phone to activate the intercom. She paused, then retracted the hand. "One moment, Mr. Prime Minister." She rose and moved to the closed door separating her office from the president's.

"Mr. President, please excuse the interruption, but the prime minister insists on seeing—"

Dootkasy's patience snapped and he pushed past the aide and into Meklis's office, stopping the woman midsentence.

"I need a moment, Mr. President."

"Sariev, what is the meaning of this?"

Dootkasy loathed Meklis Oskonbaeva all the more for calling him by his first name instead of his title, especially with the others present, Chief of Police Emil Abirov and Boris Gubuz, head of Internal Security. Dootkasy was in the first meeting with these men and a few others; apparently he wasn't wanted in this one.

"I need a moment, Mr. President."

"I'm busy right now, Sariev." He motioned at the others. "As you can see."

The president and prime minister roles were a point of friction. The president appointed the prime minister, something which made previous prime ministers little more than lapdogs. Dootkasy made a lousy lapdog. The men never liked each other and were political rivals over the past ten years. Dootkasy wasted no energy fooling himself into believing that he was chosen because of his leadership expertise but because of his influence with opposition parties. Meklis pledged an open government bent on healing rifts and ending corruption. He failed on both counts, but to his credit, not for lack of trying.

"Yes, Mr. President, I am aware of that but I have news you need to hear."

"News? What kind of news?"

"Privacy is required, Mr. President."

Meklis shook his head. "We have our hands full right now, Sariev. Can't it wait?"

"Sir, if it could wait, I wouldn't be here." He grew weary of the word play. He turned to Gubuz and Abirov. "Gentlemen, may we have the room?"

The vermin looked to Meklis for permission. He nodded, and the men rose.

Dootkasy draped his words in a tone of concern. "Please stay close, gentlemen. The president may have need of you in a moment."

The men excused themselves and the administrative aide closed the door to the office, leaving the two most powerful men in Kyrgyzstan alone. The office. Twice the size of Dootkasy's but, in his mind, filled with half the power.

"Sariev, this had better be good." Meklis did not offer his PM a seat.

"I'm sorry to say there is nothing good about this."

"News about the riots?"

"In a sense, but more pressing." Dootkasy pointed at the president's desktop computer. "May I, sir?"

Meklis narrowed his eyes but rose from his large executive chair, giving Dootkasy access to the device.

"I received this moments ago. It should have come to you first, but I haven't had time to find out why it didn't." He inserted the flash drive into the USB port. "This is the only record of the event I know of although it was broadcast live." He brought up the video but waited to hit play. "You may want to sit down for this, Mr. President."

The impact of the statement showed on Meklis's face. He did as Dootkasy said, lowering himself into the chair.

Dootkasy tapped the return key and the video began to play.

The female reporter.

The sporty red car.

The sudden appearance of a white van.

The abduction attempt.

The silver sedan rescuing Jildiz.

The gunfire. The wayward bullet fired by a man with a machine gun.

The blood and brains spatter of the reporter hitting the camera lens.

Meklis crossed himself, something Dootkasy couldn't recall the man doing before.

The video ended and Dootkasy removed the video from the computer monitor. He left the flash drive in the computer for the moment.

"Look at me, Mr. President."

Meklis didn't move. Time for a more personal approach. "Meklis, my friend, look at me."

The president raised his head. His skin was pale, his eyes wet, his body resembled a rag doll. "How . . . I mean . . . is she . . . dead?"

"No, sir. At least I don't think so. I've been able to determine that your daughter and whoever helped her get away, I don't know if . . ." He pretended to falter. "This is difficult. I don't know if there are injuries. May I ask when you last heard from her?"

"Early afternoon. She was meeting with someone. We had tea before she left."

"Forgive me for asking, but I am trying to help. With whom did she meet?"

"The woman from the United States. The military foreign affairs officer. Lennon. Amelia Lennon."

Dootkasy spoke softly. "This may be important, Mr. President. Who asked for the meeting?"

"I don't know. Why would that be important?"

"Sir, I will admit to being a little more suspicious than most. It is my Russian background. I am my father's son and he had difficulty trusting anyone." He drew a breath as if the next words took work to expel. "I wonder if the Americans are behind this."

"The Americans? Certainly not. They need us."

"But they are on the verge of losing rights to the Manas Airport. With the resurgence of al Qaeda in Afghanistan, they need the base all the more. Although they have been drawing down troops in Afghanistan and Iraq, they are still mired in their wars. With Iran feeding arms to Iraqi dissidents, hostilities are sure to break out again and you did say you were leaning toward revoking the Americans' lease."

"That's . . . um . . . that's why Jildiz was meeting with the American. They have developed a friendship and she wanted to personally tell her of my inclinations. She felt she owed the woman a face-to-face talk. Something without lawyers and diplomats."

None of this was news to Dootkasy but he needed to keep up the appearance. "The driver who came to her rescue, could that be the American negotiator?"

Meklis shook his head. "I don't know. All I saw was the car. I couldn't make out the driver."

"I understand, but I had to ask." Dootkasy raised a finger to his chin.

"We have to find her. I need Emil and Boris in here." He stood.

"Just a minute, Mr. President."

"We don't have minutes, Sariev. My little girl is in danger."

"I understand, and I want you to know I have people working on it. Right now. I set things in motion the moment I received this."

"You? I should be the one—"

"No, Mr. President, you shouldn't." He put a hand on Meklis's shoulder, gently pushing him back to the chair. "Listen to me for a moment, then you can do as you see fit."

"Make it fast."

"There are many questions. This looks planned to me. Somehow, someone knew the road your daughter would be taking." *Easy enough with the right spies and lookouts.* "Why do that? What do they have to gain? Why do this in the middle of riots?"

"Do you have answers?"

"Not yet, Mr. President. If she has been abducted, then someone will contact you. Maybe for a ransom. Who knows? Perhaps to force you to make a political concession. Maybe for some other reason. There are a dozen groups who hate your administration—" *A mistake.* "I should say, *the* administration. I don't need to tell you how common this is in our history. I can tell by your surprise at this video that no one has contacted you."

"True."

"If they have her, they will. If they don't, then she's somewhere on the streets, alone."

"Not alone. Someone came to her aid."

"Perhaps, Mr. President. Assuming the Good Samaritan isn't part of the plan—a diversion to buy time."

"I see."

"There is more." He started to speak, pretending to search for just the right words. "Mr. President, I am normally a man good with words, but I'm not sure how to phrase this. May I speak plainly for a moment?"

"Yes."

"You are now compromised and compromised at the worst time." Dootkasy moved to a chair, sat, and leaned forward to rest his elbows on his knees. "If you allocate police to find your daughter—which is my first inclination—you will be seen as putting her needs above the other citizens endangered by the violence in the streets. The same is true if you send soldiers to search for her. If we lose this building again, as we nearly did in 2010, then you will be blamed for valuing your daughter over country."

"What father wouldn't?"

"Not every father is the leader of a country in crisis."

"What do you suggest?"

"I would not suggest this under any other circumstance, Mr. President. I have not had time to think this through, so I make this statement only as a suggestion to consider. When I leave, I will send in Gubuz and Abirov. Consult with them. Call in the leader of your party and discuss this with him if you wish. There may be details I'm overlooking."

"The point, Mr. Prime Minister?"

"Let me take the lead on this. I already have men headed to the scene. They are good men. People I served with when I was an officer in our army. This way, you can keep police and soldiers protecting government buildings and other key areas. We've already lost phones and cell service. If this riot is as well organized as it seems, then we can expect to lose power too. Think of the problems that would create. The police and soldiers must be used to protect these installations and government buildings."

He leaned back in the chair. "Now the words I don't want to say. If your daughter is or has been abducted, then you will be . . . compromised. Any state decision you make will be suspect."

"Your suggestion?"

"And at this point, that is all it is, Mr. President." He sighed. "You may wish to consider transferring state power to me until your daughter is safely home."

"You cannot be serious." Meklis's face flushed.

"Please understand, Mr. President. I am not thinking of myself. This goes beyond our past political squabbles. This is your family. By transferring power to me you will be taking the advantage away from the abductors." He rose. "You will need some time to think about this. Please know I am here for you. I will inform you as soon as I hear from my men in the field." He moved to the door. "One more thing, Mr. President. If the person in the silver sedan was indeed the American negotiator, then she is either part of the plot or a victim. If she is a victim, the U.S. military will send people after her."

"They have been told they cannot interfere in our civil matters. That is part of our agreement."

"Yes, sir, of course. But remember, this is not a civil matter to them. This Lennon woman is probably CIA or military. In either case, people are going to go searching for her."

"If they know about the problem."

"Sir, we know. And if we know, we can bet they know."

Dootkasy walked from the office he felt was rightly his.

IT WAS AMELIA'S WORST fear. She did her best to block the rear door, the one she took a sledgehammer to, but she couldn't disguise the damage. Her hope was that anyone passing might blame the rioters for the destruction, but as yet, the mobs hadn't reached this area. On the one hand that was good; on the other it meant the busted door here and the broken window in the hardware store opposite the alley might raise the attention of the guy searching for them.

When the teacups hit the floor and the boxes began to scrape along the storage room floor, Jildiz gasped. Amelia clamped a hand over her mouth, harder than she intended, then immediately relaxed her grip. She put her mouth by Jildiz's ear. "No noise. Calm. Focus. Do as I say."

Jildiz nodded and Amelia lowered her hand and gently pulled Jildiz from the chair. The woman shook but kept silent. Keeping her head low, she led Jildiz back into the drug prep room where the pharmacist bottled his pills for clients, the same area where she found the rescue inhaler for Jildiz.

"Stay low. Stay here." Amelia's statement was barely audible. She made sure Jildiz had the box cutter.

"What are you going to do?"

"I have no idea." Amelia scooted along the floor, rounded the counter, and moved into the consumer area of the store, scanning the shelves for an idea, anything that could be used as a weapon. She grabbed a plastic bottle and a can of something she thought might be baby formula but didn't take time to read the label.

She continued her rapid search. She had only moments. The person or persons at the back door would make a cautious entry. That would give her only a few, precious moments. First on the agenda: lead them away from Jildiz's position. Her eyes scanned the shelves but there was so little light now. She strained her memory, trying to recall what she saw earlier.

She heard footsteps. Slow. She heard breathing. Low. Masculine. Her heart revved. Hands shook. *Calm. Focused. Wait. Advantage rests with the one hiding. Wait. Wait.*

An item on one of the shelves caught her eye: small, plastic, toy-like flashlights, the kind a child might like, or a woman might keep in her purse. They rested in a display box. The flashlights were not wrapped and probably wouldn't cost more than a buck back home. It was too light to be a weapon but she had another idea.

She positioned herself at the end of one of the shelving units closest to the front door, and stayed low as she unlocked the front door, hoping that she could hold off the intruder long enough for Jildiz to sprint to safety—if there was such a thing.

Raising her head, she peered over the counter and spied two large dark forms. Two men. Her heart sank. She had been lucky with the group of young men in the alley. There was no doubt these guys were bigger and badder, and probably trained. Most days, Amelia was glad to be a girl. At the moment, she wished she were larger and stronger. Wishing wouldn't get the job done.

Amelia switched on the small flashlight, letting its beam paint the floor, and inched back. She unscrewed the metal cap from the plastic bottle and waited. Seconds passed like eons.

She heard one of the men snap his fingers and assumed he saw the light. Crouching, she listened to the approaching footsteps. If they were trained men, then one would follow the other, or come around the back side. She hoped for the former.

The footfalls stopped. She guessed the man was just around the corner of the shelf unit. He'd be armed. He'd be tall. He'd be on edge.

She leaped up, screaming like a banshee. A tall, thick-necked man jumped and his eyes widened, which made them better targets. Amelia squeezed the plastic bottle and a thick stream of rubbing alcohol covered the man's face and filled his eyes.

He screamed and brought a hand to his face.

Amelia stepped closer.

She kicked hard. She kicked low.

The man doubled over. She took the can in both hands, raised it high, and brought it down on the base of the man's skull. He teetered for a moment then crashed face-first to the floor. The fact he did nothing to break his fall told Amelia the man was unconscious the moment the can cracked his brain pan.

One.

Her head snapped back; pain blazed through her scalp. In the two seconds it took to dispatch the first man, the second came from behind and seized her hair, lifted and pulled hard, snapping her head back. More pain ran down her neck. Muscles threatened to separate from sinew. She reached for the hand, tried to turn, but it was all too late. Before she could think she was being pulled back. A second later she slammed into the glass storefront. The large panel of tempered glass rattled against its jambs. The impact forced the air from her lungs.

He pressed his body to her back, pinning her to the glass. "Where is she?" Kyrgyz. Voice rough; anger filled.

She didn't answer. The man pulled her head back then slammed it into the glass again. She had no power to stop him. *Run, Jildiz. The back. Out the back. Run.* She tried to will her commands to her friend in the back of the pharmacy.

The man swore at her and put his face next to hers. She cut her eyes to see him. He was dark, unshaven. He grinned, revealing holes where teeth should have been. His breath smelled like fish left on a hot, sun-drenched dock. He pulled back and replaced his face with the barrel of handgun.

She heard the hammer *click*. The bullet was three inches from her temple and just a few ounces of trigger pull from being on its way.

He started the question again but never finished. Amelia heard a hallow thud, like a ripe cantaloupe hitting the floor. The man with the bad teeth was no longer behind her. Something was pressing at her heels.

She spun.

At her feet rested the limp form of a gorilla-sized man. Standing next to him was the trembling form of Jildiz holding a fire extinguisher. "I-I thought this might be more effective."

"Wow." Amelia looked at the red fire extinguisher. She couldn't be certain but she thought she saw a dent in the cylinder. A thin stream of blood trickled from the man's nose.

"Did I kill him?"

Amelia looked into the man's lifeless eyes. "Of course not." She took the man's handgun and searched his body for an additional clip. Sure enough, he had one. She didn't recognize the weapon but it reminded her of an old Baretta 92.

A sound erupted from the first man she attacked. A squawk. A bit of static. He had a radio.

Amelia relieved him of it.

CHAPTER 16

MEKLIS ASKED THE LAST adviser to leave his office to close the door behind him. The moment the man did, Meklis brought his hands to his face and rubbed his burning eyes. When he first became president, when he and his wife first walked into the wide expanse of his office, he felt power, joy, and a sense that he could make a difference in his beleaguered country. He came to the position with his eyes wide open. He held no illusions that everyone would love him; that the populace would rise in unison and bless his name. He was in his early sixties, far too old to be so delusional.

Since his days at university he was a student of world politics. Few were the number of leaders who could maintain a satisfaction rating over 60 percent. Most were overjoyed if half of their citizenry agreed with the administration. When he first took office, his approval rating was near 80 percent. Now it hovered near the 40 percentile. He achieved the first number by promising economic reform, more jobs, better education, lower inflation, and better health care. He could have stolen speeches from the British prime minister or the American president, changed the language and context, and no one would know the difference.

He saw a difference—felt a difference. He was not political by nature. He preferred the calm and quiet of a university library to the shouts and cheers of a political rally. He entered politics a decade and a half before at the urging of friends and family. "You can make a difference. You can bring our country into the twenty-first century."

He listened and, against his instinct, chose to believe their words. To be sure, he tried to make things better and made some progress, but progress cost money. Lots of money. Kyrgyzstan had so little of it. Government money came from only three sources: taxes, bonds, and loans from countries like Russia and China. China was rolling in cash and bought the majority of Kyrgyzstan's bonds, just has they had with many countries including the United States. China, in Meklis's mind, was conquering the world one loan and real estate purchase at a time. Russia lacked the wealth of China, but they provided loans for road and school improvement. None of that was cheap. Since the 1920s, the country had been a vassal of Russia. That ended in 1991. Now they were becoming an economic slave to China.

By the end of his first year as president, Meklis felt like a man swimming the Baltic while shackled with handcuffs and leg irons. He could make a little distance but the waters would swallow him soon enough.

Still he tried. He brought conflicting parties together, going so far as to appoint Sariev Dootkasy as prime minister. It drew the two largest parties together but gave Dootkasy more power in the legislature than Meklis was comfortable with. That was the trade-off. He didn't like the man. What was the American poker phrase? "The man has an ace up his sleeve." It didn't take long before Meklis learned to believe half of what the man said. Aces. Dozens of aces up his sleeve.

Meklis lowered his hands and stared at the seating area where he often sipped tea and met with members of the government. It seemed so empty; so unimportant. Once he felt a sense of power, but the riots in the streets—not just in Bishkek but in three other cities—and the news about his missing daughter made him feel as helpless as a newborn.

When Dootkasy suggested Meklis abdicate—no, kings abdicated and he was no king. When Dootkasy suggested Meklis *resign*, he saw it as a power play, a way of taking advantage of a series of horrible situations, but the more he thought about it the more it made sense.

Within minutes of Dootkasy's departure, Meklis called his head of internal security and the chief of police for Bishkek back into his office. He also summoned a few other advisers. The moment they sat, he blurted the news.

"They've taken my daughter."

There was a moment of silence then a chorus of "Who?"

"I don't know." Every word spoken seemed to bring the hot tears and icy fear to the surface. "We have video." He told them of Dootkasy's visit and then showed the video. It was greeted with gasps and curses.

Emil Abirov was the first to get down to business. "When did this happen?"

"I don't know."

"I'll find out. We can contact the reporter's news organization. There are other ways to track the time. I know the street. I'll send men in to search for her right now."

"Do you have men available?" Meklis studied the man.

"I'll pull some off crowd control. I can also pull some away from government buildings—"

"No."

"Excuse me, Mr. President?" The police chief looked confused.

Meklis rubbed his forehead. His skin felt hot; his soul cold. "The Prime Minister is correct. I can't allow that. If others are hurt because my daughter has taken precedence . . ."

"Has there been contact?" Boris Gubuz was the calmest man in the room, but his face seemed to have aged a decade in the last few minutes.

"No, Boris. We think she's on the run with the one who rescued her. The car in the video was found a few blocks away from the incident."

"Who found the car?" Gubuz asked.

"Some people the prime minister knows."

Gubuz looked to the side as if deciding where to spit. "Did the prime minister have a suggestion?"

Meklis gave an agonizing nod. "He thinks I should transfer power to him until Jildiz is rescued or . . ." He swallowed hard. ". . . until the matter is resolved."

"I am not surprised." Gubuz was never a fan of the prime minister. Over the last year he tried to resign his position because of the man. Meklis called upon his loyalty to encourage him to stay. The president held no hope of keeping him after the next election.

"I'm afraid he has a point." General Nurbeck Saparaliev spoke softly, sounding more clergyman than leader of soldiers.

"What are you saying, General?" Gubuz looked stunned.

The general stroked one of his bushy eyebrows, something he did before delivering an unpopular opinion. "Mr. Secretary, you have children. Correct?"

Gubuz stiffened. "You know I do. You do too."

"Yes, three, all adults now. They are my greatest joy and fear." He looked at the floor as if seeing his next few words in the carpet. "I have trained myself to create and evaluate situations I might face as a military general. I've created scenarios ranging from an attack from eight different countries, to a military coup. Since the uprising in 2010, I've been preparing for another riot. It is one reason we were able to secure Ala-Too Square so quickly."

"So, God forbid, we have to evacuate key personnel from the White House." Meklis spoke what everyone already knew.

"Yes, sir. My point is this: the one scenario I've struggled with the most is the abduction of one of my children. I can send men in dangerous situations without hesitation but . . . my children . . . my grandchildren." He turned to Gubuz. "If it was one of your children abducted, what would you do?"

"Find them."

"How?"

"I would find a way."

Saparaliev looked away again. "I've said those very words, Mr. Secretary, but I've seen too much to leave it at that. The question isn't finding, but finding them alive and unharmed. Could you do your job knowing your next decision could set up a chain of events that might lead to great harm to your child?"

Gubuz set his jaw but spoke softly. "I am not insensitive, General, but the well-being of our nation supersedes personal loss."

"Brave words, Secretary Gubuz. Could you utter them again if three or four fingers of your child arrived in a box?"

Gubuz blanched.

Saparaliev seemed to shrink a size. "I've wondered what I would do. We don't know who the abductors are but if they are religious extremists or Russian mobsters or . . ." He took a breath. "We are an ethically mixed country. We are religiously mixed as well. Sometimes those stresses turn violent. Extreme Islamics have been known to cut the nose off women caught in adultery. Imagine getting that mailed to you." He looked at Meklis. The word and gaze made him shudder.

"That is uncalled for, General!" Gubuz shouted.

Saparaliev didn't respond.

"No, it's not, Mr. Secretary," Meklis said. "He is being frank, painful as it is to hear."

"I take no pleasure in it, my president, but I am of no use to you if I am not honest. Forgive me."

"There is nothing to forgive, friend." Meklis gazed at the drape-clad windows. Outside, police, building security, and military prepared to meet an advancing mob. "You said you thought about what you would do should someone kidnap one of your children. What decision did you reach?"

For the first time since meeting the man a decade ago, Meklis saw tears in his eyes. Saparaliev was a career soldier, the son of a career soldier, the grandson of a decorated career soldier. He once said the general was made of granite with molten steel for blood.

He never saw him blush, hesitate, or lose his temper. He certainly never saw the man weep.

In the moment it took Saparaliev to answer, the general straightened his back, stiffened his neck, and narrowed his eyes. "I would resign the moment I confirmed the abduction. I would do so, sir, to keep myself from doing something I shouldn't."

"You're not suggesting the president would compromise his position—"

"Yes. I'm suggesting that everyone in this room would do the same. The only solution for me would be to pass my responsibility on to the next highest officer."

Gubuz shot to his feet and began to pace. "I can't believe I'm hearing this. We can't pass the country to the prime minister. I do not trust him. He received the position as a compromise."

"I am a military man, I am not allowed to have such opinions."

"It doesn't matter why I appointed Sariev to the position, he has it now." Thoughts ricocheted in Meklis's mind. After a moment of swatting at them like a man swatting at a swarm of gnats, he said, "There is something else. The prime minster believes the person who helped Jildiz is Amelia Lennon, the diplomat negotiating the American side of the Manas Air Base. They were having a late lunch. If that is true, then the Americans may have sent a team to recover her."

"How would they even know?" Gubuz raised a hand. "Never mind. They would know the same way we know." He returned to his seat. "They would not do that, Mr. President. They have no right to send military forces onto our soil without our permission."

"Yes, they would," the general said.

"You can't be sure."

"It is what I would do, Mr. Secretary."

Gubuz's face turned red. "That's a violation, a breach of our agreement. If word of this gets out the antigovernment proponents will have an even bigger reason to riot." He ran a hand through his hair.

The phone/intercom on Meklis's desk sounded. He rose from the sofa, left the conversation area, and walked to his desk. He answered, listened, then said, "Thank you." Retrieving a remote control from desk, he turned on a small flat-screen television mounted to the wall a few feet to the left of his desk. "Gentlemen." He waved them over.

The television was set to the local news station. On the screen a male reporter stood a few meters in front of a burning car. Meklis could see several bodies on the asphalt, each ablaze.

". . . repeating, the vehicle behind us is believed to belong to the American military. We have reports that the bodies belong to soldiers posing as citizens. The cause of the fire is unknown as is the reason for American soldiers being in this part of the city . . ."

"God help us all," Gubuz said.

A moment later the car's fuel tank burst, sending orange and yellow flame crawling into the sky.

NASIRDIN TANAYEV WAS TWO blocks away from his destination when his radio crackled. "Three to One." It was Rasul.

"Go One."

"Done. Proceeding to next location."

"Understood. One out."

Rasul was on his way to the pharmacy, his arson job finished. Rasul was Nasirdin's most faithful operative. They served together as mercenaries in several conflicts. He never questioned orders; never hesitated. He did as he was told without debate. He was also vicious, unhindered by a conscience and thrived on dirty work. He was the kind of man rogue generals and dictators needed to fulfill plans of domination. Rasul had no such plans, he just enjoyed what others found reprehensible. In that, he and Nasirdin were brothers. Rasul was more ruthless; Nasirdin more intelligent. Both were fine with the distinction.

Nasirdin raised the radio to his mouth again. "Six, report."

Nothing.

"Six, this is One. Report." Still nothing. "Five, this is One. Report." More nothing. Concern mingled with anger. As Nasirdin neared the back door of the pharmacy, he set his Zastava M92 to full automatic and made certain the thirty-round magazine was properly fitted. It wasn't like his men not to respond but fate had turned against him. What should have been a simple grab-and-go kidnapping turned to ashes in moments. The one thing certain in the life of a mercenary was uncertainty. Sometimes it seemed the simpler the mission the more could go wrong. Even the devil stubbed his toe now and again.

He moved down the dark alley until he found the damaged door his men reported. Across the alley was the broken window. This was the place.

The rear door was partially open like a narrow opening to a cave. He had no fear of the women, but he did have concern that one of his thick-headed men who couldn't answer a simple radio call might mistake him for a soldier or police officer and shoot before thinking. If so, he wanted to be ready to put a bullet in the middle of their chests before they could do the same to him.

Leading with the M92, Nasirdin entered the small pharmacy.

Just inside the door he saw a few shelves and a pile of boxes. A storage room. He kept the barrel up. Was there someone else in here? Had the women found help? A dozen scenarios raced through his brain, most of which ended with gunfire.

He steadied his pulse and did his best to peer through the dim room. Although not shrouded in complete blackness, the place was dark enough to make quick movement inadvisable.

He paused and listened and heard nothing. No whimpering. No sobbing. No talking. Nothing.

Slowly, Nasirdin reached to his radio and tapped the talk button twice. He heard two quiet pulses from the shopping area of the pharmacy. No one responded. Nasirdin eased into the area and saw several aisles, and a long counter. Someone could be hiding behind any one of them.

Where were his men? Their last communication said they had found the women, but nothing since then. Light from a streetlamp pushed through the glass storefront. A small light washed the floor at the end of one of the counters.

Something else was on the floor. Two large, dark shapes. Nasirdin moved forward slowly, his ears straining for any sound, his gaze scampering around the room. He saw a large form on the floor, then a similar one a short distance away. The front door was ajar.

He didn't approach the forms on the floor. He knew what they were. First he searched the store and found it empty. Only then did he return to the front of the store where his men lay unmoving. He picked up the tiny, plastic flashlight and tried to piece together what may have happened. He couldn't be certain but it didn't matter. His prey was gone, after besting two of his men.

He shone the light on the first form. The man stared back through unblinking eyes. Next to him was a fire extinguisher. He examined the device and saw bits of scalp and hair—hair that matched his man. He moved to the other man. He was curled in a near-fetal position. A large, damaged can of baby formula rested near his head. Blood dripped from his nose and ears. He, too, was dead.

Nasirdin swore in two languages, then spun on his heel, and kicked the first dead man in the ribs again and again until he heard bones snapping. "Fools! Imbeciles! He turned to the other man and stomped his head, then swore some more.

He walked away and calmed himself. How long had it been since they first announced they found the busted door? How long did it take him to deal with the men found by Rasul? He then added the time it took him to travel by foot to this spot. Twenty to thirty minutes. They had as much as a half-hour lead.

He snatched his radio. "One to Three. Come up the street side."

"Street side. Understood."

"Run."

"Running."

Ten minutes later a sweating Rasul arrived and listened as Nasirdin explained the situation. As usual, Rasul showed no emotion. He walked through the store then studied the men. "They did all this?"

"Some of it. They killed them. I may have contributed after the fact."

Rasul nodded. "Understandable." He returned to the front door. "Where was the light?"

"On the floor. At the end of this counter."

Rasul tilted his head as he studied the situation. He walked around the bodies, and bathed the light on the floor. "Blood smears."

"They left them both bleeding."

Rasul shook his head. "This is near the spot where you found the light. One of them is still bleeding."

"Not enough."

"Well, we will have to see she bleeds some more." Rasul looked Nasirdin in the eyes. He was one of the few men who dared to do so. "We have another problem. One of the radios is missing. So is his Grach."

Nasirdin grew angry with himself. He should have thought to check that. Each of his men carried a tactical radio. "Grach" referred to a Russian Yarygin PYa MP-443 pistol. This meant the women were now armed with a 9mm pistol carrying seventeen rounds in the magazine. They also had a radio.

He chewed the information. "They can't call for help on the radio. We have the frequency locked down. But they can monitor our transmissions." He paused. "Maybe that's not so bad."

"HOW ARE YOU DOING?" Amelia pulled Jildiz down another alley searching for a new place to hide. What she really wanted to do was make it into one of the mobs. She knew enough of the country's history to know the last major riot had protesters marching on the White House, the center of government. That's just where Amelia wanted to take Jildiz, but getting there wasn't going to be easy. So far, she was able to avoid splinter groups of rioters, although she had that run-in with a small group of men. She was lucky to get away. That was the problem with men, they never expected the woman to fight back like a warrior.

But the plan was hampered by gunmen chasing them and Jildiz's asthma made worse by tension, fear, and smoke-filled air. Her ability to run was extremely limited. Jildiz couldn't run because she couldn't breathe.

Jildiz took another hit of the rescue inhaler, leaned against a dirty wall, and tried to draw even breaths. She pulled the front of her blouse up to her nose, trying to filter the air.

"Tell me you can't overdose on that stuff, Jildiz." Truth was, Amelia needed a break as well.

"No chance. It's safe."

She looked at the woman. "You're lying to me, aren't you."

"I didn't know I was that transparent." She used the inhaler.

"What should I know? About an overdose I mean."

"You have enough to worry about."

"Tell me, girl."

"You know, you get pushy when gunmen chase you. You should get help with that."

Amelia tried to look firm, put out. The expression lasted only a moment. She laughed, more from tension and exhaustion than from the humor in Jildiz's statement. "I need help with many things. More than I care to mention. Now answer my question."

"The medication is albuterol based. Too much leads to chest pain, high blood pressure, heart palpitations. Occasionally death." She pushed away from the wall. "The same symptoms as being chased by killers."

CHAPTER 17

NORMALLY, COLONEL DANNY WEIDMAN would be comfy in his bed but there would be no sleeping tonight. He had no problem assigning duties to his leadership staff. He did it all the time. It was what good leaders did: bring up better leaders. Conditions, however, demanded his attention.

He was Army born and bred. He started life at Fort Bliss, born to an Army cook father and high school teacher mother. Years later he had graduated in the middle of his class at West Point and wished he had graduated higher. Still, twenty-two years of applied work in the Army made him a full bird colonel. Not bad. Still he held no illusions that a brigadier general star was in his future. He had hopes of retirement in the next two years. He wished he could retire this minute.

"Ready, sir." The aide activated the conference screen. The face of Colonel MacGregor appeared.

"Thank you, Corporal. I'll take it from here. I'll call if I need anything."

"Yes, sir." The corporal left the room.

"They look younger every year, Danny." MacGregor looked like he was trying to conjure up a smile but the corners of his mouth were too heavy.

"You got that, Mac. The kid's a whiz with electronics."

"Aren't they all? I'm starting to feel like a dinosaur."

"Yeah, I know the feeling." Weidman bit his lip.

"Just say it, Danny. It won't taste any better but you'll be done with it." Colonel Mac leaned closer to the camera.

Weidman pulled his shoulders back. "Local media is saying the bodies of American soldiers have been found burning along with a car. They had video."

"Confirmation?"

"No. I would have to send in another team and I have it on good authority the bodies are being removed."

"Good authority?"

"The prime minister called after the news aired the story. He expressed his sorrow and the regrets of his nation but snuck in a jab about American military running rampant through the streets of Bishkek. I started to offer a demonstration of what his city would look like if we were running rampant." Weidman took a moment to swallow. Mac was right, bad news tasted bad. "He described the bodies as being men wearing balaclavas, helmets, dressed in black, and carrying American weapons."

The video connect conveyed Mac's pained expression. He didn't jerk, didn't react, but an ocean width and half a continent of distance couldn't hide the emotional agony. Mac's only physical response was an increase in his blink rate. "Did you confirm it was an Army team?"

"No. Of course not. I denied the whole thing." He pressed his lips together. "There's more. Apparently, the prime minister raised Cain with the embassy and they called the president. I'm under orders not to allow any other teams onto the streets."

"That doesn't sound like Huffington," Mac said. "He's always been on our side. He owes us. We saved his skin and that of his wife, not to mention the leaders at a G-20 meeting in Europe. This isn't right."

"Not by a long shot, Mac. I know it; you know it; but our hands are tied. I've had to shut down flights over the country. We're focusing on work-arounds, but no matter what direction I send up a craft, it will fly over Kyrgyzstan dirt. I am effectively grounded. Which is just as well. I'm putting troops to work protecting the perimeter of the base and the aircraft. I don't think it will come to this, but we may have to defend our assets. We're not real popular with the locals. It's always been tense, but this last year has been worse."

"You said it was the prime minister who contacted you? Not the president? That's a bit odd, isn't it?"

Weidman shook his head. "Sorry, Mac, but no. President Oskonbaeva has his hands full. He has riots in at least three cities, it appears several mobs are moving in on the government building, and someone tried to kidnap his daughter. He has the PM doing a lot of the communication work."

Mac tilted his head back and looked up. Weidman wondered what he saw on the ceiling. "I know the answer but I have to ask." He looked back into the camera. "Radio contact?"

"No. The team is using hand radios, no man-pack. They're line of sight mostly and we're too far away from the Bishkek to get a decent signal. If we were allowed to fly over the city, I could get a chopper within range in minutes."

Mac rubbed his face hard. Weidman thought the spec ops commander would peel the skin from his skull. "The Army has trained me for many things. I thought Ranger training was the worst thing a man could endure, but I was wrong. This is. I've had to deliver bad news before, but these boys—these men—they were like sons." He stared at the table in front of him. "J. J. has . . . he's got twins on the way. Jose has enough kids to start his own school." He paused then began to swear in an unrelenting stream of obscenities. Weidman let him rant. He had a right to. Sometimes cursing was all a soldier could do.

When Mac slowed the obscenities and curses, Weidman said, "Mac, I'm sorry. I wish it wasn't true. I'll be here if you need me."

"Thanks, Danny."

A moment later, Weidman moved on to the next thing he didn't want to say. "Mac, this stuff is going out over local media. That means CNN or some other news agency is going to get wind of it, if they haven't already. I wouldn't doubt the PM will make sure the world news agencies get wind of this. It's to his advantage. He would love for us to pack up and leave tonight." Another pause. "Mac, you gotta tell the families before the news does. It might already be too late, but you gotta try."

"I need confirmation, Danny. We don't have proof."

Weidman spoke softly. "Mac, we are two of the few people in the world who know we had special operators on the streets. We have to assume the dead men in the street are our boys. It's your call, but if it were me, I'd tell them now rather than let the media do it for me. I don't know your team well, but they seemed like good guys. Their families deserve to hear from the Army first."

Mac rubbed his chin. "I want you to do something for me."

"Name it."

"You won't like it."

"That's not a requirement, Mac. You know that."

"I do. I want you to pull a team together. Make it a good one. I don't care if they're Rangers or Marines or Air Force spec ops. Just get me a team."

"I'm under presidential orders not to send in another team."

"I didn't ask you to send them in, just pull it together. I'll talk to the president."

"And if he doesn't want to see you?"

Mac interlaced his fingers on the desk surface. "He'll see me."

MASTER SERGEANT ALAN KINKAID sat to the side of the desk watching his boss hear the worst news a commander could. Mac looked to his longtime aide. The man hadn't done field work in years but his body was still hard has a granite boulder. He knew for a fact the man worked out two hours a day. As much as that impressed Mac, Kinkaid's mind was more impressive. He was a skilled administrator and had almost a sixth sense about things. Quiet, unassuming, Kinkaid was the only one who could keep Mac grounded.

"We're going to DC, Sergeant. Make it happen."

"Yes, sir. When would you like to leave?"

"Ten minutes ago. Get us on the president's docket."

"That might be difficult, sir. He's bound to know you'll want to speak to him."

Mac rose and fixed a hot gaze on Kinkaid. "Master Sergeant, make this happen. I don't care whose fingers you have to shoot off to bring it about. Clear?"

Kinkaid stood. "Crystal clear, sir."

Mac started to leave the communication room in the Concrete Palace situated at Fort Jackson. "I'm going to go to my office and try to figure out a few things, like how I'm going to tell Tess and the others about this."

"Sir? Something isn't right here."

"You can say that again."

"No, sir. I mean, yes, sir, but I mean something doesn't track."

"What?"

Kinkaid shrugged. "I don't know, sir. I feel like I'm missing something. I just don't know what."

"You can figure it out on our way to DC. Now get hopping, soldier. I'm not feeling patient."

"And if the president won't see us?"

"Then I will stand in the middle of the public area of the White House and refuse to leave until he does or he orders someone to strip the eagles off my collar."

"BINGO," J. J. SAID. "Back us up, Junior."

Pete slowed, then threw the vehicle in reverse. "Whatcha got?"

"I'll tell you when to stop."

"Got it, Boss." Pete focused on the side mirrors, moving backward slowly.

"Stop. There, that door has been compromised. There's her mark. Lower right of the door." He keyed his radio and passed the news to Aliki and the others. He ordered them to the street side of the building and told them to hold their position. "We're going in." He pulled his knit mask over his face, flicked off the safety on his M4A1. He trained extensively with the weapon but was used to carting the longer, heavier M110 Semi-Automatic Sniper System. That was when he was the team sniper. As Boss, he was required to lead his team into the close-quarters works. Mike Nagano was the guy with the big gun now.

"Ready?" J. J. asked Pete and Jose.

"Hooah," they whispered.

"Let's rock."

J. J. exited the vehicle with Pete and Jose on his heels. He dropped his night vision goggles in place and took careful steps. He approached the half-open door. Pete and Jose were just a few feet behind him forming a tight line.

Aliki's voice came over his ear set. "Boss, Joker. Front door looks unlocked."

"Roger that. Stand by."

Taking a deep breath, J. J. plunged in, the barrel of his M4 leading the way.

"CHECK HIM FOR ID." J. J. felt a moment of disappointment. He was certain he had found the women. That certainty evaporated the moment he found the two bodies on the floor and the open front door.

The team swept the building in moments and found evidence the women had been there: open packages, boxes piled by the back door, and two male corpses.

"Man, I hope this woman isn't married," Aliki said.

"She'd be one tough date." Mike Nagano stooped and patted the men down. Jose used his tactical light to illuminate the corpses. "No wallets. Civilian clothing. I bet they didn't see her coming."

"They've underestimated her," J. J. said. "I'm starting to wonder if we are too."

"How so?" Pete stood near the store front, scanning the street for activity.

"I don't know, Junior. She stays a step ahead of us."

"She has to, Boss. She and her friend are running from clowns like this." Jose examined the bodies. "Both have taken blows to the head. The guy closest to the door had the side of his caved in. My guess is someone took the fire extinguisher to him. This guy," he pointed at the smaller of the two men, "took a head pounding too. I'm just spit-balling here, but I think he took a blow to the back of the head, just above the Atlas vertebrae. The blow may have snapped his neck."

"What's that on the floor, Doc?" Aliki stepped closer.

"Baby formula, dude. Trust me, I know the smell. It's from that can. One of them killed the guy with a can of baby formula. That's gotta be a first."

"She's innovative, I'll give her that," Junior said. "What now, Boss?"

"We carry on. We know that there is another team looking for them. We saw Lennon mow down two men with her car, now two more here, so it's more than one guy. Mobsters? Mercenaries? Islamic extremists?" He rubbed the back of his neck. "There is more we don't know than what we do. I don't much like that." He looked around the pharmacy one more time. "Doc, how long have they been dead?"

"I can't be sure, Boss. I'm no coroner." He removed one of his black gloves and touched the dead man's face and hands. "He's cool but still has some warmth. His skin is still pink so the blood hasn't settled. They haven't been dead long."

"So our ladies can't be very far."

"I don't know, Boss," Aliki said. "After seeing what this woman can do, I wouldn't be surprised if she sprouted a cape and flew off."

"I've noticed something else." Jose moved to the area behind the pharmacist's counter, bent behind the divider, and then stood again, setting several items on the counter. J. J. and Aliki moved to the counter. The others kept watch by the rear and front doors. Jose shone his light on the objects.

Aliki spoke first. "What's that junk?"

J. J. took the largest of the objects. "A painter's mask?"

"Yep, well, a mask used to filter particulate matter from the air. My dad is big into woodworking. He wears one of these when he does heavy-duty sanding." He picked up a box. "Asthma rescue inhaler. I found two of these boxes. Both empty."

"One of them is an asthmatic?" J. J. thought for a moment.

"Yes, and throw in stress, physical exertion, and all that stinky air out there, it's a wonder the woman can move at all."

"So, Lennon broke into here to get meds for the president's daughter."

"And broke into the hardware shop to get the mask."

"Yep," Aliki said. "A woman like that just has to be saved."

"And we're the guys to do it. Mount up."

CHAPTER 18

COLONEL MAC AND SERGEANT Alan Kinkaid were escorted to the Oval Office, something former Chief of Staff Helen Brown did on previous visits but since becoming vice president, that job fell to someone else. In this case, Mona Willard, the president's private secretary, did the honors.

Mac stood as straight as a rifle barrel, his blue dress uniform perfectly fitted to his frame. Mac considered himself lucky because the president was in DC instead of in some other corner of the earth; and because he agreed to an unscheduled meeting, something normally requiring at least two stars and a key position in the Joint Chiefs of Staff to pull off. But he and Ted Huffington had history. Not many months earlier, the president ordered Mac to send his best team to Siberia to recover or destroy a fallen spy satellite. Before that, the same team was tasked with finding the leader behind a series of female suicide bombers. In the course of that mission, the team saved the lives of the president and his wife. They also saved the lives of twenty key leaders of some of the world's most powerful countries. He was sure that was the only reason he was able to elbow his way into this meeting.

"The president has been expecting you." Mona was a pleasant, unflappable, middle-aged woman.

"It was good of him to see us on such short notice." Mac walked with purpose, his cap tucked under his arm.

"He wondered what took you so long."

He turned to look at her. "So long?"

"He told me to expect your call any minute."

"Really? Interesting." Mac looked at Kinkaid. "And here I thought you were some sort of genius."

"Even geniuses get lucky sometimes, sir."

"Let's hope it holds."

Mona led them to her office and opened the door to the adjoining Oval Office and stepped aside. She closed the door behind Mac and Kinkaid.

President Ted Huffington sat behind his desk. He was on the phone but waved them in. He motioned to the seating area at the center of the room. Sofas and white leather chairs were situated around a blue carpet with the presidential seal woven into its center. They stood, waiting for the president to finish his phone call.

"Just give it some thought, Mr. Speaker. Once, just once, let's present a unified budget effort to the public." He listened. "Mr. Speaker, the public is weary of both of us. This is my last term. After that, I'm going to write books and make a fortune on the speaking circuit. You, on the other hand, still have years of opportunity before you. Let's be unique. Let's be bold and get a workable budget on time." He listened some more. "I know you have to talk to your party leaders. I expect that, but . . . Let me be frank: Instead of asking for permission, take the bull by the horns and tell them what's going to happen. Be the dog, not the tail."

He rolled his eyes. "Thank you, Mr. Speaker. My best to your lovely wife." He hung up then rose from his chair. "And to think I wanted this job."

When Huffington stood, Mac and Kinkaid came to attention.

"As you were, gentlemen. Please, sit."

The president lowered himself into one of the padded chairs. He looked a half-decade older than the last time Mac was in this room. The world continued to be a troubled place; the country continued to teeter on economic collapse; and party infighting was never more intense. One thing Mac enjoyed about the Army was its structure. Orders were given; orders were followed. In politics there were no orders, just ideas and desires batted back and forth like a tennis ball. Mac had no patience for it.

"Thank you for seeing me so quickly, Mr. President."

"I knew you'd come. I owe you a meeting." His eyes softened. "I-I was sorry to hear about the lost team. Colonel Weidman tells me it was J. J.'s team."

"Yes, sir. We have two issues. First the FAO Amelia Lennon is still missing and we need to recover her. Second . . ." He closed his eyes for a moment. "Second, I want the bodies of my team back."

"I can't send another team, Mac. Technically, they should not have been there in the first place."

"With all due respect, sir, there are many missions where we went where we were not welcome."

"I'm well aware of that, Mac. I called for a few of those, but every situation is different."

"I understand that, sir, but every mission has one thing in common: they're conducted by brave men who love this country more than their own lives."

Huffington closed his eyes for a moment and Mac realized two things: one, he had crossed the line; two, he didn't care.

The president opened flint-like eyes. His jaw had tightened. He spoke softly. "Mac, I admire you, I respect you, and I consider you an important adviser. I like to think you and I are friends, at least as much as our positions allow, but I want to advise you against playing the patriotism card with me."

"Sir—"

"I'm not finished." Those words had more heat. "It took me a long time to decide to run for president. It seems like forever ago but I never gave a second thought to the hatred I would face, the lies, the political backbiting, the media misrepresentation of my policies, or the fact I might one day be assassinated. Water off a duck's back. What did give me pause was the idea of me sitting behind that desk over there giving the go-ahead to a suicide mission. For weeks I wondered if I had the spine for it. It turns out I do. I find no pleasure in it, and yes, it has kept me up at night. That doesn't matter, no one takes this job unless they can send men to their deaths. You know what that's like, Mac. You've had to do it." Huffington brushed an imaginary piece of lint from his dark trousers. "Do you know the difference between our work, Colonel?"

"I believe so."

"The way I see it, you focus on a mission. Well, in your role as head of spec ops, you focus on several missions. Your objective is success in the field. You get in and get out, hopefully safe and sound. You don't have to be concerned with the long-ranging ramifications. I do. I have to deal with the other heads of state. My decisions and responsibilities don't end with a mission. They continue and the ramifications can resonate for years to come. I'm dealing with problems left over from a president two administrations back."

"I know your job is difficult, sir, and I have no desire to make it worse, but we need to finish the mission and get the bodies of our men back."

"You will not send another team in, Mac. Nor will the SEALS nor any other spec ops group."

"Sir, these are men you know—"

Huffington shot to his feet. "That is enough, Colonel. Do you think a part of me didn't die with J. J. and the others? He and Tess were married right out there." He pointed out a window to the Rose Garden. "I was at the wedding, remember? J. J. and the others rescued the son of my former VP. Don't think for a moment I've forgotten that. I know every one of their missions in detail. I care about those men. I care about their families, and yes, I believe this country owes them. I would ask for their bodies back but that would mean admitting that we were running a military operation in a country considered an ally, one that provides a strategic base of operations."

"I do understand the importance of Manas, sir. I've been there many times."

"But what you're forgetting, Mac, is that the base is needed for more than what we're using it for now. Sure, we need it to stage the delivery of men and equipment to Afghanistan, but that's not all. Our presence in that country is winding down but you know as well as I that terrorist activity is on the rise. It was what killed the team members of the men now in J. J.'s unit. Again, info you already have in pocket. What you may not realize is that we need that base for problems on the horizon."

Huffington returned to the sofa and sat. "Pakistan grows more distant. Too many American drone attacks on their soil. It's their fault for letting terrorists set up camp there, but nonetheless, we may have a problem with Pakistan in the near future. That's just one problem. Throw in unrest in the Baltic nations, unsettled peoples in several other Central Asian countries, and then you'll see why it is so important for us to keep Manas open. The Russians want it. The Chinese want it and have offered a huge chunk of change to have us evicted so they can move in. We don't need that."

The president continued. "Kyrgyzstan is a troubled, impoverished nation with an unemployment rate that makes ours look infinitesimal. It is a key country in the region, important to Russia and China. Most of the population hates us. Yet, I doubt one in fifty people on an American street could find the place on a map. I doubt half of Congress could find it. It's hard to get additional funding for operations in a country most people don't know exists."

"Yes, sir." Mac had much more to say, but he knew a brick wall when he ran face-first into one. "The FAO?"

"Captain Amelia Lennon." The president said the name as if making sure Mac understood how much he knew about the happenings. "Her service jacket is exemplary. A good soldier. A good diplomatic asset." He took a breath. "I've been led to believe that local law enforcement is conducting a search for her and the president's daughter."

"Do you believe that, Mr. President?"

Huffington didn't answer straightaway. Then, "No. The government has too much on its hands at the moment."

"Do you know who killed our team?" Mac pressed the words through clenched teeth.

"Not yet, but when I find out . . ." Huffington crossed his legs as if relaxing in front of a Washington Nationals televised game, but the posture could not hide the tension in his body. "Last year, when your men were in eastern Siberia, I was an inch and a half away from sending a Navy cruise missile to destroy that satellite—the satellite your men found. It would have killed them all." He looked at the carpet. "I still get chills thinking about it. Still, I would have done it had the team failed." He looked into Mac's eyes. "I would have sacrificed them for the mission and carried on." He lowered his voice. "Mac, I wish I could do what you asked, but I can't."

The president stood, indicating the meeting had ended. Mac and Kinkaid stood.

"Mr. President, if I may." It was the first words Kinkaid had uttered since shaking hands with his commander in chief. "I have a favor to ask."

Mac looked at his aide. Normally the man was a mute in such meetings unless called upon to speak.

Huffington raised an eyebrow. "Say it."

"The news video showing the bodies of our team. Something doesn't fit."

"Like what?"

"I don't know, sir. This is one of those 'gut' things. Could you get someone to analyze the video? The Army has some specialists, but I'm thinking a police agency."

"You're thinking the FBI?"

"They're the best at analyzing video of crimes; we're better at analyzing battle scenes."

The president's eyes narrowed. "And you want me to do this on a hunch?"

"Yes, sir, I do."

"You good with this, Mac?"

"Yes, sir. Master Sergeant Kinkaid's hunches are better than most men's logic."

"I'll see to it."

MAC STARED OUT THE window of the Cessna UC-35A corporate jet as it knifed through the air. The low roar of the engines normally relaxed him, but this trip the sound was a major annoyance. His mind tumbled like a shoe in a clothes dryer, bounding from the meeting with the president, to an unnamed street in Bishkek, to the horrible, soul-shredding work ahead of him.

The president had a point but that didn't mean Mac had to like it. The president had bigger issues, but Mac refused to look past the loss of six good men and the people they left behind. On the other side of the jet sat Kinkaid, his hands folded in his lap, his head forward, his eyes closed.

"Sleeping, Sergeant?"

Kinkaid's eyes snapped open. "No, sir."

"It looks like it."

"Prayer sometimes looks that way."

Mac felt a moment of remorse for his comment. Kinkaid had been Mac's aide for several years and he knew the man went to church on occasion but that was it. Just recently, he learned the man was more committed than Mac knew.

"Maybe you should have prayed before the team was killed." The comment was harsh, but Mac's patience was gone. Maybe he had been "in this man's Army" too long. Maybe he was getting too old. He progressed through the ranks and served in his share of special operations. Being on mission was, in some ways, easier than sending operators into danger. He would rather lead a team than conduct operations from a desk, but he was too long in the tooth to keep up with the young guys. He was the fittest and youngest fifty-something man he knew, but keeping up with guys in their mid-twenties was just this side of impossible. "Sorry."

"No need to apologize, sir. For the record, I did pray for them before the mission. I pray for all the teams."

"Yet the team is dead. And J. J. was a dyed-in-the-wool Christian. Does God not know where Bishkek is?"

"He knows, sir."

"Then why . . . never mind. I'm just looking to vent."

Kinkaid chuckled. "That's what I was just doing, sir. Venting."

"You said you were praying."

"I did, and I meant it. I had a few things I wanted to say to God. Not that He didn't already know how I feel about things."

"Does it do any good?"

"I think so. A man can't keep things from God, so I figure it's best to be honest."

"You Christians amaze me. You see so much bad in the world yet you still think there's a good God."

Kinkaid gave no sign of offense. "We also see a lot of good."

"Such as?"

"Men willing to sacrifice themselves in an effort to help others. Sacrifice is the heart of Christianity. Jesus was the ultimate sacrifice, all the apostles sacrificed their lives—all but one was martyred. The early church was persecuted. The streets of Rome were lined with Christians on crosses. I have no expectation that my faith will keep me from trouble."

"Then why have it at all?"

"To strengthen me in trouble. Faith helps me soldier on."

Mac looked away. "So you're not bothered by the loss of the team."

"Bothered? Yes, sir. I'm heartbroken. I'm furious. I feel helpless. Faith changes none of that. It just changes me."

"If you say so." A few moments passed in silence. "I don't want to be misunderstood, Sergeant. I have great admiration for you. I could not do what I do without you."

"It's my honor, sir."

"Ha! I doubt that. Some people think you should receive a Purple Heart just for working with me."

"For what?"

"Psychological wounds, I suppose."

Kinkaid grinned. "I'm not that fragile, sir. I'm afraid you're stuck with me."

"And you're stuck with me, for now."

"Sir?"

"Never mind." He decided to change the subject. "Asking the president for a favor after I ruffled his feathers took some nerve."

"That was the best time to ask, sir. I figured he needed something to give us, a sign of conciliation."

"Maybe." Mac wasn't feeling conciliatory yet. "What makes you think something is amiss with the video?"

"I wish I knew, sir. I . . . When I left high school, I was drifting. Wasn't sure what I wanted to do with my life. I took a few classes at the community college. I took architectural drafting in high school and liked it okay, so I took a college-level class. Landed a part-time job at a firm that specialized in residential subdivisions. It was a grunt job but I got to do a little drafting. The architect was old school, did all his drawing the old-fashioned way with pencils instead of computers. Good training for me really. Anyway, I was trying to figure out a roof—"

"Figure out a roof? You mean where to put it?"

"No, sir. I'm pretty sure the roof goes on top." He smiled. "A lot of people don't realize that drawing roof plans on a house that has odd angles and the like can be tough. When you draw a set of working drawings, you're taking three-dimensional thoughts and putting them on a two dimensional surface—the paper. Not everyone can do it. I sure had a problem with it. Anyway, I thought I had it all figured out when one of the project managers walked by and looked over my shoulder. 'Wrong,' he said. I disagreed. I was sure I had it right. Again, he told me it was wrong, but when I asked him to show me my mistake, he just shrugged. 'Beats me.' He walked away."

"So the guy was just yankin' your chain."

"No, sir. He was right. I messed up. It took me another hour, but I found my mistake. The roof could never have been built the way I drew it. When I asked him how he knew, he shrugged again. He was big on shrugging. He said, 'You do this long enough and sometimes you just know.' He said it was a subconscious thing. A man can recognize that something is wrong without knowing what it is."

"Instinct."

"I suppose. I feel the same way about the video. There's something wrong but I can't identify it. Maybe the FBI can coax out a clue, something to help us identify the killers."

Mac let that sink in for a moment. Such knowledge would be good, but it wouldn't bring the team back. "How long until we land?"

Kinkaid looked at his watch. "I figure fifteen minutes tops. Is there something you want me to do?"

"Yes, I want you to make a couple of calls. Get Chaplain Bartley to the office. Give me enough time to change into my daily uniform. I'll start with him."

"Perhaps we should have another chaplain there, sir."

"Good idea. See if his commander is available. Set it up for his office. Neither man is clear to enter the Concrete Palace."

"Yes, sir. May I attend?"

"Yeah, I'm gonna need you." What he didn't say was, *I don't want to do this alone.*

CHAPTER 19

RASUL DIDN'T HAVE MUCH use for other people. Most were annoyances at best, enemies at worse. A flame of admiration did flicker for one man: his boss Nasirdin Tanayev. He was vicious and smart, two qualities Rasul admired. That opinion dimmed when Nasirdin ordered him to stay behind and watch the pharmacy instead of helping him find the women. Sure, other men were called in, but he wanted to find the women. Killing men was fun, but killing women, well that was dessert.

Directly across the street was a shoe store. He slipped to the back alley, found an access ladder, and worked his way up to the flat roof. He found a spot near the front parapet that concealed him but allowed him a view of the street below. Nasirdin's logic was simple enough. "We know there's a team of soldiers out there. They will be better armed than we are. Sooner or later they will find what we did. Stop them if you can."

He was right. A panel truck pulled down the street and stopped a short distance away, out of sight from the pharmacy front window. Three men exited and took positions. Men in black. Helmets, weapons. They moved like a trained squad.

They didn't enter the building. They just waited. Three targets waiting for a sniper, but Rasul didn't have a rifle, just a handgun. He might be able to take them down, but one miss and those left standing would open with automatic weapons fire. That would be bad. He needed to be patient and smart like Nasirdin.

Something else bothered him. The three weren't making entrance. That made him think other soldiers were coming in the back. That's how he'd do it. The men, the ones he left burning in the street, said there were six men. That had to be it. Three in the front; three in the back. That also meant there might be another vehicle. Easier to search the streets.

Rasul forced himself to be patient, a Herculean task but being outmanned and outgunned helped. Moments passed slowly, then the intruders walked in the front door. Body language said the others had checked and cleared the interior. Rasul had an idea. He scampered from the roof and to the alley. He then eased to the street and, keeping the truck between him and the pharmacy window, moved to the driver's side of the vehicle. He stayed low. It wouldn't do to be seen while he had no place to run. If that happened, he decided he would empty his weapon before they put him down.

Rasul pulled a large, military-style folding knife from his belt, opened it, and studied the tire. His first plan had been to send the blade into the sidewall but he feared the sound might attract attention. He thought for another moment, then put the blade at the base of the fill stem. The knife cut through it easily. He cupped his hand over the air stream, muting what little noise it made. He repeated the process on the driver's side rear tire, then scrambled back across the street and to the alley. He jogged south two blocks, crossed the street and moved north again. Just as he expected there was another vehicle in the alley behind the pharmacy.

He approached slowly, keeping his eyes on the broken door. He kept his 9mm level at the door. If one of the men came out, he could down him and flee. He spent a moment wondering if he could surprise them and take down all six men without getting killed. He doubted it. He focused on the tires.

AMELIA AND JILDIZ MADE it another half mile before Jildiz needed to rest again. They stayed in the alleys. The streets were too well lit and cars could move freely along their paths. While vehicles could navigate the alleys, they had less room to do so. Amelia used the time to study the radio she took off the body of one of the attackers. It was commercial grade and bore the mark of a Chinese maker: TYT.

"Clever. It's programmable."

"Can you program it to call for help?" Jildiz was wheezing again. Amelia waited for her to pull out the inhaler but she didn't, no doubt conserving what she had.

"It's password protected." She felt the glimmer of hope fade. She tried to put a positive spin on things. "At least we can listen to them."

"I haven't heard anything."

She was afraid Jildiz noticed that. The radio had been silent except for the one transmission: *Pereklyuchatel*—"switch" in Russian. She assumed her pursuers had predetermined frequencies to use should a radio fall into the wrong hands.

If they made a switch in frequency, then it meant they knew a radio was missing, and that means they found the pharmacy, and that meant they found the bodies, one of which she knew was dead. Maybe both. She hadn't taken time to check pulses.

"How are you doing?"

Jildiz looked up. "Orangey."

"Orangey . . . peachy?"

"I pride myself on American slang. I guess I'm not at my best."

"I think you're remarkable, girl. You put me to shame."

Jildiz bent forward, resting her hands on her knees, drawing breath. Each inhalation came with pain. She winced. "I'm slowing you down. You should go on and leave me."

"Yeah, like that's going to happen."

Jildiz straightened. "I am being serious. I'm growing weaker. Breathing is more difficult. It's me they want. I don't think they know who you are."

Jildiz's spirit of self-sacrifice raised tears in Amelia's eyes. Gently, she touched Jildiz's chin and turned her face toward her. "I'm not leaving you. The only way they get to you is through me. Besides, I'm expecting a big payoff."

"Payoff. You want money?"

"Nope, I was thinking of a great big bronze statue of me in Ala-Too Square. You know, my beauty captured in well-crafted bronze. A toga. That's it. I'll be wearing a flowing toga and pointing to the sky with one hand and holding a hair dryer in the other."

"Toga? Hair dryer? Amelia, you are a very strange woman."

"What? I think it would be an inspiration to your citizens."

Jildiz smiled. It was one of the best things Amelia ever saw. Humor kept courage up. She looked around. "I lost my marker. I don't know. Maybe that's a good thing." She put marks on the back door of the pharmacy. Whoever found the bodies would have seen it. Leaving new signs might be a bigger detriment than help.

She ran scenarios through her mind and none of them seemed good. She tried to isolate her biggest fear and realized there was more than one. Top of the list was being found by the attackers. They couldn't be all that far behind and every time she stopped so Jildiz—crippled with asthma—could draw a few more breaths, she gave time for the black hats to close the distance. For all she knew, they were just a block away. Second, she was working under the assumption that rescue was on the way, something she didn't know for certain. Third, she was now armed but one handgun against two or three automatic weapons wouldn't be much good. That was another problem: three made the initial abduction attempt but she cut down two of them. Then two other men found them in the pharmacy. That meant reinforcements arrived. How many? How well armed? Trained? Did they have night vision goggles?

The pursuers had the advantage. Hunters always did. A game hunter faced little danger unless they came too close to a wounded and cornered beast. She was feeling wounded and cornered.

Her most recent plan was to join one of the mobs; hide in plain sight. If they were lucky, there would be police attempting crowd control. The idea was genius, but she found no crowds. If they followed a similar pattern to the riots of 2010, then they would be moving to the government building. That was still miles away: too many miles for the ever-weakening Jildiz. She had to get the woman out of the toxic air, give her time to rest. She needed a place where she could set up a small bunker. They might get them, even kill them, but not before someone took a round or two in the head.

"We need to keep moving."

MAC HAD WORKED WITH Chaplain Paul Bartley on several occasions although he never stepped into the chapel for a typical service. He knew the man's history. He knew he entered the Army intent on being a Ranger. Unlike his twin brother J. J., he washed out in the second week, but not for lack of trying. Bottom line, he washed out of the sixty-one-day training. There was no shame in it. He might not have been Ranger material but he was a persuasive man. He was able to extend his enlistment and take college courses. Seminary and officer training followed. He spent the last few years as one of the many chaplains serving at Fort Jackson.

Missing the Ranger mark did not mean the man was a poor soldier. He did tours in Afghanistan and Iraq, ministering to troops in the field. He had a reputation for friendliness and straight talk. He also had a heart the size of a tank, something Mac witnessed firsthand when Eric Moyer's daughter was kidnapped while he was on mission. Moyer was the previous team leader for the unit J. J. now led.

Mac was thankful for one thing: Bartley and J. J. were fraternal twins. He didn't look like J. J., something that would have made this all the more difficult.

Chaplain Bartley entered the spare office in the admin building, followed by another chaplain. Both wore daily work uniforms, both had Army chaplain emblems over their right shirt pockets. Mac noticed a cross on Bartley's uniform; a Star of David and a stylized Ten Commandments tablet on Colonel Joel Rubin's. Rubin was the new Fort Jackson command chaplain.

Both rose when Mac walked into the room. For a long moment no one spoke.

Bartley looked white as concrete and his face as hard. Rubin looked as if he had been awake for a week. Mac exchanged glances with Kinkaid, who didn't look any better. Seconds passed as Mac tried to find the words to begin. Should he thank them for coming? Stupid idea. They were ordered here and if anyone on base could guess why they were summoned, it was these two. Mac thought of the advice he gave Colonel Weidman, "Just say it, Danny. It won't taste any better but you'll be done with it." Advice was so much easier to give than follow. Mac opened his mouth to speak but Bartley beat him to it.

"When?"

Mac should have guessed, part of their job was delivering the very kind of news he was bringing. "We don't have a specific time. Sometime this morning our time. Evening theirs."

"How?"

"Unclear, Chaplain. We assume gunfire. It's still being investigated."

Bartley's face reddened and he shut his eyes for a moment. A tear trickled down his right cheek. "The team? All gone?"

A beat. "Yes."

Another second passed. Mac didn't rush things. He had delivered news like this before. He lost men before, but never a whole team.

"May I ask where?" Bartley's right hand trembled a moment then stopped. Mac didn't have to strain to guess the kind of battle going on between the man's ears.

"You know I can't reveal . . ." Then took a noisy breath. "This doesn't leave the room, Captain. Clear?"

"Perfectly."

"Kyrgyzstan. Bishkek. The capital."

"Where the riots are going on." It was a statement, not a question.

"Captain . . . Chaplain, you should know that I can't give details but I can tell you they were on a rescue mission. He died trying to save lives."

Bartley nodded. "He once told me if he died in the field, he wanted to do it doing something noble. I guess he got his wish." He opened his eyes. They were flooded. "Bodies?"

"We're working on that. It's complicated."

"It always is. Will another team be sent, Colonel?"

"We're working through channels to get their remains—"

"I was thinking about the rescue mission."

Mac leaned back in his chair and rubbed his chin. "No. I've been overruled."

"There aren't many people who can overrule you, Colonel." Bartley drew a hand across his cheek, removing another tear.

"This guy can." Mac leaned over the table. "Chaplain, I admired your brother. I passed over several people with seniority to make him team leader. There are many great men in the Army but only a handful like him. I have no children. The Army has been my life, my family. If I had a son, I would want him to be just like J. J." Mac's eyes burned.

"Thank you, sir. He . . . he thought the world of you. He prayed for you daily." This time Bartley let the tears fall. "He once told me you had the most difficult job in the Army. Going into battle, he said, was easier that sending others in."

"Thank you for sharing that." Mac looked at Kinkaid. He sat like he had rebar in his spine. He always did. The only evidence of emotion was the trail of tears. *Brave men cry.*

"Has Tess been informed?"

"You're the first. I've learned she's home and not at the War College this week. I'm headed there next."

Rubin spoke up. "Let me do that for you. You have your own emotion to deal with."

Bartley shook his head. "Thank you, Rabbi, but no. She's my sister-in-law. I need to be there for her. Then I'll tell my parents."

That almost undid Mac.

Rubin's voice was kind but firm. "I could order you not to go." He waited for Bartley to respond. "You'd go anyway, wouldn't you."

"Yes, sir."

"BOSS, I THINK SOMETHING is wrong with the Joker's truck." Pete stood at the pharmacy's front window and looked down the street. They stopped a few meters away from the entrance. "I think it's leaning to one side."

J. J. stepped to the widow. He snapped around and pointed to Aliki, Nagano, and Crispin. Then with two fingers, he motioned to the back door. He repeated the motion with Pete and Jose, this time pointing to the front. Aliki's team was on the move before J. J. finished the second set of gestures. J. J. keyed his mike. "Go."

He snapped the door open, M4 directed to the left, then the right, then up to the roof. He saw no one; saw no movement. His team put distance between themselves to keep from being one target.

Weapons raised, they trotted to the vehicle. Jose moved to the driver's side; Pete took the opposite; J. J. worked his way around to the back. He scanned the rooftops again, then set a hand on the rear door handle. Pete and Jose were at his side, barrels pointed at the door. J. J. gave a nod then swung the door open. His men had the barrels of their weapons in the opening before he could pull the door to the stops.

"Clear," Pete said.

Jose returned to the side of the vehicle. "Two flat tires, Boss."

"Boss, Joker." The words poured into J. J.'s head from the ear set.

"Go."

"Two flat tires. Someone cut the stems."

"Roger that. Same here. We've had company. Take your team north for two blocks then come around to our position. We'll do the same to the south."

"Roger. One other thing, Boss, and you ain't gonna like it. CONNIE is gone. We've been robbed."

"Standby." J. J. looked in the van Aliki had been driving. To his relief, he saw Crispin's kit. "Hawkeye, your toys are still here. I want you over here double-time."

"On my way, Boss."

It took only a moment for Crispin to make his way from the alley, through the shop, and into the street. He didn't acknowledge the others. Instead, he leaped into the back and knelt by his bag of tricks. Using his tactical light, he rummaged through the gear. "It's all here. Why did they take CONNIE but not this? I mean this stuff is uber special."

"My guess is that it was one guy. Several men might have taken us on. One guy would just try to slow us down. Your kit is a tad awkward to carry."

"You got that right, Boss."

"Not only that," Pete said, "but the store front window gave us a view of the van. Not the side with the flats, but he might not have wanted to risk being seen. We had no direct view of the alley."

"Great," J. J. said. "Colonel Mac is gonna make me pay for that thing. I should've posted a man at the door." *I've got to learn to think ahead more. How did Moyer do this?* "Junior, I want you and Hawkeye on one of the roofs." He looked at Crispin. "I assume the roof would be a better advantage for you to work your magic."

"It would, Boss."

"Can you do this in the dark?"

"No sweat."

"Then get your skinny butt up there. I want you to scan the area. Keep an eye out for the bad guys. The women have to be fairly close. Doc, how far can a woman with asthma run?"

"If she's having an attack—and I'm guessing she wouldn't have broken into a drugstore unless she had a big need for meds—with this air and the stress she's under, well, I don't think she can go very far."

J. J. pointed a finger at Crispin. "Find her, Hawkeye."

"Yes, Boss."

TESS PUT DOWN THE novel and stretched. She was wasting the day and loving every minute of it. Sometimes a woman just needed some downtime. After her coffee chat with Lucy, she returned to the apartment and planned her day: read, snack, nap, snack, read, watch a stupid movie, and then snack. That evening she would go out for dinner, treat herself to a romantic comedy at the theater while gorging on buttered popcorn, return home, sleep, and start a new diet tomorrow. Yep, the plan was inspired. This was a perfect day.

There was a knock at the door.

She rose and a powerful sense of worry settled in her stomach. Odd.

Slowly, Tess opened the door and saw Colonel Mac and J. J.'s brother. Commanding officer and chaplain.

Everything went dark and the floor rose to meet her.

CHAPTER 20

TESS HAD NO IDEA how she made it from the apartment's front door to the sofa, but there she was: on her back, a blurry ceiling above her, someone was holding her hand and rubbing her arm.

"Stay still." Familiar voice, one that brought more fear. Not danger, just the crushing ache of sadness. Everything inside her hurt, as if someone cored her out, blended her internal organs, and poured the goo back inside.

She blinked and the ceiling came clear. So did the voice. Paul Bartley sat on the coffee table and held her hand. At the foot of the sofa stood Colonel Mac. Another man she didn't recognize stepped into view holding a glass of water. Why did people offer water at difficult times as if it were a magical elixir?

"Slow, even breaths, Tess." Bartley spoke softly but the strain in his voice was easy to detect. She faced him. His eyes were red and swollen. An athletic man who enjoyed the outdoors, he wore a year-round tan. He looked ghostly.

Tess pulled her hand free and raised it to her face. She didn't want to see; didn't want to feel. No one spoke the news but they didn't need to. When a man's commanding officer and one of the base chaplains show up at the door without an invitation, it could only mean one thing.

"When?"

"A short time ago," Bartley said. "I heard about it less than an hour ago."

"It would have been early morning our time," Mac said.

"And you're just now getting here?"

"That's my fault, Tess," Mac said. "I had to make a trip to DC."

"The president knows?" She pushed herself up. The room spun like a top. It took a moment for things to settle.

"Yes."

"Here, drink this." The strange man, dark complexion, dark kind eyes, held out the glass. She took it. As expected, it didn't help. "Who are you?" She looked at his uniform and recognized the chaplaincy badge.

"This is Colonel Joel Rubin. He's the command chaplain of Fort Jackson."

"I'm sorry to meet you under these circumstances." His voice was kind but it was clear he had said those words more times than he could count. "I am very sorry for your loss, Dr. Rand."

"Bartley. I'm a Bartley these days." She handed the glass of water back. "Kyrgyzstan?"

"You know I can't discuss such things, Tess." Normally those words would have been snapped out, but Mac seemed to choke on them. Tess aided Colonel Mac several times, providing information that might be useful to teams in the field. It was an odd relationship. Only her expertise allowed the Army to look the other way while the wife of a team member gave advice to a man who sent her husband into impossible situations.

"I'm not asking, Colonel. I know J. J. and the team were doing training at Manas. I'm guessing the rest. Am I wrong?"

Mac didn't respond.

"I didn't think so. Okay. I've prepared myself for this. I married J. J. knowing this could happen." She stood and swayed for a moment. "I'm not the first wife to go through this. I'll miss him of course. He was the . . . love . . . I'll be fine. I-I need to make plans . . . plans . . . his parents." She paused, then raised her hands to her face again. It began with a whimper, then a sob, then a scream muted by her hands.

She tried to quell the storm of sorrow, to tame the unrelenting hurricane of grief. Her head spun. Her knees gave way but she didn't fall. Paul Bartley stood in front of her, his strong arms wrapped around her, providing the strength that had abandoned her. She made one effort to push away but it lacked power and conviction.

She needed to be held; needed the support of someone as wounded as she.

The sound of sobbing filled her ears. It took a second for her to realize the deeper tones came from Paul Bartley.

In a small apartment, in a medium-sized city, in a small state in a large country, on a planet in the corner of countless galaxies, the universe collapsed.

"NO GOOD, BOSS." PETE'S voice poured through the earpiece.

"You know how unhappy bad news makes me."

"I do, that's why Weps is gonna finish the story."

A moment passed before Nagano came on. J. J. looked down the street from his position at the intersection just north of the pharmacy. He could see the van in the street with two of his soldiers hunkered over one of the flat tires. At the south intersection he could see Aliki scanning the streets. So far, no movement.

"Boss, what Junior is too chicken to say is the spare from the other vehicle won't work. Different size, different lug nut configuration. Different makes; different countries."

The plan was to use the spare tires from both vehicles to get one up and moving. A good idea gone bust.

"Understood."

"What now, Boss?"

He had no idea. "Joker, pull back to the vehicle." J. J. turned and double-timed it down the street.

They gathered around the vehicle. J. J. looked at his men. "Okay, this is how I see it. Whoever did this was alone or maybe had just one partner. Had there been a team of them, they might have taken us on, or set up sniper positions and popped us as we came out. A trained sniper might have given it a go, but the odds would be against success. Two or three men would be needed to make things work."

"It also means the guy isn't packing a high-power automatic. He could have gotten my team or yours."

"Yep, but not both. That was his problem. The question is: Is he coming back with some pals? I don't like standing around here. Right now, we're nothing but good target practice."

"So what's the call, Boss?" Pete asked.

"Everyone on the roof. I want to check on Hawkeye. He should be up and ready to go."

"Boss, I recommend we split the team. Let's not put all our eggs in one basket." Aliki stood close to J. J. and seemed to be focused on J. J.'s face.

"Agreed. Joker, you, Weps, and Junior take up a position on one of the roofs. Pick one with good cover. I'll join Hawkeye and Doc. Maybe we can see something from an elevated position. Go."

The men hustled into the dark. J. J. found the access ladder to the roof over the pharmacy and made his way up. With each rung he rose, he thought of Tess and the babies. A sense of ill ease percolated in him. He was a man of faith but he was not superstitious, nor did he believe in ESP.

So why was he so worried about her?

TESS MADE COFFEE. SHE didn't want coffee. Didn't want tea. She offered both to Bartley. He wanted nothing. She knew what she was doing: finding stuff to do to fill every second; to avoid every thought. It was futile. She burst into tears every five minutes. When she wasn't crying, Bartley was, not as loudly, but with as much conviction.

"I let my parents know," he said. "I called them before coming over here."

"How are they doing? Sorry, dumb question. What I mean is . . . I don't know what I mean."

"You're asking how they're dealing with the news."

"That's it. My brain is muddled."

He took a ragged breath. "Everything is muddled." It took a second before he answered the question. "They've prepared for the phone call. Every Army parent does. Doesn't make it any easier, but at least they have a script running in their head about what to do in that moment. I spoke to Dad. He's made of granite. Mom, eh, not so much."

"That had to be the most difficult phone call ever." Tess moved out of the kitchen and to the sofa. She fell to the cushion.

"I went into minister mode. That helped me get through it."

"Minister mode?"

"Ministers, especially chaplains, are called on to deliver the worst kinds of news. If you don't know the people involved it's a little easier, but it is never easy. After awhile, a minister learns to invest everything into the one they're helping. They have to if they want to be of any value, but what they never tell you is, we do it to shield ourselves from ourselves."

"And that works?"

"It's a temporary measure, but it helps. You see it when a mother busies herself taking care of the children. Thinking about them helps her deal with her own pain . . ."

Tess bolted to her feet and moved to the window, turning her back on Bartley. She placed both hands on her belly.

"I'm an idiot, Tess. I'm sorry."

"You didn't do anything wrong."

"Yes, I did. I made a careless statement without considering the situation." He stepped to her side and put his arm around her shoulder. She could feel his hand shake. "I guess my brain is muddled too."

Tears escaped her eyes: rivulets of sorrow.

"You won't be alone, Tess." There was tremor in her brother-in-law's voice. "You have family. You and the kids will have me."

"I know, it's just . . ."

"I'm not trying to be a replacement for J. J., but you are family. You are the sister I never had. When J. J. married you, he improved himself and our family."

"I feel so lost." She looked at the carpet. "I used to be so independent, so focused on what I want. J. J. was such a surprise. I put myself through college and graduate school. I earned my PhD and I thought that was the greatest thing I could do, then I met J. J. He became my world. Now, I'm pregnant and that has changed my outlook on everything."

She looked up again, staring out the window, seeing nothing. "I've become an expectant mother and widow within a few months of each other. How wrong is that?"

"Very wrong. Life has never been fair. Not this life anyway."

She blinked back a few more tears. "I've tried to pray, Paul, I can't get the words out."

"Me either. Prayer has always been the first thing I turn to. I can't seem to get that to work."

"Has God abandoned us?" Tess avoided eye contact.

It took longer for Bartley to answer than she expected. She assumed he had a ready answer to a question he must have heard a hundred times.

"Faith is a wrestling match, Tess. At least it is for me. J. J. always seemed better able to trust God. I have always had to work through the theology of it."

"And you're the one who became a chaplain."

He forced a smirk. "Go figure. No, I don't think God has abandoned us. You are solid in your faith. I've seen it. So I'm not telling you anything new here, but the Bible never says we will be protected from trouble. We are promised wisdom and courage in times of trouble. Christians suffer like everyone else."

"I feel abandoned."

"Of course you do. You have a right to feel that way. Truth is, I'm more than a little angry with God right now. I've told Him so. Not much sense in pretending otherwise."

"Did He respond?"

"You know I don't hear an audible voice. God could do that if He wants but He's never done it with me. God speaks louder than that." He lowered his arm and put his hands in his pockets. "When I told God how furious I was over this I got the impression He was saying, 'I know.' No condemnation, just a sense of love and tolerance. He understands."

"Do you think we'll ever understand?"

"Not in this life, Tess. Not in this life." A few moments passed. "Do you want me to call your parents?"

"No, I'll do it. I'll call from the phone in the bedroom."

He nodded. "I'll be here when you're done."

"How long do you think it will take for Chaplain Rubin and Colonel Mac to visit the other families?"

"A couple of hours at least. I can't be sure."

"I need to call them. Especially Lucy."

"Why Lucy?"

"We had coffee this morning. She felt something was wrong. I assured her the team was safe. I never imagined being so wrong."

CHAPTER 21

THE SITUATION ROOM IN the Kyrgyzstan capital of Bishkek was filled with new technology. Under his leadership, President Meklis Oskonbaeva saw a rise in the technology sector of his country. The process was slow and taxing but headway was being made. Jalal-Abad State University and the Kyrgyz Technical University produced world-class engineers and computer experts. Communications in the country advanced remarkably, and to be fair, Prime Minister Dootkasy helped make much of that possible. It was Meklis's dream to see his country join Japan, Korea, China, and the United States in technology fabrication. In June of 2011, the parliament passed legislation to build a high-tech park like one built in Belarus.

As a sign of his interest in such matters, Meklis had the White House equipped with computers and software developed in-country. That included a modern situation room with flat-screen monitors and communications that allowed him to converse with other heads of states or monitor news from a number of international news agencies. He didn't fool himself into believing the control center came anywhere close to those in more developed and richer countries.

As he walked in, his team of advisers rose from their chairs. Sariev Dootkasy was among them.

"Please be seated." Meklis took his place at the head of a long and wide table large enough to seat twice what was there. "Emil?"

Chief of Police Emil Abirov shifted in his seat. "No word on your daughter, sir. That could be either good or bad news. I have received no communication from abductors."

The report dropped a hot coal in Meklis's stomach. He said nothing. He was afraid the dam holding his emotions back would crumble. He encouraged Abirov to continue with a nod.

"Sir, I'm afraid that I have not been able to assign any men to search for her. The crowds are growing. The number of fires have multiplied. What started as debris and tires being burned in the streets is becoming arson. Several buildings have been set ablaze. I have every man on the force helping with crowd control and the protection of other government buildings. I have requested help from departments in other cities but they have riots of their own." He stopped suddenly.

After a moment of silence, Dootkasy spoke. "Tell the president the rest of it." His voice was even and devoid of accusation or criticism.

"It pains me to say it, but some of my officers have joined the protests."

"What?" Meklis wondered if he heard right.

"I am sorry to report that some of my street officers are aiding the protesters." Abirov slumped in his seat.

In an unexpected show of support, Dootkasy came to the man's aid. "I am not surprised." He immediately held up a hand. "That is not to say anything bad about Abirov's leadership. I was just thinking of Arab Spring, when citizens rose against their government. Egypt for example, Libya, and so on. Military and police often sided with protesters."

"It's treasonous," Boris Gubuz said. He brought a fist down on the table to make his point.

Dootkasy nodded. "Yes, it is, but treason is in the eye of the beholder. To those in power—like us—it is treason; to the man on the street it's revolution, perhaps similar to our country's history. You are all familiar with the 1916 revolt against the Tsarist empire. One in six people in our country died. One in six. Some of those were our grand or great-grandparents. The United States War of Independence was viewed by the colonists as a fight for freedom, but the British saw treason. Which was it?"

"You defend the protesters, Mr. Prime Minister?" Meklis kept his voice low.

"No, Mr. President, I do not. I am on your side. Yes, we have different views of policy, but I am very aware of who appointed me to this position. I'm merely trying to paint a broader picture. We have made great strides forward, but not enough to help the people in the streets. Our unemployment makes us the poorest of all the former Soviet republics." He leaned on the table and steepled his fingers. "I am simply saying we tend to see the protests as criminals run amok; they see it has a patriotic act. Is that what it is? Not to our minds, but it is to theirs. These are not hooligans burning cars after a sports match. They riot for a reason."

"It still sounds like a defense of protesters." General Nurbeck Saparaliev's tone was harsh.

"I'm sorry you see it that way, General. I am not here to defend them and I think you are doing a magnificent job. My goal is only to bring to this table another side. But you will find I stand with you. Sometimes I think revolt is in our blood."

Meklis returned his gaze to the police chief. "You have more?"

"I do, sir." He picked up a remote and activated a large, flat-screen television. Several smaller television monitors surrounded the large screen. "I have a video feed from our police helicopter. The pilot provides an aerial platform to see the activities in the streets." The city was dark, with only the dim glow of old street lamps dropping puddles of light to the streets below.

Meklis watched as the helicopter did a slow circuit over the city. Fires burned in the street and he counted at least five buildings on fire. A high-intensity spotlight flooded the pavement. People, who had been dancing around the fire as if in some pagan ritual, turned their faces skyward.

"The numbers have grown," Abirov said. "Estimates vary but there may be as many ten thousand already on the streets and the numbers are swelling. We could see twenty or thirty thousand soon. By sunrise . . ." He tossed his hands up. "In 2010 there were over 1,000 injuries and eighty-eight dead. Who knows where this will lead."

The copter expanded its circle, taking in more of the troubled city.

"Have you used the helicopter to search for my daughter?"

Abirov was slow to speak. "Some, sir, but we haven't found anything encouraging."

"What do you mean by 'some'?"

"I've sent the helicopter over the area where the attempt to abduct your daughter occurred. We did a sweep of the area but saw nothing. Unless she is on the street or in an alley, we won't be able to see her. We hoped she would have heard the helicopter and shown herself, except . . ."

"Except what, Emil?"

"Like you, sir, I have watched the video several times. We know they were being pursued. Perhaps . . ."

"Say it, Emil." Meklis uttered the words with a conviction he didn't feel.

"Perhaps she and her rescuer have been caught. Perhaps they are hiding. If the street wasn't filled with such turmoil, I'd have a police unit on every street searching every building, but . . ." He sighed. "I need the helicopter to guide our men on the ground."

"I can have a military helicopter in the air to replace the police one," the general said.

"A military aircraft flying over the citizens?" Dootkasy rubbed his chin. "I'd worry about violence, Mr. President. We know there are some anarchists in the crowds. A military flyover might incite more violence. I also have to ask what happens if some anarchist opens fire on a military aircraft? Does it fire back? Are we at that stage yet?" He rapped lightly on the table. "I'm with you in whatever you decide, Mr. President. I will do my best to make certain the parliament understands your reasons."

The comment sounded insincere. "Thank you, Sariev."

DOOTKASY HAD NO WAY of knowing if Meklis believed him or not. It didn't matter. The president was losing his grip on the government. Dootkasy had many followers in parliament and many more in the streets. Within five minutes of the end of the meeting, he would make certain someone fired on whatever helicopter circled overhead. A few incidents like that and Abirov would have to ground the craft. If need be he'd have Nasirdin bring the craft to the ground.

J. J. MOVED TO the northwest corner of the pharmacy's roof. "How goes it, Hawkeye?" The young soldier had his kit open and J. J. saw the same quad-propeller unit Crispin used to show off with at the base. That seemed a week ago but it was only a few hours ago.

"Good, Boss. I'm using the quad. It can handle wind gusts better." He looked around the roof. "I'm gonna have to watch the power lines. I figure I'll take it to about 500 feet. It's undetectable at that altitude. I'll be running live video. Of course, if they're inside a building, this thing won't be much good."

"It's all we have at the moment. I want you to keep an eye out for black hats. Time to earn your nickname. Get that thing going."

"Roger that, Boss." The fan-like propellers came to life and a moment later, the device was hovering six feet above the roof. "Gotta love that stabilization. Pick a direction, Boss."

"North."

Crispin pushed a lever with his thumb and the device shot up several hundred feet and then eased north.

"How much can you see in the dark?" J. J. asked.

"Unlike commercial remote control vehicles, I can add night vision. That's what took me so long to get airborne. I had to swap out the micro camera."

J. J. gave a reassured nod. "I don't care what the others say, Hawkeye, I'm starting to like you."

"Gee, thanks."

"Doc. Get your eyes on."

"Got it, Boss. I'll take the south and east sides of the building and leave the north and west to you."

"Just as I planned it. The others are doing the same."

J. J. looked north and saw dozens of fires, flashing police and fire department lights, all of which glowed eerily against the smoke-filled air. The wind carried the mixed voices, shouts and screams of thousands of protesters. "So this is hell," he said to himself.

TESS KNEW SHE SHOULDN'T. It was unwise at best; foolish at worst. It could only hurt her, but she had to do it. After disappearing into her bedroom to call her parents and leaving Paul Bartley to fend for himself for a few minutes, she turned on the television and tuned to a cable news network. Ten minutes and six commercials passed before the professionally dressed and made-up news anchor said, "I must warn you that this video is graphic and not fit for children. Earlier today, a news station in the Central Asian country and former Soviet Republic Kyrgyzstan reported that six U.S. military men were killed on the streets of Bishkek, the country's capital."

Video began to play. Bathed in the light of street lamps and the camera's spotlight was the burned remains of a sedan. Around the base of the car were several blackened corpses.

Tess staggered into the master bath, dropped to her knees, and vomited in the toilet. When the retching ended she fell to her right side, her head resting on the floor between the tub and toilet.

The poison of deep pain exploded from her in convulsive sobs.

CHAPTER 22

DOOTKASY GREW MORE IMPATIENT with each minute that passed. He assumed there would be difficulties along the way, but not for a moment had he considered the failure of his men to capture a single woman. Now there were two women on the run and one was more than she seemed. He could not imagine Jildiz breaking into buildings and killing two armed men. She was a tough negotiator, a woman of singular dedication and a keen mind, but she was not violent. Amelia Lennon was a different matter. She worked as a diplomatic aide but he long suspected she was CIA and if not that, then some kind of military intelligence. In one way, he admired her, which made her pending death a tad less enjoyable.

The night was wearing on. The women needed to be found and soon. There were still the American soldiers to deal with. For his plan to continue toward success, he had to be proactive. He called his aide Apas Isanov.

"Yes, Mr. Prime Minster?"

"I want you to get a message to our people in the field. Have them spread this news: A bounty will be paid to anyone who finds and delivers the two women to me. Payment will also be made for the location of the American soldiers."

"Do you care about the condition they are found in?"

It was a gentle way of asking, "Dead or alive?"

"I would not be upset if they stumbled upon the bodies. Make sure Nasardin knows of the offer. I don't want him killing people who are trying to help."

"Yes, sir. Of course. However, he will not be happy about the offer. I'm certain he will fear the loss of his bonus."

"His happiness is not my concern. He has failed several times already. He will get paid if he finds the women and paid even more if he kills the soldiers. Understood?"

"Yes, sir. I understand completely." Apas shifted his weight. "May I ask about the president, sir? Has he taken your advice to release power?"

"Not yet. I can sense his conflict. He wants to govern, he wants to find his daughter, he doesn't want to be considered a coward."

"If only the abduction had worked as planned. You could have used Jildiz as leverage or at least removed his most pressing reason to stay."

"All the more reason we need to find her fast."

Apas nodded and left the spacious office.

JILDIZ LAY ON HER back in the sleeping compartment of an eighteen-wheeler they found two miles from the pharmacy. She wasn't asleep. The struggle to breathe kept her awake. Amelia could see the strain on the woman's face. Maybe it was the smoke-dimmed light of the streetlights, maybe it was the exertion, maybe it was fear, maybe it was all those things and a dozen more that made the pretty Jildiz look fifteen years older than she did at their late lunch.

The truck was old and looked as if it had been driven around the world several times. Still, it was a port in the storm and they were lucky to find the driver's door unlocked. Had Amelia been alone, she could have easily jogged the distance to the White House, but she was not alone; if she hadn't been watching Jildiz driving in front of her, she'd be back on the base with her feet up and wondering what her next move would be to save the air base.

If. If. If. If never changed anything. She refocused her attention. First, she checked the side mirrors again and saw nothing moving behind her. The mirrors were an asset. Next, she scanned the area in front of her and saw only an empty street, although she could see movement of crowds some distance away. For a time she thought the crowds could be their salvation. Maybe they could blend in with the protesters, use them as human camouflage. Now she was having doubts. Her instincts didn't like the idea. Things nagged her. Things like cell and landline service going out at the same time but radio—and she assumed—television still functioned. Somebody was up to something.

What other choice did she have? Jildiz was having trouble walking more than a block or two. Running was out of the question.

Amelia turned her attention to the handgun she lifted from the attacker in the drugstore. It was a 9mm, semi-automatic, clean, and fairly new. She smelled the barrel. Just gun oil. It hadn't been fired recently and the previous owner took good care of it. She popped the magazine and took note it was full. She chambered a round, double-checked the safety, then set it on the seat next to her. Again she checked the mirrors and the surrounding area.

The cab rocked as Jildiz rolled over. The curtain separating the cab from the sleeper parted slightly. "You're still here."

"Of course, where else would I be?"

"I dozed and had a dream you left me behind."

Amelia cocked her head to steal a glance at Jildiz. "It was just a nightmare, Jildiz. I'm not leaving you."

"It didn't seem like a nightmare. It seemed right. Leaving me was the right thing to do. I told you that in the dream."

Amelia studied the stick shift and the pedals. "Did my dream self agree?"

"Yes. You said thank you."

"I'll have to talk to myself about that. I'm not leaving." The cab jiggled again. "Hey kid, go easy on the movement. This thing's suspension was old before we were born. I don't want our friends to have reason to investigate."

"Sorry."

"Don't be. You didn't make the truck." Amelia ran a hand under the dashboard. Her fingers found wires. Wires to what she didn't know.

"What are you doing?"

"I'm thinking of hot-wiring the ignition."

"Hot-wiring?"

"I don't know what the Russian or Kyrgyz word is for it, but it means to start a vehicle without the key, but I have a problem. I don't know how to do it."

"That disappoints me. I thought you knew everything."

"I do, just not how to hot-wire a thirty-year-old truck."

"They don't teach that in American schools?" The curtain closed.

"I majored in armed robbery." Amelia tugged on the bundle of wires. "I have two brothers but both grew up reading books instead of swiping cars for fun. How's a girl supposed to learn?"

She yanked the wire harness free. Several strands of wire were bound together by electrician's tape. Someone had been doing home repairs. "Jidiz, is there a flashlight back there?"

"I can't see much. There's an overhead light—"

"Don't touch that. It might give away our position. Just feel around."

"I can't find one. I found a . . . fire extinguisher. I'll never look at these things the same way."

"You earned a black belt in fire extinguisher. You did a good thing."

"Doesn't feel like a good thing."

"Feelings don't matter right now. Just survival. We can get weepy later." Amelia looked around the cab and found a plastic box between the seats. It had a top with hinges. The equivalent of a glove compartment. She opened it: maps, an apple well on its way to cider, and a flashlight. "Found one. Truckers always travel with a flashlight."

"I didn't know that."

"I don't know it either, I'm just trying to convince you I'm smart."

"I already believe that. Um, won't we have the same problem with the flashlight as the overhead light?"

"Yes, I'm thinking about that. What about a tool kit? A truck this old has to travel with a tool kit."

"Nothing. Could it be outside?"

Amelia hadn't taken time to investigate the truck beyond seeing that the cab was empty and the door was unlocked, but Jildiz had a point. She couldn't remember where or when but she had seen a compartment on the side of trucks like this. "I'm going to check."

"Is that wise?"

"Probably not." Amelia looked at the small overhead cab light, found a switch, and turned it to off. She exited a dark cab into a dark night.

"BOSS, WE GOT COMPANY, coming up from the south. Street side. Half a klick." Doc's voice was calm as if describing a play made on a baseball field.

"Down," J. J. ordered. He dropped to a crouch then scrambled to the south end of the building. He dropped his NVGs and the world turned digital green. He glanced across the street and saw Aliki's team spaced along the parapet wall, barely visible in their black helmets and balaclavas.

"Need me, Boss?" The whispered question came from Crispin.

"Negative, stay with the program."

A mob of fifteen young men and several middle-aged guys moved up the street. Several carried bottles of booze. *A gang of rioters? Looters? If so, they'll pass by.*

They didn't pass by. They saw the crippled van and slowed, then they did something that chilled the team leader: they split into two groups on a hand signal from one of the older men. Several produced handguns.

Slowly, the armed men advanced on the vehicle. J. J. looked at the roof where the other half of his team took position. He saw Aliki looking back. Neither activated their radios. They didn't need to. The only solution was to wait. They could dispatch the mob in short order. Truth was, J. J. could do it without help. A simple sweep of his M4 on full auto would leave corpses everywhere. If the rest of his team did the same there would be nothing but human-burger left. That wasn't their mission. Killing civilians would cause four hundred kinds of trouble. However, should the group turn their attention to the roof, then it would turn into a really bad day.

Wait.

Watch.

Be ready.

"Check north," Aliki whispered through the radio.

J. J. did and saw another group of about the same size coming their way. He pointed at Doc and motioned for him to check the alley. Doc moved like a cat across the gravel blanket roof. It took only a glance.

"One group, from the south, armed. I make it to be fifteen strong."

"Roger that. Stick there." J. J.'s brain spun like a jet engine. *This isn't coincidence.*

Another whispered voice. "Boss, Hawkeye. Got her! Whoa!"

AMELIA SLIPPED FROM THE cab, and found a small door with a chrome clasp, or what might have been chrome at one time. Definitely a storage locker. A locked storage locker. "Oh sure, leave the cab open but lock up the tool compartment. What kind of moron does that?"

A sound. Odd. Slightly distant. Fuzzy.

She kept one hand on the locker and reached for the 9mm in her coat pocket.

Buzzing. Electric.

She spun and leveled her weapon ready to unleash a body mass shot, but there was no one there. She swept the gun to one side then the other. Nothing. Just the buzzing noise—from overhead. She looked up and saw a small device hovering a couple of yards away and twenty feet high. Amelia snapped the weapon up and sighted on the thing, ready to squeeze the trigger.

She hesitated. *What the . . .*

The device dipped its front end then brought it up again as if bowing. Then it moved to the truck, descending to the door. Amelia watched, both fascinated and fearful. It moved from the door then back again, repeating the action several times.

The thing is telling me to get in the truck. How can . . .

It hit her. A surveillance drone. The only question was, was it friendly?

Amelia crawled back into the cab with a big decision to make.

CHAPTER 23

THE KNOCK ON THE door sounded firm but not intrusive, as if the visitor wanted to be heard but felt guilty about it.

"I'll get it," Bartley said and moved from the small kitchen table.

Tess let him. The weeping stopped for now leaving her a husk, weak, and barely able to think. The image of the burned car and corpses repeatedly played in her head, an image that became more graphic with each replay. She no longer saw bodies burned beyond recognition—she saw J. J. Tess considered her imagination an aid in her work. She could read reports about military actions and see them unfold in her mind. There were times when her imaginings resembled hyperreal dreams—something she could live without.

The door released a tiny squeak as Bartley opened it. Tess hoped it was a salesman who could be sent away. It wasn't. She recognized the voice.

"Chaplain. I'm glad you're here."

"Come in, Sergeant Major."

"It's just Eric these days."

"And I'm just plain ol' Rich."

Tess rose and stepped to the lobby in time to see two familiar people cross her threshold. Eric Moyer was a man who, although fit, looked a decade older. He wore gray slacks and a blue polo shirt. Next to him stood the behemoth Rich Harbison. His size earned him the nickname Shaq, like the seven-foot one-inch basketball player. The large black man wore a patch over one eye, an eye lost on his last mission.

Willing herself to be strong, to remain composed, to show an emotional stability she didn't have, Tess looked into the eyes of her husband's former team leader. "Eric. You didn't need to come. I know you're busy." *Stupid words.* She couldn't come up with anything else.

"Yeah, I did. I . . . Nothing could keep us away."

"You two were always J. J.'s friends." The past tense kicked down the emotional walls. Tears rose. Tears fell. Sobs followed and without quite knowing how, she found herself in the arms of Eric.

He said nothing. No one did. The only sound was the closing of the front door. Minutes had no meaning. The apartment seemed to recede and Tess wondered how many times and how long a woman could cry.

When she looked up she saw tears in the eyes of Eric and Rich, two of the toughest men she knew. Somehow that brought a wave of comfort. "Doesn't make sense to be miserable in the foyer when we could be miserable in the living room."

"You were always the smart one of the family," Rich said. "And J. J. would have agreed with that."

"Yes he would," Tess said. "I made him utter that very phrase three times a day."

They laughed through the tears.

Once in the larger room, Rich moved to Bartley and threw his arms about the man. A taller than average man, Bartley looked tiny in Rich's arms. "We haven't forgotten you, Chap. How you holdin' up?"

"You want the truth or a lie?"

"Nuff, said, sir."

"You're no longer in the Army, Rich, you don't have to call me sir."

"I am a wonderfully complex man with deeply rooted habits."

The talk was light but the mood dark. They took seats. Bartley sat next to Tess on the sofa, Eric took a side chair and Rich pulled a chair from the kitchen. The easy chair in the living room remained unused. Apparently, Rich assumed it was J. J.'s. He was right.

"Tess, I have no words. I've been on this end of things before but . . . well, J. J. was different."

There it was again: that horrible past tense.

"We're here for you, Tess. You too, Captain. You ask, we'll do. I don't care what it is."

Can you bring J. J. back? Out loud she said, "Thank you. J. J. considered you more than fellow soldiers. You are . . . were his friends."

Eric teared up again, but kept the grief in check. "My position kept me from getting as close to him as I would like. Oh the pizza parties and barbecues were one thing, but being team leader required I keep a certain detachment."

"He knew that. His greatest fear was not being half the team leader you were, Eric."

"I recommended him for the job because I thought he'd be better than I ever was." He drew a finger under his nose. "I can't help feeling partly to blame."

"Why?" The statement stunned Tess. "Because you bumped him to team leader?" She leaned forward. "You know better than that, Eric. He would still have been on the team even if the brass put someone else in your spot. You have no reason for feeling guilty. He died doing something he felt was important."

"Guilt doesn't follow reason, Tess. At least not with me."

"I shoulda . . ." Rich cleared his throat. "I should have been there for him." He looked away, eye contact being too painful.

"You didn't choose to retire, Rich. Neither did you, Eric. Injuries and the attack on Eric's family made early retirement necessary. I know that."

Eric shifted in the chair as if sitting on tacks. "Tess, I want you to know you can ask anything of us and we'll do it. I don't know, um . . . I don't know what your financial situation is. I know J. J. made diddly. I don't know what the War College pays instructors or what you get for consulting. That's none of my business, but Rich and I make a good living now. The security firm that hired us is generous."

"Big time generous," Rich said. "We get five times the coin we got from Uncle Sam."

"If you need help with the funeral, travel expenses for family, cash to tide you over until Army pays out death benefits, you let us know."

Rich jumped in. "We're not talking a loan here, Tess. We want to do something to be helpful."

"Thanks, guys. I think I'm okay, but I'll keep your offer in mind. I can't speak for the other families. Some of them will need more help than me. I don't have a family . . ."

"Yet," Moyer said. "That's what I'm talking about. You need something for the twins—"

"How did you know I was having twins?"

Rich grinned. "You sure you're married to J. J.? He did everything but put the news on a billboard. I think he called everyone in the white pages."

A smile crept across Tess's face, surprising her. "That's J. J. He had a lot of teenager left in him."

"And a lot of man too." Eric seemed to drift to a time and place only he knew.

Tess wrestled with a question. The "wife" side of her felt she had a right to know; the "military expert" part told her she didn't. She ended the debate.

"Eric, how much do you know?"

The question pulled him from his distant thoughts. He exchanged a glance with Rich. "I was read off once I signed my retirement papers. I'm not in the loop anymore. Colonel Mac can't tell me anything."

"I've only been a soldier's wife a short time but I've been rubbing shoulders with the brass and intel agencies for half a decade. I also know about the security company you work for. They have a reputation for knowing things they shouldn't."

Moyer chewed his lip for a moment. "I have made a few calls. Don't ask with whom." He chewed his lip again then directed his attention to Bartley. "Captain, this is awkward. I wonder if you wouldn't enjoy a little stroll outside."

"I'm not going anywhere, Eric. I want to hear what happened to my brother."

Moyer left his lip alone and started pulling at his ear. "I understand, sir. I would want the same thing if I were in your shoes." He took a deep breath. "The firm I work for has many connections and I still have a few friends . . ." He trailed off as if the last part of the statement shouldn't have been uttered. "How much do you know, Tess?"

"I know the team went to Manas Air Base in Kyrgyzstan to do some training and to meet the two new members of the team. From there, they were supposed to fly to Germany so Crispin could demonstrate the new field remote-piloted vehicles."

"So far, you're right on the money. Crispin is an expert in nano and miniature air vehicles used for field work. He's become the golden boy of the surveillance technique."

"Man, I miss busting his chops," Rich said. "He was such a great target."

"Go on, Tess. What else do you know?"

"For some reason they were pressed into a mission. I know there are riots going on in Bishkek, Talas, Osh, and other cities. I saw . . ." The tears in her eyes felt as if they had been drawn from a pot of boiling water. She took a deep breath and looked at the ceiling. Someone told her a person can't cry while looking up. It sounded like nonsense then and it felt like nonsense now. Still . . . "I saw a news report—"

"Oh, Tess," Bartley said. "I thought we warned you of that."

"I'm not in my right mind, Paul."

He took her hand and gave it a squeeze, delivering a message words were inadequate to convey.

"Anyway, the reporter said the attack happened in Bishkek. I guess that makes sense, since that's the closest city to Manas Air Base."

Moyer looked at the chaplain. Tess had enough experience with the military to know he was uncomfortable revealing information he shouldn't have and doing so in front of an officer and a man of the cloth. Moyer was making a sacrifice for Tess.

Moyer cleared his throat. "A lot of my information is coming from winks and nods, but I do have some solid info. My sources say the team was dispatched to achieve two goals: find and recover an FAO named Amelia Lennon; second, if possible, to rescue a VIP with her."

"VIP?"

"The Foreign Affairs Officer is an Army-trained captain. Highly trained. Which is one of the problems. She knows how to hide. The VIP is the daughter of the Krygyzstan president. She's a Western-trained lawyer and the lead counsel for her country on the Manas Air Base problem." He described the news video and the abduction attempt including the graphic details of Amelia's use of a car to mow down two armed men.

"So they were on a rescue mission?" Hearing it again gave Tess a bit of relief. Dying on a mission was bad, but dying for something that didn't matter was worse. J. J. joked that his greatest fear was dying stupid, like forgetting his parachute when leaping out the back of a VC-22.

"Yes. He died doing what he loved. He died trying to save lives."

Tess could only nod. A wad of grief was stuck in her throat.

"Has another team been sent?"

Eric leaned back in silence. His eyes drifted to Rich.

"No," Rich said. "At least the best we can tell. Word is the Kyrgyzstan government has forbidden any U.S. involvement on their soil. All forces are confined to Manas." He folded his hands. "It is our belief the team was sent out very soon after they got word about the abduction attempt. Cell and landlines are down. A message could have been sent by e-mail, but e-mail can be ignored. We have a source that says the locals sent a personal messenger to the base commander. By that time the team was already active."

"So the FAO is on her own?"

"For now." Eric grimaced as if the words were soaked in green bile.

"So the local government has police and security searching for the women?"

Eric shook his head. "Possible, but doubtful. They have more on their hands than they can handle."

"But what about J. J.'s body, Eric? We can't leave him on the streets. They wouldn't allow another Somalia, would they?" She didn't need to explain the reference to the men in her living room. They all saw followers of a Somali war lord desecrate the bodies of slain soldiers downed in Mogadishu. The thought of it made her sick to her stomach.

"It's a different group of people, Tess." Eric didn't sound convinced by his own words. "I can tell you this. Colonel Mac paid a visit to the president. He's one of the people who can get a hearing almost anytime."

"That's because we saved his fanny in Italy," Shaq said. "That and he has strong emotions for the team and for you, Tess."

"But the president said no."

"Correct."

"So his hands are tied and my husband is left dead on a Bishkek street."

"Officially, yes, his hands are tied. Unofficially, well, he's been known to make up a new rule now and again."

"Whatever happened to the Ranger creed? What happened to never leaving a fallen comrade?"

"We agree with you, Tess." Eric rubbed the back of his neck. Tess could see the tension in the man's face. "We're just not in a position to do anything about it."

"I understand." Tess rubbed her temples. "It wouldn't be fair to risk more lives."

"Don't say that, Tess," Shaq said. "That's what men like us do and we're not alone. This isn't finished yet."

"It is for J. J." Against her will, against her desire, she began to weep again.

Three male voices joined her.

Big men cry.

CHAPTER 24

THIS STINKS.

The assessment wasn't profound but accurate. Moments before they located Captain Lennon and the president's daughter, the team found itself on separate rooftops watching their vehicles burn like a pyre. The numbers had grown. J. J. estimated they were outnumbered ten-or-twelve-to-one. At least a third of the men were armed, some with military-grade weapons. He couldn't be certain, but the body language of some of the men indicated they were military or paramilitary trained. Just one more burr under his saddle.

His team had the advantage of position, gear, and night vision. They could easily open fire and take down every last one of them but they were civilians. There were more Army rules prohibiting the killing of civilians than J. J. cared to remember. Then there was the ethical problem. He could never live with himself for ordering an ambush on civilians, no matter how stupid they acted.

This was not a new problem. There were many cases in military history where a mission was abandoned and personnel lost because hostiles hid behind the skirts of civilians, women, and children. For now, all J. J. and the others could do was wait and watch. He hoped they would tire of torching vehicles and move on. Helpfully they wouldn't graduate to setting buildings on fire—such as the buildings he and the others were on.

He slipped along the gravel-dressed roof, moving down the centerline of the building, making it all the more difficult to be seen from the street below. He stepped next to Crispin. "Still got her?" He whispered in the young soldier's ear.

"Yep. She's still in the cab of the eighteen-wheeler."

J. J. looked over Crispin's shoulder. "I don't see her."

"It's a sleep cab. I think she crawled back there to stay out of sight."

"How long can you stay airborne?"

"Not long. At this distance and running four props, a GPS, a transmitter, and a camera I've got maybe another twenty minutes air time assuming the winds stay down."

"This may take longer than that."

"I've thought of that. I'm thinking of parking it on top of the trailer."

"Will you be able to scan the area from there?"

"No, Boss. The camera is on the bottom of the device. Once I set her down on the trailer, all I see is a whole bunch of nothing."

"Understood. Okay, park it but I want you to do a quick survey every five minutes."

"Roger that, Boss."

"I need you to break out another toy. I need something silent."

"Can do. What do you want it to do?"

"I want to know if more people are headed this way."

Crispin frowned. "Now there's a scary thought." He thought for a moment. "Okay, I have just the thing, however, I can't operate both units at the same time. I'll set the quad down and break out the beach ball."

"Just make sure you're not seen or heard."

"Will do, Boss."

J. J. returned to his observation corner thankful they got Crispin's gear out of the back of the vehicle before the mobs flowed in. *I could use a break here, God. A really big break.*

AMELIA SAT ON THE mattress in the sleeper portion of the cab. It was roomier that she expected but still a tight fit for two grown women. Jildiz lay on her side at the back of the compartment, wheezing with each breath. Amelia sat cross-legged on what space remained, stroking Jildiz's hair in an effort to keep her calm. The woman was showing more courage than Amelia had a right to expect. She knew Jildiz wanted to inhale another hit on the rescue inhaler but resisted the urge. What she had was all that was left. Calmness and rest were the best treatment now. Amelia wondered how to get her to a hospital. Unlike other major cities, Bishkek did not have a choice of major hospitals. There were a number of clinics, but she doubted any would be open. Jildiz needed a real hospital and Amelia knew of one a few miles north of their location. All she needed to do was find a way to get Jildiz there without killing her, or being killed by their pursuers.

She released a mirthless chuckle.

"What?" Jildiz breathed. She didn't bother opening her eyes.

"When I awoke this morning I had only two concerns. One, that you would tell me you were selling out to the Chinese."

"Selling out? That is harsh."

"Sorry. I get irritable when people try to kill me. I never had any patience with that. What I meant was, you'd tell me all my fine negotiating skills came to no good."

"And the second?"

"That you'd make me eat horse meat besh barmak."

Jildiz smiled. "I almost did. That or goat's head. I know how you Americans love a nice roasted goat's head."

Amelia leaned against the wall of the sleeper compartment. So tired. She felt tapped: no energy, sore muscles, two flesh wounds, all combining to like a terminal illness, and an overpowering sense of depression. The latter had been lifted by the sight of the small surveillance drone. She didn't know who was on the other end of the controls but she planned to kiss him full on the lips.

"How long do you think before they get here?" It was as if Jildiz was reading her mind.

"I don't know. It shouldn't be too long. I assume they have transportation. I can't imagine them searching on foot. They would have been deployed from Manas. There's a good number of miles between here and there. I haven't heard a helicopter overhead. You know, that's odd. Why isn't there a chopper up there looking for you?"

"The riots. We don't even know if my father knows about all of this."

"I imagine he has his hands full."

Jildiz rolled on her back. Her breathing seemed to have eased. "There's a chance he's had to flee. Last few times riots broke out, the government buildings were breached. Security is better, but untested."

"You mean, your father may be somewhere other than the Kyrgyzstan White House?"

"It's possible. It was a riot that caused President Kurmanbek Bakiyev to flee the country for Kazakhstan and then on to Belarus."

"I see. Can I ask a question?"

"Well, I was going to get my nails done but I can spare a few minutes."

Amelia smiled. "Humor's a good sign. Would he leave without you?"

"Yes." Jildiz's answer came without hesitation. "We discussed the possibility. I don't live with my parents. I have a home outside the city. Since our country has a history of violent protests, I thought it best to insist he and Mother flee should it ever come to that." She rolled back to her side again, taking deeper breaths. "I never thought the day would come. My father has been the most progressive president in the last fifty years. He communicates well with voters. I always felt he was loved. It appears I was wrong."

"No head of state is loved by everyone. In my country, criticizing and making jokes about the sitting president is a national pastime."

"I thought baseball was the national pastime."

"It used to be. It's football and NASCAR these days."

Jildiz closed her eyes. The conversation seemed to be taxing her lung's limited ability. Amelia decided to risk another question. "Do you know of anyone who might have the power to initiate the protests?"

"My father has few enemies."

"You only need one."

Jildiz opened her eyes again. "I suppose that is true. Yes, there are several political opponents and elections are not far off."

"But would they have the kind of influence to plan a set of protests that would bring out thousands and knock out phones, but leave radio and television stations operating?"

"I don't know who could do that. Well, maybe Prime Minister Dootkasy. He has fingers in every pie."

"Would he do such a thing? Would he try to have you abducted?"

"I do not like the man," Jildiz said. "I don't trust him, but he already has great power, what would he gain?"

Amelia gave that a moment's thought. "Does he have the same power as your father?"

"No, but my father appointed him. Why would he turn against someone who has shown so much trust?"

"Et tu, Brute."

"Shakespeare . . . you think Dootkasy might be the Brutus to my father's Caesar?"

"Not Dootkasy necessarily, it's just that most revolts start at the hand of someone close. Of course, it might be coincidence. Somehow though, I don't think so."

"I'm sorry, Amelia."

"For what?"

"For being such a weight. You could be home with the doors locked, not hiding in an old truck—"

Amelia's hand over Jildiz's mouth muffled the last word. Jildiz's eyes widened. Amelia raised a finger to her lip with one hand and retrieved the 9mm with the other.

She tilted her head to point an ear to the front of the vehicle.

Silence.

She was sure she heard something.

TESS WAS ALONE NOW. All alone.

Chaplain Bartley was the last to leave and only after he asked a dozen times if she would be okay. Moyer and Rich left five minutes earlier. The three were going to make the rounds, visiting the wives and families of the other team members. Colonel Mac and Chaplain Rubin had a head start on the grueling, mind-melting duty. That was as it should be. Tess told Bartley he should go home and deal with his own grief, but he refused. "I have to see the others. It's my duty as a minister and as their friend."

Tess didn't argue.

The apartment seemed emptier than ever before, even emptier than when the landlord showed her and J. J. the place. It had no furniture then and smelled of fresh paint and carpet shampoo. It didn't take them long to settle in and start calling the place home.

She selected the furniture. “There’s no way I’m letting a guy who considers travel in a troop carrier First Class pick out furniture.”

“You are a wise woman.” His eyes twinkled when he said it. She wasn’t sure eyes could really do that, but it was how she remembered the event. “Babe, all I need is a place to put my fanny, something to put my feet on, and a sixty-five-inch high-def, flat-screen television.”

“Did you say, ‘sixty-five-inch’?” She remembered putting a hand on her hip.

“Of course not. Sixty-five inch? Really, I said, sixty-inch.”

“Sixty.”

“Don’t be silly, I said a fifty-five-inch television. I’m not greedy.”

“You know there’s only 900 square feet in this apartment, right?”

“Not to worry, Babe. I’ll pick it out. You won’t have to do a thing.”

Tess tried to look stern but was sure she failed. “It is my wifely duty to say that we can use the money for more important things.”

“You could watch all those cooking shows on cable.” He offered a cheesy grin.

“You know I’m a lousy cook. I don’t watch shows like that.”

“I know—I mean, you’re being too hard on yourself. Okay, how about this? Think about how good the History Channel and the Military Channel will look. That’s right up your academic avenue. In fact, I bet we can even write the expense off our taxes, you being a professor at a military college and all.”

She lifted her hands in surrender. “Okay, okay, you win.”

"Great. Thanks, Babe. You're gonna love the sixty-five-inch set . . ."

His voice faded, replaced by the sound of her sniffling.

His voice would never return. Gone forever were the quips. Gone forever the stupid jokes. Forever lost were the gentle words of endearment and the small voice he used when they prayed together.

Gone.

Forever.

Killed by a mob on the other side of the world.

Did they understand what they took from her? Would they ever know they stole her love, her heart, her longing, and the only man she ever loved? Would they? Would there be justice? Would the perpetrators be made to pay for their crimes? Or would they, like so many, escape justice?

Anger welled in her. Anger became fury. Fury became hatred.

Hatred? Was she allowed to hate? Did her Christian faith grant her at least a few moments of seething spite? Would God hold it against her if she detested those who not only killed her husband but burned his corpse? Or would He allow her to voice her bitterness like the psalmists who wrote scorching, bile-laced, imprecatory psalms?

Tess recalled the first time she read one of the harsh psalms. She had assumed all the ancient lyrics were of the same nature: joyful, full of praise, words of godly praise. Some were far from the realm of soft and cuddly. She picked up the Bible resting on the coffee table and found Psalm 69:24. She read aloud, "'Pour out Your rage on them, and let Your burning anger overtake them.'" Another two verses down: "'Add guilt to their guilt; do not let them share in Your righteousness. Let them be erased from the book of life and not be recorded with the righteous.'"

Hard words.

Harsh words.

Accurate to her feelings. She wished that very thing. "God, You know who they are; You know what they did; You know where they are. Pour out Your judgment upon them. Make them pay. Make it hurt. Make their pain lasting and intense. Punish them, Father. Hurt them. Destroy them slowly . . ."

She drew a hand beneath her runny nose. "I want them dead."

Hollow words.

"I want them to burn in the fires of hell."

Empty words.

"God, please make them suffer. Do what I cannot: inflict them with the greatest pain."

She didn't believe herself.

She tried to continue but couldn't muster the hatred. Why wasn't she furious? Why wasn't she ranting and calling down fire from heaven? Why? She had every right to wish the killers a painful demise. It was even in the Bible. The words she just read were recorded in the Bible and have been read for three thousand years.

Tess was too smart to keep lying to herself. She knew imprecatory psalms were not examples of how to pray, but illustrations of the pain and fear people—even people of faith—endured. God was the Judge, not her. Still, she had a right to her hatred, except hatred never came. Just emptiness. Perhaps she was too emotionally taxed to juggle more emotions than the dominant sorrow.

Setting the Bible down, Tess slipped to her knees, rested her elbows on the sofa seat, and folded her hands in prayer.

"Heavenly Father . . ." It was a two-word prayer, the rest of the petition was delivered in unspoken emotion.

Tess knew two things: prayer didn't require words; prayer spoken into the cushion of a sofa in an apartment in Columbia, South Carolina, by a crushed, pregnant woman was heard in heaven.

CHAPLAIN PAUL BARTLEY PULLED to the side of the road on his way to Lucy Medina's home. Odd, he always thought of it as Jose's home. He pulled to the side because he could no longer see the road ahead of him. He found a side street in front of an elementary school empty for the evening and leaned his head on the steering wheel.

At first he feared someone would see him.

When the tears came, he ceased to care.

CHAPTER 25

J. J. TURNED TO see Crispin set what looked like a basketball in the middle of the roof. He crawled on hands and knees to reach the center. J. J. had seen everything in Crispin's bag o' tricks so he knew he wasn't looking at a piece of sports equipment. Although difficult to see in the dim light, he had seen it in full illumination and it was the craziest device he ever viewed. At a distance the "ball" looked solid, but up close it proved to be a sphere made of horizontal and vertical plastic ribs. Inside were the brains and senses of the surveillance device. Also inside were a pair of counter-spinning propellers driven by a small electric motor. The thing was not fast but it was agile. The original design came from a Japanese research company, but several military contractors were hard at work on something similar.

"Binkster," as Crispin liked to call the device—J. J. failed to fathom the man's need to name his equipment—rose slowly, straight up then at an altitude of 500 feet eased to the northeast. By plan, Crispin programmed the device to move slowly so it didn't catch the eyes of the growing mob below.

One of the benefits of Binkster was its ability to operate without a human controller. Crispin could input a GPS location and the drone would fly there. It could even sense solid objects in its path and steer around them. It had its greatest usefulness searching inside a building while soldiers remained safely outside avoiding hidden combatants or booby traps.

Crispin watched the small video monitor. J. J. turned his attention to the crowd in the alley. Their numbers were thinning. He saw several walk down the alley and around to the street to join their pyromaniac pals. He already received word the alley side of Aliki's building was clear.

J. J. glanced back at Crispin and saw the man staring back, motioning him over. J. J. scampered to the middle of the roof. "What's ya got, Hawkeye?"

"Nothing good, Boss." He held the remote with the embedded video monitor so J. J. could see it.

The sight of a small group of men moving down an empty street. It wasn't the sight of the group that bothered J. J.—there were six of them—it was the way they moved. Each man was armed with an automatic weapon although they wore no uniforms. Three moved down the east side of the street; three down the west. They moved like a military unit, clearly searching for something. They peered in shop windows and tested doors to see if any were open. If they were looters, they would be breaking windows. These men were not looters, they were a search team. Good guys? Bad guys? In the chaos that was Bishkek, J. J. couldn't tell.

"Doesn't look good, Boss." Crispin whispered the words.

"How far?"

"Based on GPS, about a klick, but using streets we'd have to transverse a klick and a half. Maybe a little more."

Great, a mile of open streets with roving gangs between us and them. With full gear they were looking at a ten-minute double-time advance. They could never get there before the armed men did. The only hope was the men would ignore the truck. Based on the way they were rattling doors they would check the semi.

"What should we do, Boss?"

J. J. wished Eric Moyer was here. He always seemed to know the right thing to do and when to do it. But he wasn't here. J. J. was Boss. The brass had expectations of him; his men needed instant decisions; and two women needed his help. This thought steeled his spine but the thought of his pregnant wife waiting for him melted his resolve.

In high school he had a friend whose father was a firefighter, the only other career apart from the Army J. J. ever considered. He loved to hear the man tell stories about everything from brush fires to fire-engulfed buildings. He relished every tale of rescue and auto accidents. Then his friend's father told him of his first call: a crib death. "There was nothing we could do. The child had been dead far too long. I was a rookie with a wife but no kids. My fellow firefighters had kids. They were a mess. I was left to keep an eye on the mother and father until the sheriff arrived. It's like being on suicide watch. People do strange things when confronted by sudden tragedy. It was sad then, but I couldn't understand why all the more experienced firefighters were outside smoking and avoiding eye contact with each other. Then Jim here was born."

J. J. remembered the man pausing. "I used to check his breathing every night before going to bed. If I had to use the head in the middle of the night, I would slip into his room and lay my hand on his back."

It was a sad story but this was the first time J. J. understood. He was never hesitant to run to the sound of gunfire; never reluctant to enter the fray. Things changed. He wasn't just a soldier any longer; he wasn't just a husband; he was a father to unborn twins and that put a hitch in his step.

"Boss?"

J. J. looked into Crispin's eyes, nodded, then activated his radio. "Joker, Boss."

No response.

He tried again. "Joker, Boss." Still nothing. He was about to make a third attempt when the Samoan's whispered voice came through the ear piece.

"Go, Boss."

"Hostiles are moving in on our target. Time to hit the road. Is your street side still clear?"

"Roger that, Boss."

"Good. Now listen up . . ."

GREAT, HE'S GONNA THINK *I fell asleep over here.* Aliki wanted to slap himself but didn't want to explain the self-abuse to Mike and Pete. He moved to the center of the roof and motioned the others over.

"Boss says we're bugging out. Black hats have found the girls, or are about to. We go in as two teams. They will approach the semi from the north; we'll come in from the south."

"What do we do if we run into locals?" Nagano asked. "Some of those guys are packing serious heat."

"Orders are to avoid contact whenever possible. We are not to engage civilians unless they are armed. Deadly force is authorized if necessary."

"So we toast anyone pointing a barrel our way," Pete said.

"Roger that. We have to get off this roof quiet and fast. I want everyone sharp-eyed and on their game. We are severely outnumbered here. Clear."

"Clear." Mike and Pete said in unison.

"Junior, get eyes on the alley. I want to know if it's still clear."

Pete shuffled to the rear parapet. He hadn't made the steps before Mike moved closer and punched Aliki in the arm. Hard. "What's with you, dude? If I hadn't alerted you that Boss was on the horn, you'd still be up here picking at your teeth."

"I'm fine. I let my mind drift."

"Don't give me that, Joker. We've been pals for too many years. Is your hearing getting worse?"

"I'm fine, really."

"I can only cover for you so long, dude. You gotta know that."

"I know it, Mike. You did me a solid. I owe you big time."

"You got that straight. There's no such thing as a stupid hero, just a dead one. You have a problem, you let me know. Clear?"

"I think I have an extra stripe you don't, Mike. Don't push our friendship too far."

Nagano started to speak, but bit back the words. Instead of speaking he hustled to the alley side of the building.

AMELIA REMOVED HER HAND from Jildiz's mouth, took the 9mm in hand, and flicked off the safety.

"Get to the back," she whispered. "Slowly. Don't jiggle the cab." An impossible request. Amelia guessed the three-decade-old tractor was still running on the same suspension it rolled off the assembly line with.

Jildiz did an admirable job, slowly scooting across the narrow mattress. Amelia sat on the edge of the bed, the pistol held in both hands and positioned between her knees. She tilted her head to one side but heard nothing. Before, she was certain the breeze carried a human voice her direction. She couldn't be sure, but she was in no position to take chances.

She waited. She strained her ears. Nothing.

The cab jostled. It did it again. Amelia thought the motion originated in the back, maybe at the trailer's doors. Someone was trying to open the back. The owner? The cab swayed again. Not the owner, he would have a key to unlock the back and too much effort was being made to open the doors.

Now she heard voices, muted but clearly locals. Had she been wrong to assume the little drone was American? Americans didn't have a lock on technology.

All went silent again. A moment later the cab shook more. This time she could tell someone was trying to open the driver's side door.

Her heart began to pound and she tried to calm it by raising her weapon, its barrel near the curtain separating the driver's space from the sleeper cab. They couldn't be seen. That gave her a moment of relief. Maybe they would move on. Then again, if they were looters, they might be interested in whatever was in the trailer. In that case, the natural thing to do was check the cab for the key that would open the lock.

She heard someone try the passenger side door. Amelia weighed the most likely scenario and it wasn't good. If there were several men and they were armed, she might be able to take out one or two of them before the others opened fire. The thin metal skin of the cab wouldn't provide much resistance against copper-jacketed rounds spit from an AK-47 or similar. Crawling into the truck seemed a good idea a short time ago, now she chastised herself for being so foolish as to put them in an environment with no back door.

Was surrender better than battle? If only she knew how many men were out there. If only . . .

J. J. GAVE CRISPIN ninety seconds to pull his gear together and switch from surveillance geek to Ranger-trained soldier, something he saw the man do on several occasions. The transformation was amazing to see. Jovial, somewhat innocent, and almost always nerdy, Crispin could become a steely-eyed soldier by flipping a mental switch. Ninety-two seconds later, Crispin was crouched next to the alley-side parapet at the south end of the building, M4 poised to do damage. Jose was in the same position at the north.

Taking one deep breath, J. J. slipped over the side and slowly moved down the ladder, his back turned to the smoldering carcass of what had once been their transportation. Acrid smoke flowed near the wall with the ladder, keeping the men some distance away. J. J. didn't blame them, a burning car stunk.

Only three men remained, each smoking a cigarette. J. J. was never a smoker. Didn't like the smell or the health risks. It amazed him how these guys, with smoke overhead and eye-burning, toxic smoke still rising from the vehicle, would feel the need to voluntarily inhale more smoke. *To each their own.*

He set boots on pavement as silent as a kitten walking on a carpet, then, with his M4 leveled at the backs of the men, moved to the rear of the vehicle then around the other side. Being stealthy was to their advantage. Had they heard him and turned his way, several suppressed rounds would have rained down from the roof. That would be bad for them.

J. J. positioned himself next to the still-hot hulk and leveled his weapon at the backs of the three men. He sighted on the spine of the center man. Easier to pop the other two without moving his weapon more than a few inches to either side. He hoped he wouldn't need to squeeze the trigger.

But he would should they hear Doc or Hawkeye's descent. Of one thing he was certain: these were not nice people caught in the wrong place at the wrong time. Each had a weapon: one AK-47; what looked like an Israeli-made Uzi, one of the world's most widely spread weapons and popular among certain military groups and terrorists. If it came to it, he would be the first to go. Then the AK-47 man. The third man had a handgun holstered to his belt. He stood the best chance of living if things went south. Not a good chance, just the best of the three.

The men laughed loudly and spoke in a language unfamiliar to J. J.. Not Russian, most likely Kyrgyz. He guessed it was a dirty joke. A certain kind of laugh followed such things.

Footsteps to his side. A corner-eyed glance showed Jose two feet behind him and one foot further away from the vehicle. More footsteps. They were lucky so far. Now they needed a little more luck, or as J. J. thought of it: grace.

The plan was discussed before J. J. went over the parapet. Neither words nor signals were needed. Crispin peeled off, his large pack swaying with each step. Jose followed. J. J. fell in step, moving backward, his eyes fixed on the three.

A few rapid steps and they reached the intersection of the alley and a cross street. Crispin stopped just shy of the corner of the last shop and held up a fist. Jose and J. J. slowed and moved behind him, J. J. still focused on the men they left thirty meters back.

Crispin peeked around the corner then took one step back. Without turning he held up one finger. One man.

J. J. turned his head. A large, ruddy-skinned man, looking to be four inches taller and seventy pounds heavier than Crispin, stepped into the alley. The man was armed with an AK-47, which made him a friend of those who burned their cars. His eyes widened. His mouth opened. He reached for his weapon. Crispin's fist caught him square in the face.

The man's knees buckled for a moment, long enough for Crispin to throw an arm around the gunman's neck, pinching his trachea and carotid arteries in the crook of his elbow. Jose slipped forward and wrenched the AK-47 from the man's hands. Crispin turned and hoisted the man on his hip, letting the enemy's weight do most of the work. The choke hold cut off the man's air, keeping him from sounding the alarm and squeezed shut the arteries feeding his brain blood and oxygen. He was unconscious a few moments later.

Crispin lowered the man to the pavement, tucking him in the juncture of an exterior wall to the street. Jose ejected the magazine from the weapon and cleared the chamber of the ready round.

Seconds later they were two blocks down and headed north in another alley. Doc found a Dumpster and dropped off the AK-47 magazine. One less gun in the mix.

In the Dante-like smoke-shrouded night, J. J. led his half of the team toward the truck and prayed they would get there in time.

ALIKI URALE TROTTED AHEAD of Mike Nagano and Pete Rasor. His size was an advantage in hand-to-hand situations but running remained a challenge. During basic training and later Ranger training, he always suffered more than his companions on the long runs and hikes. He finished, usually just well enough to stay in the program. He excelled in everything else, but carting 280 pounds of muscled Samoan took work, especially if there was a pack on his back.

Their exit was smooth, waiting until they heard two *clicks* on their radios, telling them Boss and the others were down and safe. If gunfire erupted, Aliki, Mike, and Pete were to pin down the group in the street, taking out every man with a gun if they could. Those two *clicks* on the radio were sweet sounds. Now if he could only get rid of the constant ringing in his ears.

At every intersection, they stopped and peered around corners, moving only if they felt they were unobserved.

For a moment, Aliki thought they would be able to make the distance without being seen. But then two men with Chinese-made Type 56 assault rifles, a knockoff of the AK-47, both raised their weapons and one of them said something. Aliki couldn't hear it. He didn't care. He and Mike brought both men down with short bursts from their weapons.

Aliki was in a hurry. He didn't bother to see if either remained alive. It didn't matter. They would bleed to death soon enough.

The smoky air made his lungs ache and the pounding of his boots on pavement made his knees feel as if they were splintering into tiny, sharp shards. He pressed on. That's what he always did. Press on.

ONCE, IN AN UNGUARDED moment, J. J.'s previous leader quipped, "All leadership decisions are meant to be second-guessed." J. J. didn't give Eric Moyer's words much thought then, but now he not only understood the comment, he felt the weight of it. Ordering his men off the roof meant several things—life and death things. First, it meant risking discovery by an overwhelming and heavily armed force; second, it meant surrendering the high ground, and putting them on the same footing as the enemy; third, it meant—

if discovered—the end of the mission. Failing in his first action as Boss wouldn't look good in his personnel jacket.

Two things pushed him to make the call: one, to do nothing could mean the capture or death of Amelia Lennon and the president's daughter—something else that wouldn't look good on his record; second, risk was his business and the business of his team. Better they take the greater risk than the women he was tasked to save.

The armed mob was behind them and Aliki just reported their location. They were two streets over and half a klick ahead. For a big man, he made good time. That or he was making Pete carry him.

Voices. Shouts.

J. J. slowed his jog down the alley. Jose and Crispin did the same. They reached the next intersection and peeked around the corner of what J. J. took to be some kind of delicatessen. A block to the east stood three men forming a half-circle around a mother and—he strained to see details through the NVGs—two children. The children were the same height. Both girls. Both about six years old. Twins. In the street, three feet from the curb, rested a sedan that looked older than J. J.

One of the men had the woman pinned to the wall, his body pressed against her.

"Boss? We're burning time."

"Take a look, Doc." J. J. pulled back from the corner.

Jose took a quick look then pulled back. He said something in Spanish that sounded like English words J. J. tried to keep out of his vocabulary. "That won't do. No, sir. That won't do by a long shot."

J. J. could see the anger in Jose's eyes, the balaclava might conceal the man's face, but not the tension and barely subdued fury. He looked at the situation again. The man was rubbing a hand on the woman's face then moved to her shoulder.

Crispin took a turn looking. It took only a second. "We gotta do it, Boss. I don't want to live with that scene playing in my head."

"It will only take a couple of minutes." Jose bounced on the balls of his feet.

"We move quietly and fast. Don't shoot them unless they draw down on you."

"You sure you want us to hold back, Boss?" Jose said.

He heard laughter from the men that chilled his spine. "No." One more second passed. "Doc, you take the man on the left; Hawkeye, you got the dude on the right. The man with the woman is mine. Go."

J. J. pushed his NVGs up on the hinge that fixed them to his helmet. They moved from the alley into the street in a half crouch. Stealth was the order of the moment and they moved silently, aided by the distraction the men had with their partner and the woman. His hand moved to her blouse.

Every nerve in J. J. body came to life, fueled by an anger he seldom knew.

It took less than twenty strides for the team to reach the attackers. It took ten seconds to put an end to their activity. J. J. hung his M4 behind him on its sling, seized the man by the back of the collar with his left hand and the belt with his right. He pulled. He lifted. The man's feet came off the sidewalk. J. J. replaced them with the attacker's face. He then dropped to a knee, landing hard on the man's backbone. In a fluid motion, J. J. had his service handgun out of the holster and pressed into the base of the man's skull. It took all of J. J.'s willpower not to tap the trigger.

A glance to the left showed Jose raising his M4 and delivering the butt of the weapon to the man's face. J. J. guessed Doc was aiming for the man's nose but he missed, catching him square in his open mouth. Blood ran. J. J. didn't want to know what the crunching sound meant.

A glance right showed Crispin could work more than a joystick. Hawkeye's booted foot caught the third attacker in the coccyx. The man arched his back, hands reaching for the sensitive, injured area then turned, his face showing pain and fury. Crispin thrust the barrel of his weapon into the man's chest so hard that the sternum made an audible crunch. He crumpled like an empty sack.

It took only moments to check the men for weapons. J. J. allowed his man up but kept his handgun aimed between his eyes. The man wet himself. J. J. pointed down the street. The two men ran, one with soggy pants, one with missing teeth. Crispin's target remained unconscious, maybe dead.

Not wanting to speak, an act that might give away their nationality, J. J. pointed at Jose then to the car. Crispin went with him.

The tires on the car looked sound; the engine continued to hum. The only thing out of order was the windshield, which had fractured into a spiderweb of fragments held together by the safety glass. J. J. wanted to ask what happened but knew nothing of the language the woman might speak. That left him nothing but guesswork, and best guess was the men threw something at the car, shattering the windscreen and making it impossible to see. The woman pulled over, the worst thing she could do.

Jose removed his Benchmade Nimravus knife and drove its four-inch blade through the shattered bits of glass and the plastic laminate that was holding it together. He repeated the action until he had a hole large enough to put his hand through. He began pulling the damaged windshield out in pieces. Crispin caught on and stepped in to help.

J. J. turned to the woman. She looked thirty-five or so. Tears covered her cheeks. He could see a bruise forming on each check and J. J. wished he'd dumped the man harder. His eyes moved to the children who huddled next to their mother. They were twins with the same light hair and the same terror draped on their faces. Mother pulled them close. Their expressions reminded J. J. of how he must appear to them: armed to the teeth, helmet, face covered in a black mask. J. J. wanted to pat the children on the head but figured they had been manhandled enough by strange men.

Taking a step back, J. J. gave a gentleman's bow and motioned to the car. The woman moved from the wall where she had been pinned and took a trepidation-filled step. J. J. moved away, put enough distance between them to help her feel safe. Crispin and Jose did the same.

She put the car in gear. J. J. waved. The children waved back. He wondered if his kids would be that polite and that brave.

Jose stepped to J. J.'s side. "We did a good thing, Boss."

"Yes, yes we did."

Jose chuckled. "Did you see our baby? I'm gonna have to be careful how much I tease him. Wow, what a move."

"I'm not the baby of the group," Crispin said.

Jose ignored him. “I think we’ll have to give him a new nick. Maybe Hawkeye 2.0.”

“I like it,” J. J. said.

“I don’t,” Crispin said, but his voice carried a tone of good humor.

“Let’s go. There’s more bad guy butt to kick.”

CHAPTER 26

BISHKEK CHIEF OF POLICE Emil Abirov arrived at the front gate of the Transit Center at Manas Air Base ahead of the approaching crowd, but not by much. He traveled in the police helicopter which landed on the commercial side of the airport, an area separate from the portion used by the American military. He arrived after giving difficult advice and making hard decisions.

His resources were limited and the danger greater than he could recall, even worse than the 2010 riots. Crowds were moving on key government facilities, the American Embassy, the White House, and several key business centers. Already several police cars were set on fire and at least three military vehicles. Eight policemen were wounded, two of them seriously, and Abirov had no reason to believe the worst had passed.

The smoke-darkened sky made Bishkek seem more like purgatory, and he feared purgatory would become hell. Even here, north of Bishkek, the air stunk of smoke. He wondered how many toxins he had inhaled over the last few hours.

A police cruiser waited for him near the helipad to take him around to the American-leased portion of the airport to the access road used to enter the military compound. Abirov was in a bind, stuck, as his grandparents used to say, between the devil and the deep blue sea. On the one hand a city to protect, but the airport also fell under his jurisdiction. No matter where he was, he felt he should be somewhere else. When at the White House, he wanted to be on the streets with his men; when on the streets with his men, he wanted to be overseeing the protection of the Manas International Airport. His forces were spread too thin. He did not have enough men to secure all the areas in need of police protection.

The army was proving useful but they were tasked with protecting hospitals, key government buildings, and now the airport. It was made clear that only a few resources would be used to protect the American portion of the base. It was a political decision no doubt influenced by Prime Minister Dootkasy. The thought of the man turned Abirov's already gymnastic stomach.

Abirov slipped into the front seat of the police car. Jantoro Kalyev, assistant chief of police, was behind the wheel. The dome light revealed a man who had aged five years since breakfast. Jantoro had been an officer for twenty-five years and was two years from retirement. The years of police work sped his aging. His head seemed too thin, his hair too white, his eyebrows too unruly.

"Could you see the crowds from the air?" Jantoro sounded grim.

"Yes, I estimate they are twenty minutes away. Two groups. I estimate fifteen hundred. Maybe more."

"Will we be getting more men from the army?"

"No. Not on this side of the airport. Everything around the airport is secure. We are to maintain the crowd a hundred meters from the Americans."

The car moved down a side street near one of the runways. Abirov could see armed American soldiers forming a perimeter around the military aircraft.

Jantoro shook his head. "We do not have the manpower for that. A crowd the size you mentioned will easily run over us. Does the order not to shoot still hold?"

"It does. There are still those who think police and military opened fire on civilians in 2010. The president wishes to avoid that."

"Would the president like to come here and help us?"

"That's enough. We do as we're told."

"Yes, sir. My apologies. I'm a little tired."

"I'm frightened too, Jantoro." He stared into the near dark and wondered when he would see his home and family again. "I want you to pull our men back. We will set up a line fifty meters south of the entrance. The Americans will undoubtedly have men along their fence and at the entrance. Since communication with them is limited with the phones down, I have brought one of our radios for them to use. Have you seen soldiers at the base?"

Jantoro gave a brief nod of his narrow head. "They are staying out of sight, perhaps to avoid agitating any protesters who show up at the gate, but I have seen vehicles being moved in place and armed troops taking up positions behind buildings closest to the front gate. They have also moved two large trucks across the road. I think they expect the crowds to rush the gate."

"It is wise to be cautious."

The drive ended a few minutes later with the car stopping at the front gate. A pair of large men in U.S. Army uniforms and carrying automatic weapons stood at the entrance gate. Abirov had no doubt other eyes were on him. He was glad he was in uniform.

He approached the men. "I am Chief Emil Abirov." He hoped his English would be clear enough. "I would like to speak to Colonel Weidman."

"I'm sorry, sir. The base is closed."

Abirov conjured a smile. "Yes, I assumed that to be the case. I still need to speak to him. He needs to speak to me."

"Sir, the base is closed."

"There are fifteen hundred people a short distance away. Your commander might want to hear that from me rather than from the mob. Unless you want to make that decision for him." Abirov didn't blink. One of the soldiers did.

"Wait here, sir."

The soldier stepped to the guard building. Abirov could see him making a call on a field telephone. He returned a few moments later. "The colonel asked if you would mind waiting a few moments."

Abirov chose not to comment. Of course, he would wait. It was why he approached them.

It took less than five minutes for a uniformed man to arrive in a Humvee. He was accompanied by two well-armed military police. Colonel Weidman walked with authority and determination, his face blank of all expression. Abirov steeled himself for verbal assault. The man had to be angry. He was facing a base closure under his watch. A bad way to end a career.

"Chief Abirov." Weidman held out his hand. "I'm sorry for the delay. It seems my attention is needed in many areas today."

"As are mine, Colonel. I am under orders of the mayor of Bishkek and our president to provide what aid I can. As you may know, riots have erupted throughout our country, the worse being here. With the telephone system down I thought it best to bring you up to date and offer you this." He offered a handheld radio.

"I've been exchanging e-mail with the president's office." Weidman kept his hands to his side.

"Yes, sir. I am aware of that. The radio is so you can monitor our transmissions." When Weidman hesitated, Abirov sighed. "Colonel, it is just a radio, perhaps a little more primitive than you're used to, but it is still useful. I assure you, it is not a bomb." A second later he added, "With all due respect, sir, if I were here to assassinate you, you would already be dead. Do you agree?"

"I do." Weidman took the radio.

"Thank you, sir. Now, I need to give you some information . . ."

KAZIMIR VILNOV CARRIED A sign calling for the expulsion of "American Squatters." Other men and women carried signs broadcasting similar sentiments, some more critical that others. Some started a chant, "Ugly Americans leave our beautiful home." Privately, Kazimir agreed. Nothing would please him more than to see the Americans take their war planes and arrogant soldiers to some other part of the planet. It was an opinion he kept to himself. It was inappropriate for a Bishkek police officer to voice such ideas. The sign he carried was part of his cover. Putting plainclothes officers in the midst of protesters was a tried-and-true technique to monitor events from inside and to identify instigators. Protesting was one thing; violence was another.

"Ugly Americans leave our beautiful home." He chanted loud enough to be heard by those around him, but not so loud he couldn't hear what else was going on. Hearing was less useful than seeing. He scanned the crowd, frequently moving from one part of the mob to the other. He eyed their behavior, their dress, their expressions. Mostly he watched their eyes.

Protesters tended to look in the direction they were walking or at the people by their side. If a leader was present as in this case—a young man with a megaphone at the front of the pack—most eyes gazed his way. Terrorists and criminals shifted their eyes frequently, often looking at cohorts who might be some distance away.

Clothing was important too. Summer in Bishkek was mild, even at night. There was no need for long, heavy coats. Briefcases, sports bags, and the like were always a concern.

So far he only saw average citizens, unemployed workers, teenagers looking for excitement to inject into their lives. Mothers carried small children. The crowd was a cross section of what Kazimir saw when the city was normal and quiet.

There was nothing ordinary about tonight. That protests occurred was no surprise to him or anyone else in law enforcement. They trained for it for several years. Every officer had a role. Some of his compatriots were in uniform and very visible. That was by plan. Others worked undercover. There were three other officers in this crowd and a dozen more spread throughout those marching on the government buildings. Far too few for his liking.

A motion to his right caught his eye: just a woman repositioning a toddler on her hip. Another motion to his left: two men in a scuffle over their place in the queue. Bystanders pulled them apart before fists could be clenched.

A noise behind. Someone brought a long plastic horn and was blowing it like a fan at a soccer game. Kazimir returned his gaze to the woman with the child. She was young, early twenties he guessed. The child couldn't be older than three. The same age as his daughter. Her image flashed on his mind as did those of his wife, his six-year-old son, and his widowed mother who lived with them. He would have preferred to be with them rather than in a mob that seemed to be closing ranks around him, making it hard to breathe.

A short distance down the road the yellow glow of high-pressure sodium lights used by the military base diluted the darkness. They weren't far from the south entrance. Another hundred yards and he could see the flare of flashing red lights. The uniforms were ahead of them.

The mob slowed and Kazimir's heart quickened. Push just met shove.

Again his gaze danced around the group. In a marching crowd like this, new faces appeared every few seconds; suspicious ones could disappear in a moment. The angry men were side-by-side again, this time walking like old friends. Ideology could make friends of enemies and enemies of friends.

The mother held her position but two other mothers with children on hips joined her. Between angry shouts they smiled, enjoying the excitement the march brought to their home-bound lives. Kazimir knew what it was like to live with a woman who felt chained to the home by children—

A new face. Bearded. Long hair like an old Russian mystic. While others kept their faces lifted, this man kept his head down. He stared at the ground, alone in a crowd of over a thousand. He didn't chant. Did not pump his fist in the air. More disturbing, he wore an overcoat. Stains and several unraveling seams said the coat was old, older than the man who owned it.

"Did you hear?" A man in his forties with a face scarred by the sun touched Kazimir on the elbow. "They have brought in a fire truck. Maybe from the air base. We might get wet." He smiled, showing a gap where two incisors had been. "Pass the word on."

"Thank you. Yes, I will."

Kazimir regained sight of the man in the overcoat. He was moving forward, elbowing his way through the crowd.

He reached inside the coat with his right hand.

Gun? Worse, a bomb?

The man shoved an elderly woman to the side. That settled it for Kazimir. He dropped the sign and pressed his way forward, trying not to draw the vocal ire of the protesters. He needed to surprise the man.

He failed.

"Don't push!"

The suspect looked behind him and his expression told Kazimir he had been spotted. The man drew his hand from the coat and Kazimir saw a cylindrical object.

"Bomb! Bomb!" Kazimir shouted loud enough to hurt his own ears. No time to think. No time to form a plan. No chance to question his actions. Kazimir sprinted forward, the image of his family in mind.

Screams poured from the front of the group and rolled over the heads of the crowd. An unfamiliar sound. People began moving back. A careful step or two at a time then with a quicker pace.

Kazimir pushed against the human tide. So did the overcoat-man.

"Bomb! Bomb!" Kazimir knew there would be a panic but his warning might save a few lives even if it caused a few injuries—

Something white flew through the sky then fell on the crowd. It was cool and slimy.

He pressed forward, closing the distance.

The slime continued to fall but in greater amounts until it covered persons and pavement. Kazimir slipped in the material, falling to a knee, driving it into the road and launching fiery bolts of pain up his leg and back. He pushed to his feet and continued the pursuit, working his way between fleeing protesters.

The man with the cylinder in his hand fell to the ground hard, his feet unable to get traction in the goo. He pushed to his feet, turned, and raised the object over his head.

Kazimir plowed forward, leaping with arms outstretched but unable to get the position necessary to launch himself as high as he needed. Instead of reaching the suspicious object he had to settle for the man's throat.

Both tumbled to the ground as a hundred pairs of feet raced past. His momentum landed Kazimir on top of the bomber. He was crawling over the man's frame before the fall was complete.

He let go of the man's neck.

He pinned the arm with the cylinder.

He stretched for the object: a metal cylinder with a red button. It reminded him of a spray can, but a kind of spray can he had never seen before.

The man struggled to get a finger to the button.

"Drop it! Police. Drop it!"

The man continued to struggle. He brought a left fist to the right side of Kazimir's face but his position on the ground, surrounded by slippery foam, deprived the punch of any real power. He tried again, but Kazimir ignored it as he did the first. He was focused on one thing: keeping the man's finger off the red button.

Kazimir had no sense of time, or of pain, or of his own life. The button. Just the button.

One finger touched the top of the can, then the side of the trigger, then the top of the button. Kazimir took hold of the finger and pulled it back and then back more until he heard the knuckle snap.

A scream.

Kazimir twisted the broken finger, ignoring the howls of pain. Then he yanked as hard as his position would allow and it allowed plenty.

The cylinder dropped and Kazimir snatched it.

A wave of white, fire-retardant foam swept over him.

CHAPTER 27

AMELIA WONDERED IF HER pounding heart had enough power to break her sternum. It was as if the muscular organ was trying to make good its escape. Jildiz pushed herself to a sitting position on the sleeper cab mattress. Pulling her knees to her chest, she remained quiet just as Amelia told her to do. Still she wheezed and, to Amelia's heightened senses, it sounded as if the woman had a three-pack-a-day habit.

She heard something else. The sound of the rescue inhaler. Amelia worried about an overdose but she couldn't make Jildiz take back the inhalation of medication. It was done now and that egg couldn't be unscrambled.

The cab jerked to the right several times as if someone were trying to rip the door from the hinges. Then a voice spoke in Kyrgyz, "Look. The wiring is hanging low."

Amelia cringed. She had pulled a portion of the wiring harness from beneath the dashboard in a useless attempt to figure out how to hot-wire the vehicle.

"It is old. What do you expect?" A different voice. Older. Harsher. Muted by the metal frame of the truck cab.

"No one would leave it that way. It would be in the way. We should check inside. The key to the back must be in there."

"That doesn't matter. We are not here to loot. We are here to find the women. I don't want to explain why they got away when you're holding stolen goods. It would not go well."

"I'm not afraid."

"That is because you are stupid. We have wasted too much time here."

There were other words Amelia could not work out. She assumed the man at the driver's side window was mumbling under his breath. She strained to hear more.

"The curtain to the sleeping area is closed. Do you want to explain why we did not search it? That would not go well either."

"Do it quickly."

Something hit the side window. Once. Twice.

Then came the sound of the door opening.

ALIKI WAS SUCKING FOUL air like a man surfacing from the bottom of the ocean.

"Too many cupcakes, Joker?" Nagano touched his elbow, making the big Samoan turn.

"Hey, Weps?"

"Yeah?"

"Shut up."

"Roger that, Joker. Shutting up."

They slowed as they reached the intersection of the target area. Aliki sighted down the street. In the green haze of his NVGs he saw an old eighteen-wheeler and several men around it. One searched beneath the trailer, one stood to the side, one stood on the driver's side running board peering into the window. He keyed his mike. "Joker, Boss. We are on site."

"Report." J. J. sounded nearly as winded as Aliki felt.

"I make five hostiles, all armed, all men. They're giving the truck a good going over."

"Any sign of our friend?"

"Negative. What's your ETA?"

"We're five minutes out."

Aliki pressed the earpiece further into his ear to overcome the unending ringing in his brain. "Roger, ten minutes out."

Weps shook his head and held up five fingers.

J. J. came back immediately. "Negative, Joker. Five, I say again, five minutes. Confirm."

"Roger that, Boss. Five minutes. Orders?"

"Sit tight until we are in place unless the bottom drops out."

"Understood. We'll sit—Standby." Aliki watched as a man raised the butt of his AK-47 and started pounding the driver's window. "We have a situation. They're making entrance."

"Understood." A second later. "Go."

J. J. LENGTHENED HIS stride. Five minutes wasn't much time on the clock but in a gun battle it seemed just an hour short of eternity. He pressed on, moving as fast as his boots and gear would let him. The part of his brain not involved in assessing the situation and weighing options chugged out a prayer.

Ten strides later the sound of gunfire echoed down the streets.

FIRST SHE SAW HIS hand take hold of the curtain. Then she saw his ugly face and smelled his cigarette-laced breath. His eyes widened first at seeing two women behind the curtain. His Asian face split into a yellow-toothed smile, which disappeared when he saw the barrel of the 9mm. He was close enough to see the rifling. He jumped back and fumbled with the AK, a weapon never designed to be wielded in the cramped confines of the tractor trailer.

She felt a half-second of guilt for having the advantage of surprise.

Then she pulled the trigger.

ALIKI HEARD A MUFFLED *pop*, a pop sharp enough to be easily recognized by a man who had fired a dozen different high-powered weapons in his decade and a half of military service. His hearing was too damaged to put a size to the caliber but good enough to know it was a handgun with a kick.

The body of the man who broke the window slipped from the cab and fell to the curb. He made no attempt to get up. If Aliki's guess was right, the man's days of getting up were done. "We going, Joker?"

Not Nagano's voice. Pete's. He turned. Pete repeated the question. "We going? They need help." Aliki turned his gaze to Nagano and saw anger.

"Of course. Watch your cross fire."

Nagano swore then stepped in front of Aliki, leveling his M110 Semi-Automatic Sniper rifle down the street. "Stay to the east of the truck. I'll take this side."

PETE WAS MOVING FROM the alley into the street and making his way forward, his M4 aimed and his finger applying one ounce less of the necessary pressure to pull the trigger. He heard Aliki move up on his right. Pete had a bus load of questions but lacked time. Everything else would need to wait. The men in front of him were all that mattered at the moment.

Two of the men on the sidewalk backpedaled and raised their weapons to fire at the truck cab, clearly intending to punch more holes in it than Bonnie and Clyde's Ford. His peripheral vision caught a glimpse of Nagano aiming his sniper rifle down the sidewalk.

There was a *pop* and one of the men staggered back two steps, his hand raised to his chest. Pete had seen it before. The high velocity of the copper-jacketed round passed though the gunman as if he were made of paper. He looked at his hand, then down the street. His automatic rifle dropped barrel-first to the concrete. He followed it down.

His companion looked confused for a moment as his brain tried to make sense of what he just saw. It took only a second for him to match the effect to the cause. He spun, raising his weapon. The head shot didn't give the man time to aim. He joined his friend on the walkway.

That made three on the ground; two on their feet. For the moment they had the advantage. Nagano had cover, Pete and Aliki didn't.

Advance. Weapon ready. Eyes forward. Advance with caution. Advance with purpose. Forward into the teeth of the beast.

When Nagano dropped the hammer on the second man, his pals scooted to the front. Pete saw that. He also saw one had a radio. A dozen other men or more might be on their way. He knew of a mob of armed men not far away. He watched them torch their vehicles.

This had to be done and done quickly.

THE ACRID SMELL OF spent gunpowder permeated the small space. Amelia made the shot she had to make. The sight of flesh and blood splattering the windows and seats sickened her and had she the time, she would have emptied her stomach. She chose to retreat farther back into the sleeper cab, pressing against Jildiz, shielding her.

Then came a different sound. A shot . . . rifle . . . big rifle. Then another. That was followed by several bursts of familiar automatic fire.

"Down." Amelia pushed Jildiz down on the mattress and covered her body with her own. She might be hearing the weapon fire of friends. She prayed she was right.

J. J. CAME UP a block south of his other men. The original plan was for half the unit to approach from the south and the other half from the north. That would have given them advantage over the men at the truck. It was close to impossible to fight soldiers from the front and the back simultaneously. Even the best plans rarely survive the first contact with the enemy. The sound of gunfire was louder and closer.

J. J. signaled his men to slow then surveyed the street. He saw Nagano advancing toward the truck, the M110 shoulder high. In the middle of the street Pete and Aliki approached from the other side. They were exposed with no shelter between them and the gunmen. Every few steps, Pete's weapon spit out a burst of fire, pinning the enemy at the front of the semi.

It took only a few seconds for J. J. to access the situation.

One of the gunmen popped up, his AK-47 over his head, and squeezed off a burst. It was a blind shot, the man not wanting to make his head a target. The rounds missed Pete and Aliki, but not by much.

"With me," J. J. ordered, and began a sprint around the block. Long strides. Fast feet. The sound of bootfalls behind him. He keyed his mike. "Coming up on your left."

There wasn't a response. He didn't expect one. His men had their hands full.

The trip around the block felt too long, too far, but only a few minutes passed. J. J. didn't need to see it. He knew what the team was doing: approaching slowly, keeping the men pinned down.

They stopped at the corner. "We're in position. Hold your fire."

J. J., Crispin, and Jose stepped into the open, their weapons at the ready.

Another glance showed J. J. the position of two men, each with AK-47s, each hunkered in front of the truck's radiator. It didn't take an expert in body language to see the fear they were fighting.

"Hold your fire." J. J. repeated the command and moved quietly into the street. He didn't need to turn his head to know Crispin and Jose were with him, one three feet to each side. Five steps later, J. J. placed the muzzle of his M4 behind the left ear of one of the gunmen. Jose did the same. Only their eyes moved.

Crispin grabbed the man closest to him by the hair and pulled him to the ground, kicking away the automatic rifle. Jose matched the maneuver, then stepped back, his weapon trained on the man's back.

"Clear." J. J. whispered into the boom mike. Pete, Aliki, and Nagano arrived moments later. Pete searched the captives for weapons, removing a hunting knife from one, and a switchblade from another. J. J. motioned for Pete and Nagano to escort the men into the nearest alley. He had two motives for this: first, he wanted to limit the men's ability to hear him speak English; second, to keep them from seeing the condition of the women when they exited. They had been traumatized more than enough.

Moving to the driver's side of the truck, J. J. paused long enough to gaze at the dead men on the sidewalk. "Weps do this?"

Aliki nodded. "My boy can shoot."

"Head shot and body shot. I was looking forward to giving him some pointers. Maybe I should let him school me."

"Two rounds; two down. That's how he likes to do it. You were a sniper, you know how conservative you guys are with the ammo."

"Were?" J. J. knew what Aliki meant and tried not to take offense at it. His former nick was Colt—like the revolver—a name he took pride in.

"You know what I mean, Boss. You da man, now. I didn't mean anything by it."

Again Aliki seemed extra attentive, staring at J. J.'s masked face as if reading lips. "What about the third man? You get him?"

"Nope, but he did leave the cab of the truck in a way I doubt he expected. So I'd make your next step carefully."

"I plan to." J. J. looked at the shattered window and the open door. He removed his balaclava, stepped over the corpse with the large hole in its head, and knocked on the side of the sleep cab. "Somebody here order a pizza?"

It took a moment, but a weary female voice came from inside. "Maybe. What's on it?"

A moment later, a dark-haired, pretty woman with a streak of dried blood down one side of her face exited the truck. J. J. had to move to the opposite side of the truck so the women wouldn't have to step over the body or see the carnage done by Nagano's M110. Such sights hardened J. J. and he didn't want them to see it.

Amelia Lennon looked tired, battered, and shaken. She also looked like she still had enough fury left to whip them all in some hand-to-hand. The president's daughter looked five short steps from death's door. Her breathing was labored and she had trouble standing erect.

"Master Sergeant J. J. . . ." He stopped and gazed at Amelia's companion. "They call me Boss. The mountain standing next to me is Joker."

Amelia introduced herself, an unnecessary act. She then introduced Jildiz.

Jildiz took two inhalations then forced out a weak sentence. "As a representative of my country . . . (breath) I must remind you that you have no right to . . . (breath) conduct a military operation on our . . . soil." She then stepped forward and wrapped her arms around J. J.'s neck, sobbed for a moment, then pulled back far enough to kiss him on each cheek.

"That's it, Boss, I'm telling your wife."

"Okay, but she's been known to kill the messenger."

"Never mind."

"Doc, give them a quick checkup. Joker, establish a secure perimeter."

"We don't have much time, Boss. I think one of the bad guys got a call off on the radio."

"I'm assuming he did. We need transportation." He triggered his radio. "Junior, I need you."

A moment later he appeared at J. J.'s side.

"Do you remember your misspent youth?" J. J. nodded in the direction of the truck.

"How did you know about that?"

"I know everything about you. Think you can crank that beast up?"

He shrugged. "Electrons are electrons; ignitions are ignitions. I've never hot-wired a truck but something that old can't be too complicated."

"Do it and do it fast."

Pete smiled then looked at Amelia. "Nice to meet you." He scrambled into the truck.

NASIRDIN AND RASUL WERE two blocks north.

"They found them." Rasul's words were venom soaked. He fidgeted with his handgun.

Nasirdin understood the emotion. The American team did what he could not. He had no idea how to explain that to the man who hired him.

"If we can't have her, we just kill her."

"She's no good to our employer dead. No. We must do something else."

"Let me kill one of them. The other woman. She is unimportant."

"Patience. This isn't over yet. The Americans have us outgunned. We wouldn't last very long. Besides, we have other people to take our risk."

He lifted the radio to his lips and gave a command.

CHAPTER 28

CHIEF OF POLICE ABIROV stared through a two-way mirror at the man handcuffed to a metal eyebolt, mounted to a metal table, bolted to the floor. The police and army explosive experts declared the cylinder he was arrested with was not filled with explosives. What they could not declare was what was in it and no one thought it wise to open it and find out.

The prisoner refused to cooperate. He hadn't spoken since his arrest. In the interview room he refused to look at his inquisitors, refused offers of food and drink, resisted threats. He was afraid of someone more powerful than the police.

Kasimir, clean and dry from his struggles in the white goo, stood beside Abirov. "He will break. In time."

"I don't think we have time, Kasimir. You may have saved many lives, but saved them from what? What's in the can? Is he working alone? Are there others in the crowd?" When no explosion occurred, the crowd returned to the entrance gate, braving the fire-retardant foam, chanting slogans and occasionally throwing fruit and rocks over the gate. "I have a bad feeling about this."

"We should have fingerprints soon." Kasimir's frustration permeated his voice.

"We need answers."

Kasimir agreed. "He isn't offering any. Perhaps after the experts figure out how to open the canister safely, we will learn what we need to know."

"Let him go."

"Excuse me, sir?"

"Let him go."

"I don't understand. We need him to understand what is happening."

Abirov looked into Kazimir's eyes. "You are a good officer. Believe me when I say I know what I'm doing. Believe me when I say, you don't want to understand."

A CONFUSED AND ANGRY Kazimir walked the prisoner to the front of the police station. Abirov walked with them. At the front door, Kazimir removed the handcuffs.

The man smiled, gave a polite nod, and said, "*Spokojnoj nochi.*"

He bounced down the steps to the sidewalk and to an awaiting cab. The cab pulled away.

"And good night to you," Abirov said softly.

"Now what?"

"Now we wait. It won't be long."

One hour later, Abirov received a phone call. The message chilled him.

Two hours later, the body of a man in a trench coat was found on the outskirts of the city. He was missing all his fingers.

Abirov was ashamed of his family's history with the Russian KGB in his country. It was one reason he chose police service. Now he felt more ashamed for the calls he made to old friends of his father's.

Now he had other calls to make.

TESS RAND BARTLEY SPENT the last hours trying to get a handle on her emotions and what the days ahead held. It was the way her brain worked. Logic, detail, and action steps were more important to her than the friends she had as a child. Oh, she enjoyed playing dress up and could still remember the thrill she felt when she first tried on lipstick. Not the childish dress up experiments with Mother's makeup, but the earnest application of color to her lips before her first *real* date with a *real* boy. She was fifteen then. By the time she was seventeen she had shed all interest in such things. She wore makeup for dates such as her junior prom, but she no longer found it exhilarating. Her thirst for knowledge replaced her thirst for acceptance.

According to her husband, her simple approach to beauty was what captured his attention. Why did that seem so long ago?

She tried sitting and staring at the walls. Her depression deepened. She gazed out the window for a full half hour but couldn't recall a single thing she saw. Once she picked up a magazine as if she were going to read. She didn't read. She drank another cup of coffee, now bitter from sitting so long. Mostly she answered phone calls from family and from the other wives of J. J.'s team.

Did she have a responsibility to them? What was wife-of-Boss supposed to do? Should she drive to their homes? Buy sympathy cards? "Dear Lucy, so sorry we lost our husbands. May God richly bless you in these difficult hours."

Great sentiment; lousy way to deliver it.

Prayer was a mainstay of her life. She rose with prayer and often conversed with God while driving or in unexpected quiet moments. She tried praying now, but nothing came. She heard others say God seemed distant in times of sudden loss. Others said He was never closer at any time than during their loss. Tess couldn't sense either condition. God seemed neither distant nor near. Had she lost her belief? She asked that question a dozen times and each time she had to admit she hadn't. Grief simply short-circuited the lines of communication. The only thing she could be sure of was her grief.

She paced a lot, wearing a path from the living room to the kitchen to the bedroom to the bathroom and back to the living room. She thought of going outside to walk, but worried she would do what she had already done a dozen times: break down into a blithering, heaving mass.

Her mind begged for something to do, something useful, productive, engaging; something husband honoring; God honoring.

She moved into the bedroom, to a small desk J. J. got when he was in middle school. It was here he paid the bills, kept catalogs of high-end racing bicycles and gun catalogs. As many times as her pacing brought her into the room, this was the first time she noticed her eyes avoided the bed. That realization burned in her mind and boiled her heart.

Breathing turned ragged again, but she was determined not to cry. Not because she was ashamed, but because she couldn't endure more. Focus. Find something.

She did. A folder tucked in the corner of the desk, beneath utility bills. Tess pushed the envelopes to the side and picked up the manila folder. Inside were a collection of items: the photo of the sonogram revealing the twins, a photo of a small party celebrating Tess's pregnancy, an article on how to save money for a child's college education, and a piece of lined paper with notes made in J. J.'s hand. There were two columns made by a line of blue ink drawn down the middle of the page. At the top of the left column were two words: "Little J. J."; the top of the right column bore the words "Little Tess." A short list of names were penned for each category. Under "Little J. J." were Aaron, Josiah, Elijah, Levi, Dylan, Adam, Paul, Jack, Eric, Rich, and a few others. Under "Little Tess" were: Crystal, Chaundel, Cloe, Gwyn, and Bailey.

Tess brought a hand to her mouth and choked back a sob. He hadn't told her he was making a list of names for the twins. On the boy side of the page were other names; names that made a lot less sense: Quincy Bartley, Poindexter Bartley, Erasmus Bartley. Reading the names made her smile. He once said when making a list of ideas it was always good to have ideas to throw away. He found some good throwaways.

On the back of the page were a few more notes. "President Levi Bartley. Dr. Cloe Bartley. Bailey Bartley, Esq. Colonel Josiah Bartley. Secretary of State Gwyn Bartley. Apparently he thought their daughter either would not marry or would keep her family name.

Returning the papers, she placed the folder back where she found it. It would be up to her to name their children.

Her gaze fell to J. J.'s Bible centered on the desktop. It was a well-worn New American Standard. J. J. had several Bible translations but he had "cut his teeth" on this one. The brown leather cover was worn on the spine so much it was difficult to read the engraving.

She sat and leafed through the pages. Scores of verses were underlined. Notes decorated the margins. She and J. J. met at a chapel service and one of her first impressions was the way he listened to a sermon, pen in hand, Bible on his lap, taking notes wherever he could find white space. She moved a finger over the notes taking in every loop, every stroke, every dot. These were written memories, the handwriting of a father to be saved for the children who would never know him.

Later, she decided, she would return to the Bible to write down some of J. J.'s favorite verses. Chaplain Bartley would need that, but for this moment she needed something else.

Tess moved from the desk to the bed, lay on her side, pulled J. J.'s pillow to her face, and buried her nose where her husband's head once rested.

ABIROV WALKED INTO MEKLIS'S office. The man had aged in the last few hours. Why not? His country was on the verge of economic collapse, unemployment topped 20 percent, there was pressure from Russia and China to oust the Americans, parliament was growing less supportive with the passing of each day, and now riots in the streets and a crowd of ten thousand surrounding the White House government building.

On his way in, which required using the underground secret access from Ala-Too Square, he saw several military and police vehicles aflame, lighting the surrounding area with orange flame and sending billows of smoke roiling into the air. A crowd mingled at the square, but his police officers were able to keep the numbers down. The real action was a short distance away at the White House. Very few protesters wanted to miss that.

Few of his countrymen knew of the secret access but no doubt many suspected it. It was not unusual for such tunnels to exist. Even the Americans had tunnels running from their White House and the buildings where Congress met. History taught government leaders around the world and through time that several means of escape were needed to have a sense of security. There were even escape tunnels created by the ancients in cities like Jerusalem. Twenty-one centuries later, the need for such things still existed.

Meklis, normally a courteous man, acknowledged Abirov with only a nod. "Before you bring me any more bad news, let me ask about my daughter—or is that the bad news?"

"No, Mr. President. We have no more word on her and—"

"I know, you have too few men to conduct a search. We've been over that, but I'm a father and I have to ask."

"How is your wife holding up, sir?"

"Not well. The doctor thinks she may be on the verge of a nervous breakdown. She never wanted me to go into politics. She feared for the family. She was right."

"You are a good president, sir. When this is over, she will recover and you will continue to lead our country."

"The people in the streets seem to disagree, my friend."

"They protest poverty, sir. Their complaints should be directed at parliament more than you."

Meklis shook his head. "It doesn't work that way, I'm afraid. I should compliment you on the use of the fire-retardant foam to repel the crowd at Manas."

Abirov shrugged. "It is a temporary measure. I have reports that the group has moved forward again and are throwing stones and other objects. The airport only has so much of the material on hand. I've ordered that the technique be used again, but that will be the end of that approach."

"Do you think they will tire of getting wet?"

"The night is warm. If this were winter, we could douse them and the cold would send them home. That would only refresh them tonight. The foam is slippery so that is an advantage."

Meklis motioned to the seats. His personal assistant entered with a tray of snacks and coffee and set it on the table in front of the long sofa. Abirov settled in a chair.

"Coffee, Chief?"

"No thank you, sir. I'll take refreshment when my men can do the same."

"I understand." The president ignored the tray. "You said you have urgent news."

"I do, Mr. President, but I have a favor to ask first. Please don't ask me how I obtained my information. I say this to protect you, not me."

Meklis's eyes narrowed. Abirov knew him to be a man of principle and law. Learning the information came from torture would only give him more problems to juggle. Abirov decided to confess to the act and resign when the city was back to normal.

"I've never been asked for such a favor before."

"I must ask it now, Mr. President. I know I am not part of your cabinet. I am a simple policeman. It is all I ever wanted to be."

Meklis looked away, his eyes shifting from side to side.

"Mr. President, I can make this easier on you. I will tell you what you need to know. I do so, because I believe your life is in danger and time is short. I will tell you I have committed a crime and I did so alone. No one in my department was involved." He leaned forward as if about to whisper but his voice remained the same. "We took a suspect into custody just outside the American side of the airport. He was in the crowd. He had a metal container which we first believed to be an explosive. It is not. The army has it now and is conducting tests. I couldn't wait for their results."

"You know what's in it?"

"Yes, and I've alerted the army and my leaders in the field. I did that on my way here. I am now telling you the cylinder is an aerosol can meant to disperse a biotoxin. Had one of my officers not stopped the man, hundreds, maybe thousands would be dead."

"How do you know this?" Meklis raised a hand. "Forget that question for now. Are you certain of your information?"

"Yes, sir. Sadly, I am one hundred percent convinced the information is accurate. It is my belief the man intended to release the material into the crowd near the entrance gate to the American side of Manas International Airport."

"To what end? Why would he kill fellow protesters . . . because the act would be blamed on the Americans. People would say the Americans used the bioagent to protect their base."

"Yes, sir. My fear is he was not alone. Imagine if someone else is successful where he failed. Or imagine if someone in the crowd a hundred meters from this very office released the toxin? Your opponents would claim you ordered the death of hundreds, maybe thousands of protesters."

"I would never do that."

"Of course not, Mr. President, but your enemies would not miss the opportunity to lay the blame at your feet. I know nothing of politics or how to lead a country, but I imagine your administration would not be able to recover. I'm certain your security would warn you that such a belief, misguided as it is, would increase assassination attempts. My biggest concern . . ." The words came with difficulty. "My biggest concern is that such a weapon can be used to end your life."

Meklis seemed to melt into the sofa. "My wife."

"Yes, sir. It is what makes biotoxins so reprehensible. A gunman has to see his victim. If the toxin made it into the building . . ."

"What do you suggest?"

Abirov couldn't speak.

"Say it, Chief Abirov."

"Sir, you need to leave the building. You and your wife."

"So you're with Prime Minister Dootkasy on this? He has suggested I transfer power to him to protect the presidency."

"No, sir. I am no friend of the prime minister. Fortunately, my work doesn't require me to report to him, or even to you, sir. I am appointed by the mayor, so I have a little more freedom to speak. My only concern is your safety. Since you've allowed me the privilege of advising you on city security, I came to you personally. I will offer whatever help your security deems necessary."

"If I leave the country, it will look like I'm running away from our problems. And if the biotoxin is released then it will look like I either called for the use of the poison, or ran when I learned of it."

"Only if people know you left the country. As far as the people will know, you were out of the building doing your job, or that security forced you and your wife to leave because that's their job."

"Lie to the people."

"Trust me, Mr. President, that will be the smallest of sins I commit today."

CHAPTER 29

"HOW ARE THEY, DOC?" J. J. sat in the passenger side of the truck cab watching Pete stripping a few wires with his knife.

"Captain Lennon is pretty good. Exhausted. I've cleaned her wounds. They're superficial by battle standards but you can bet next month's pay they're painful. She's one tough date."

"We've seen plenty of evidence for that. Jildiz?"

"Pretty bad, Boss. She needs to be in a hospital. I don't know how she stays on her feet. I did what I could, but my med kit is tailored for trauma, not asthma."

"Understood. You still have them out of sight?"

"Yes, I found a small print shop a few meters down the street. The door was open. Weps is with them. Aliki has taken over guarding our two friends."

"Good . . . wait, the door was open?"

"Well, sorta."

"I'm not gonna ask."

"You say Weps and Joker are elsewhere?" Pete lifted his head from beneath the dashboard.

"Yeah." Doc sounded puzzled.

Pete sat up. "Look, I might be wrong about this, and Boss, you know I get along with everybody. I have no problem with new guys. And I know these guys have medals up to their necks . . ."

"But?"

"But I think something's wrong with Joker. He . . . I'm not sure how to say this."

"Just say it, Junior."

"Joker seems slow, like he's hesitant, or can't hear, or both. I don't know. When we engaged the guys at the truck, he was slow off the dime, like he didn't want to step out of the alley. Like . . . like he was afraid."

"Joker? Afraid. That doesn't seem right." J. J. didn't like what he was hearing, but he trusted Junior as deeply as he trusted any man. They had been through too much not to be pals.

"Okay, maybe afraid isn't the right word. He did come out, but he stayed behind me, almost like he was using me as a shield. Maybe it's something else, but something doesn't feel right."

"As bad as Data?" J. J.'s mind ran back to a former team member named Jerry Zinsser who almost got the team killed because he kept his post-traumatic stress disorder a secret. The man saw horrible things in a firefight in one of Somalia's port cities. He was the last man of his team left standing. Although cleared by the medics, his disorder came back with a vengeance, to the point he attacked then team leader Eric Moyer. In the end, he proved indispensable to the mission's success, but it was the end of his spec op days.

"Can't tell."

J. J. recalled the info in Aliki's service jacket. He was on a team that lost most of its members. Could he be dealing with a PTSD problem again?

"Okay, let's not be too quick to judge. You said he entered the fray, he was a tad slow to do so."

"It seemed that way. I had to go around him."

"We'll keep an eye on him. Maybe his team did things differently. Just be sharp."

"Roger that."

"Now get this beast started. Doc, see if you can get that lock off the trailer door. We can't fit everyone in the cab and I don't want to leave anyone behind. You might have to get Weps to pinch off a little C4."

Pete was a good soldier but a lousy car thief: it took fifteen minutes for him to get the tractor to start. Jose was a good medic but a lousy locksmith: he needed Weps to blow the lock. The trailer was empty.

"Good job getting this beast back to life." J. J. listened to the rumble of the diesel engine. "Now tell me you know how to drive this thing."

Pete looked sheepish. "'Fraid not, Boss. This is the first time I've been inside one of these."

"Great." J. J. glanced at Jose. "Doc?"

"I'd endanger more lives than I would save. Sorry."

J. J. keyed his mike. "Anyone know how to drive a big rig?"

A moment later. "I'll give it a shot." It was Nagano, and J. J. was hoping for something a little more confident. No one else answered.

"Get up here, Weps." J. J. turned to Jose. "I want the women in the cab. I don't think riding in the back will help Jildiz any. Get the rest of the team in the trailer." Jose was gone before J. J. finished the order.

"I'm gonna check the doors, Boss," Pete said. "It won't do to be locked in the back should something go down. We need to rig something up so we can open the back without someone having to let us out."

"Good idea. Make it quick. I got the uncomfortable feeling company is coming."

Three minutes later, Nagano was behind the wheel, Amelia and Jildiz were in the sleeper cab, J. J. sat in the front passenger seat, and the team was in the trailer.

"You sure you can drive this?" J. J. let suspicion hang in his voice.

"We'll know in a minute."

"Does that mean you've never driven a rig like this?" The pit of J. J.'s stomach spiraled down. "I thought you said you could drive this."

"To be accurate, Boss, I said I'd give it a shot. No one else was speaking up so I took the truck by the horns." He examined the stick shift. "Five forward gears; one reverse. Split transmission giving us high/low ratios, so . . . ten forward speeds. How hard can it be?"

"How do you know that stuff?"

"I was a gear-head in high school. I rebuilt cars as a hobby. Got a '64 and a half Mustang." Nagano found first gear and slowly released the clutch. The beast jolted forward.

"Smooth," Amelia said.

"Thanks, ma'am."

"I was being sarcastic, soldier."

"Yes, ma'am, so was I." He found the next gear without trouble. "Wow, she may be old but she's easy."

"You had better be talking about the truck," Amelia said.

The comment made J. J. smile. "How's our friend?"

"I'm still here," a weak Jildiz said.

"Where to, Boss?" Nagano asked.

"First, let's get away from the group that torched our vans. Go around the block and head south. Put a few miles between us then we'll start for our next destination. I see three possibilities: a hospital for Jildiz, the government center, or back to base." He thought for a moment.

"The hospital is likely to be packed with wounded protesters," Amelia said. "And the only hospital large enough to provide the care and protection she needs is in the direction of the fires and protests, assuming the protests are like the last set."

"Good point." J. J. scratched his chin. He and Nagano removed their balaclavas. Two men in ski masks driving through town might garner more attention than they wanted. "Let's drive toward Manas. Stay on the outskirts of town. When we're in radio range, we'll make contact."

"You don't have an Iridium satellite phone?" Amelia seemed stunned.

"We had CONNIE but someone helped themselves to it."

"CONNIE?"

He explained about the satellite communications device. "We left it in one of our vehicles when we made entrance into the pharmacy. We went in hot so we left some things behind. Fortunately, we didn't lose Hawkeye's gear or we might never have found you."

"So you've been working without contact with Manas?"

"We often work with limited radio contact. It's part of what we do. We also have cell phones but you already know how useful those are right now."

"The embassy," Amelia said. A moment later, "Sorry, I'm just thinking out loud. The embassy is close, south of the violence, and they will be able to make radio or satellite contact with Manas. They also have a local doctor on call. We can hole up there. It's closer than the air base."

"I like it, Boss." Nagano found third gear on the fourth try.

"Me too. You can be our GPS, Captain."

"That I can do—"

The streetlights went out and a fresh darkness like a black blanket fell over the city.

NASIRDIN ROUNDED THE CORNER in time to see the semi drive slowly down the street, moving north, then turn right at the next street. Rasul raised his handgun, drawing a bead on the retreating big rig.

"No," Nasirdin ordered. "Not yet. Follow me." He ran down the street parallel to the path the truck took. He dallied enough to see the driver drag the rear tires of the trailer over the corner curb. Clearly a novice was at the wheel, and that was good news. Nasirdin raised his radio to his mouth. He finished his transmission then received one of his own. One he didn't want to hear.

He slowed, then stopped.

"What? Why are we stopping?"

"We're needed elsewhere." Nasirdin muttered.

"HEY, WEPS. I HAVE an idea. Try and keep all the wheels on the road and off the sidewalk."

"That would make this kinda boring, wouldn't it?"

J. J. glanced at the man. "Whatcha got against boring? Sounds good to me right about now. Besides, you hit another curb and the guys in back are going to come after us, and when they do, I'm going to be pointing at you."

"I'm not afraid of them."

"What about Joker?"

Nagano pushed out a lip. "Okay, he scares me a little, but the captain will protect me."

"You're on your own," Amelia said. "I'll be pointing at you too."

"As always, an innovative man stands alone. . . . Um, Boss, we got troubles." Nagano slowed and nodded forward.

The truck's headlights painted the black street and a row of armed men blocking the intersection. J. J. recognized several as men in the mob that torched their vehicles.

"Get down, Cap," J. J. said. He activated his radio. "Down in back. Prepare for firefight."

The calm voice of Aliki: "Roger that." A moment later, "What we got, Boss?"

"A line of hostiles in the intersection. Handguns and automatics. I make out about fifteen."

"We got 'em behind us too, Boss," Nagano said. "Maybe ten more. Not good."

Their luck had just run out. They had no stealth; no element of surprise. They were outnumbered three to one. It was an O.K. Corral situation where men stood a few yards from each other and started pulling the trigger, except Wyatt Earp wasn't looking down the barrels of automatic rifles.

"Boss, you got any orders?"

A second passed.

"Boss?"

J. J. took a deep breath and his mind savored three seconds thinking of his wife and unborn children. What a lousy time to die. He opened his door, propped it in position with his foot, and aimed the barrel of his M4 down the street. "Floor it."

"Floor it? Really?"

"You got a better idea?"

"Now that you put it that way . . . Flooring it, Boss."

J. J. spoke into his microphone. "Brace yourself, we're running the line."

The truck lurched forward. Then it lurched again. J. J. kept his eyes trained on the line of men determined not to fire until someone raised a weapon. Whoever did that would be the first to fall. Nagano scooted as low as he could in the seat. J. J. didn't know if the man could see the road, but the truck ran straight.

Another lurch. The engine groaned, complaining about the low gear. Somehow, Nagano managed a smooth shift.

A man with an embarrassingly thin beard brought up his weapon and leveled it in their direction, then twisted and fell as a burst of bullets from J. J.'s M4 ripped him in the chest. J. J. was through waiting, he sent spurts of hot rounds across the line. There was a word for men who stood shoulder to shoulder in a gunfight: targets. J. J. swung the weapon in an arch. Men went to the ground: wounded or just diving for cover, he didn't know and didn't have time to care.

The windshield shattered, sending spiderweb cracks along its length. The side mirror on Nagano's door exploded into shards, smacking the raised window.

The thundering sound of familiar weapons rolled forward from the trailer. The doors had been loosely tied in place so the men could open them if need arose—and it had.

Nagano hunkered in the seat. Leaving one hand on the wheel, he drew his M9 pistol and fired through the windshield, opening a small hole that helped him see and aim. He emptied all fifteen rounds in moments.

The truck continued forward, the sound of bullets striking its metal skin hitting J. J.'s ears like needles. J. J. pulled his weapon back. "Reloading."

More gunfire from within the cab. Not J. J. and not Nagano. Amelia had slipped from the sleeper cab with the 9mm she had been carrying since removing it from one of the attackers in the pharmacy.

She crouched between the seats, sending round after round through what was left of the windscreen, firing systematically, each shot spaced by a second of time. Brass casings flew through the cab and bounced around.

"I said get down!" J. J. snapped.

"Shut up, Sergeant. I'm busy." Her gun clicked dry. Without hesitation she snatched Nagano's M9 while he reached for a fresh clip. She took it and jammed it in place.

Smoke stung J. J.'s eyes; his ears hurt and he was certain they were bleeding. He leaned out the door and let loose another series of bursts.

Yep, a lousy place to die. A lousy time to die.

ALIKI LAY ON HIS belly, his weapon pointed out the back of the trailer. There were ten hostiles and he saw at least three fall within a second of the team opening fire. Next to him was Jose, working his weapon like he came into this world with it. Kneeling behind, Crispin tapped his trigger again and again, and Pete did the same.

Brass casings rolled in the trailer. Noise of gunfire in a closed space threatened to melt Aliki's brain, and he was half-deaf.

It took only moments to send those attackers still living scampering for cover.

The truck bounced and a crushed body appeared then rolled from beneath the truck. Aliki assumed they were running over the dead or those too wounded to get out of the way.

More gunfire came as they burst through what had been a line of men. Again, Aliki and the others sent a fusillade of bullets into anyone stupid enough to still be in the fight.

The truck made a sharp right, and centrifugal force sent the team sliding to the left. A moment later, Aliki could see nothing but a dark street.

"Joker, report." The voice from his earpiece sounded a mile away.

"Hold one, Boss." Aliki pushed to his knees. He looked at Pete who gave a thumbs-up. Crispin just nodded. Jose said, "I'm . . . I'm good." At least, that's what Aliki thought the man was saying. The ringing in his ears was joined by the buzzing of a hundred beehives.

"We're all good, Boss. Hawkeye wants to do it again."

J. J. LOOKED AT Amelia. "You know you frighten my men, don't you, ma'am?"

"Just adding my two cents to things."

Nagano snapped his head around. "Two cents? That was a ten-spot if ever I saw one."

"I'm gonna check on Jildiz." Amelia crawled into the sleeper.

Nagano looked at J. J. and mouthed the word, "Wow."

THE LATE MODEL TOYOTA Land Cruiser carrying Nasirdin and Rasul hurried down the street, the driver moving faster than was safe.

Nasirdin heard the gunfire fade in the distance and had a bad feeling things hadn't gone his way.

CHAPTER 30

DESPITE THE DARK STREETS, Amelia proved to be an excellent guide. They were on Prospect Mira Street despite Nagano's gear-grinding and leaking radiator fluid. The engine continued to run but with a few new knocks and whistles. J. J. wasn't much of a mechanic but Nagano was, and he looked worried every moment of the drive. Of course, the O.K. Corral kind of shoot-out might have put him a little off his game.

"Approach slow, Weps," Amelia said. "And don't pull to the gate. With all that's going on, someone is going to assume your trailer is one big fertilizer bomb."

"Then how do we get in?" J. J. squinted against the air coming through the shattered window and the smell of an overheating engine.

"I plan to ring the doorbell."

"The embassy has a doorbell?" J. J. exchanged glances with Nagano.

"Not really, but they do have video cameras around the perimeter and a good number of guards. Including a few Marines. I see a few lights on so I assume they're running on the generator."

"You guys use Marines as servants?" Nagano said. "Nice."

"Be kind, Weps. They're going to be the ones who let us in."

"I'll go with you." J. J. opened his door.

"Stay put, Sergeant. If you were in a regular uniform they might not assume you're my abductor. I'll go alone."

J. J. let her out and retook his place in the cab.

"I'm thinking of asking her to marry me." Nagano fidgeted, then fidgeted again. He stopped making eye contact. He looked at the steering wheel, the stick shift, the shot-out side mirror, and the steam rising from the front of the truck. J. J. recognized the signs. He had displayed them many times. Moving from the edge of a horrible death to a moment of quiet was always tough on soldiers. Adrenaline continued seeping into the bloodstream and the images ignored in battle refused to be ignored any longer. J. J. lived through this many times and hated it. He was surprised what pictures came to mind, images he hadn't realized he saw.

"I think you should."

"Really?"

"No." J. J. radioed the others in the trailer. "You guys still have air back there?"

"Junior needs a shower." The voice belonged to Crispin.

"He always does. Okay, listen up. We sit tight. Captain Lennon is trying to get us an invite onto embassy grounds. Apparently they're fussy about shot-up truck jalopies littering their lawn. You guys still good?"

Aliki gave the official answer. "We're good, Boss, but it ain't all that comfortable back here."

"Understood. We should have you out soon."

"Roger that."

Nagano straightened. "She's in."

Amelia walked through the front gate. "I wonder why there's not a bunch of protesters here," J. J. said.

A whispered, wheezy voice came from the sleep cab. "Most of the protesters would go to the White House or the air base."

"White House?" Nagano said. He kept his eyes scanning the area.

"Our government building."

Nagano didn't let it go. "You named your government building after our White House?"

There was a weak chuckle. "That or it could be called the White House because it is a big, white building."

"Action." J. J. pointed at the gate. Four Marines jogged to the gate. Each was armed. They continued through the gate and toward the truck. No sign of Amelia.

"They know we're the good guys, right?"

"I hope so, I'm too tired for another gun battle, especially with these guys."

The unit of Marines kept their weapons with muzzles down. A man in his early thirties came to J. J.'s side, one went to the driver's side, and the others disappeared from view. "Are you Boss?"

"I am. Who are you?"

"Staff Sergeant Larry Ryan, U.S.M.C. I've been asked to verify the safety of the vehicle and escort you to the back of the embassy. Will your men in the back of the trailer be a problem?"

"They could be, Staff Sergeant, if you open the doors without warning." J. J. made the call. "Navy is here, guys. Your back door is about to be opened. Please don't shoot them."

"Why not? You said Navy." Joker continued to earn his nick.

"I'd consider it a personal favor, Joker."

The sergeant stiffened. "I said we were Marines."

"Yeah, that's what I said. Navy."

The frown was worth the quip.

"At least we drive better vehicles."

J. J. had to smile. Inter-service banter was a tradition.

One of the other Marines came to the front. "Just as she said, Sarge: four spec ops guys. Really tired-looking spec ops guys. Looks like they've seen recent action."

Ryan nodded then looked at J. J. "This thing still run?"

"It moves, if that's what you mean."

"Very well, let's move it through the gate. I'll ride along on the running board, if you don't mind."

"And if I do mind?"

"I'll do it anyway but look really sad."

"I like you, Ryan." To Nagano. "Let's roll."

LIGHTS INSIDE THE MULTISTORY embassy were minimal, illuminating only a few windows for security purposes. The embassy, like many the world over, had interior rooms set apart from exterior walls and windows. These were secure rooms: secure electronically and physically. Too many embassies had been attacked around the world to make diplomats feel secure.

Amelia stood at the rear entrance as Nagano pulled the truck forward. It shuddered and rocked as the soldier struggled to master the clutch. Not that it mattered now. This was certainly the truck's final stop. The U.S. government would be ponying up money to replace the antique for the owner.

Two Marines helped Jildiz from the truck. To J. J. she looked two or three long strides from death. Still, she insisted on walking, which she managed with the help of the solidly built Marines.

J. J. looked up and saw a pair of men dressed in black, each with assault rifles. The place was on high alert and for good reason.

A man in slacks, loafers, and a blue dress shirt waited in the inside rear lobby, a simple room with a tile floor. His hair was thin and brown and rested at odd angles on his head. He had the look of a man at the end of a long day and facing a longer night. Next to him stood an older man with a shock of white hair and a demeanor that said "medical professional."

The man in the blue shirt spoke so softly to Jildiz J. J. couldn't hear the words. He smiled but the grin had to push through a mask of shock and concern. Jildiz and Amelia looked worse for wear and Jildiz's pallor was corpse-like.

He approached J. J. and his men. "I cannot tell you how happy I am to see you. You know, you're supposed to be dead." His voice was flavored with a Southern accent and J. J. could imagine the man standing on the wide porch of a plantation house.

"Boss, this is Ambassador Robert Lee," Amelia said.

Lee slipped an arm around her. "My friends call me Bobby, and anyone who saves someone as precious and sweet as Amelia here is my friend."

Amelia rolled her eyes.

"Sweet? Yes, sir, that was our first impression too." J. J. shook the ambassador's hand. "Jildiz?"

"That was Dr. Bryson. He retired from practice last year and I convinced him to spend some time here. We used to play golf together. Terrible on the putting green, but good with all things medical. He's kept me healthy for years." He paused. "She's in good hands, soldier. How about you and your team?"

"We're fine. Mr. Ambassador, what did you mean we are supposed to be dead?"

He cocked his head to one side as if wondering how J. J. could ask such a stupid question. "This may take a few moments. Let's go to the cafeteria and get you some food. I'll fill you in."

"I need to make contact with my superiors," J. J. said. "As soon as possible, if you don't mind."

"Phone service is out in the city and power just went out as well. Internet went down also, but we have satellite phones and a pretty decent communications center filled with radios. But first, you need to hear what I have to say."

Despite the lateness of the hour, the cafeteria staff was able to serve up plates of meatloaf, rewarmed mashed potatoes, candied carrots, and pots of coffee and bottled water. It was a feast.

Ambassador Lee poured a cup of coffee for himself then looked at Amelia, who sat at the end of the cafeteria table. "As soon as Dr. Bryson has Jildiz stabilized, I want him to take a look at you."

"I'm fine. Doc fixed me up."

"Don't make me say it twice, Amelia. In this building, I outrank you."

"Yes, Mr. Ambassador."

Lee fixed his attention on J. J. but spoke loudly enough for the others to hear. "In a moment, I need to contact the Kyrgyzstan president and you need to touch base with your superiors. So I'm going to make this quick." J. J. listened between bites of food. Halfway through the story he lost his appetite.

COLONEL WEIDMAN TOOK THE satellite phone from his aide. "Weidman." He listened for a moment. "Why aren't you dead?"

"I haven't got that far down my to-do list, sir."

Weidman chuckled, then he laughed loudly. "This has been one lousy day, but you just put a bow on it. I can't tell you how good it is to hear your voice."

"Thank you, sir. Is the base secure?"

"For now, but we have quite a gathering out front."

"I'm ready to report, sir."

"Save it, Master Sergeant. Your mission isn't over. Something's come up."

J. J. DIDN'T LIKE the sound of that. He looked around the small communications room in the basement of the building. It smelled of

warm electronics. He didn't feel ready for more shocking news. He digested the last bit served up by the ambassador. Nonetheless, he said, "Ready, sir."

"There was an attempted bioagent attack at the front gate. A sharp-eyed local cop prevented its execution and was somehow able to take control of a canister filled with a still undefined agent. The local police took the man into custody. Somehow they or the local military or Intel group got the man to confess. I have a feeling the details are unpleasant."

Weidman lowered his voice. "They learned there is more of this stuff stored away and maybe in the streets. The perp was persuaded to give up the location. You are ordered to the location to render the facility inoperable. Reload and move out immediately."

"There are active bioagents in the building?"

"Yes. It's an old Soviet-era mid-rise building not far from your location. As I understand it, the plan is to release the agent at our base, in front of the major government building, and near the embassy."

"Why would someone do that to their own people?"

"The United States isn't the only country with a domestic terrorism problem. Best guess, they plan to infect the protesters and then blame the Americans. I'm sure China and/or Russia would be happy to confirm the bug or chemical—whatever it is—was American made."

"Do I have time to call Colonel Mac?"

"You do not."

"Understood, sir." J. J. let a second slip by. "Sir, the last mission was to rescue an American in danger, this is—"

"Don't finish that, Sergeant. This is well above your pay grade. Besides, you just saved the president's daughter. We should get a little leeway. Now move."

"Yes, sir."

J. J. hustled down the hallway and up the stairs to the cafeteria floor. His men were still downing chow. "Scarf it down, men. We gotta move."

"What?" Aliki stopped mid chew.

"I'm afraid this is just halftime." He faced Lee. "Mr. Ambassador, I'm going to need a favor from your Marines. I need to borrow a little ammo and a few other things. I also need a car and a satellite phone."

"When do you leave?" Lee asked.

"Yesterday."

PRESIDENT MEKLIS OSKONBAEVA MOVED through the tunnel linking Ala-Too Square with the White House. At his side, a silver-haired beauty of sixty years walked with her head down, dabbing a handkerchief to her eyes.

"We can't leave our Jildiz," she said. She repeated the phrase fifty times and Meklis imagined he would hear it many times more. He didn't mind. A very loud voice in his head was screaming the same thing.

He explained things; explained about the impossibility of her making it into the White House and that she was most likely hiding until things settled down. "Perhaps the woman who rescued her took her to friends and she's waiting for the phones to come online again." He left out the part of the shot-up and burned vehicle the news was showing.

"This is cowardice."

"No, Love, it is not. We went over this when I took office. Presidents and key leaders have to be able to move from their offices in time of war or terrorism. Every modern national seat of government has means of escape. It is vital to maintain leadership. This is the right thing to do. The choice has been made for us."

"But where are we going?"

"To a safer place." He didn't tell her about the bioagent.

Fifteen minutes later, they, and several aides, were aboard a customized Kamov Ka-62 helicopter. Sixty seconds later they were airborne for the short flight to Kazakhstan.

Ten minutes into their northward flight a beeping rose from one of the briefcases. Meklis's personal aide retrieved a sat phone and answered. He listened. He blinked. Then held it out. "It's the president of the United States, sir."

"How did he get access to this number? . . . Never mind, they know everything." He took the phone. "I'm a little busy right now, Mr. President."

"Not too busy for this, my friend."

One minute later the Ka-62 turned and flew south.

To the U.S. Embassy.

COLONEL MAC CALLED ALAN Kinkaid into his office. "Sit down, I need advice, Sergeant, and I need it now. I just got a call from Colonel Weidman at Manas—"

"The team is alive, sir."

Mac blinked several times. "I just learned that. How did you know? You'd better not have a tap on my phone. There are special prisons for people who do such things."

"Wouldn't dream of it, Colonel." He smiled. "I just got word from the president's office. His chief of staff called. The FBI discovered something in the video." Kinkaid's smile broadened. "They discovered what was bugging me."

"Let's hear it."

The master sergeant delivered the news in short order.

"I should have thought of that." Mac rubbed his chin. "My proof is better. Colonel Weidman called from Manas. He's spoken to J. J."

Mac's aide closed his eyes for a moment, then looked up, and whispered, "Thank You."

"The news couldn't be better, Sergeant, but I still have a problem—a procedural problem."

He relayed the news Weidman had passed on, including the new mission.

"What to tell the families?"

"Exactly."

Kinkaid did as Mac knew he would. He reduced the problem to its simplest terms then listed the most likely courses of action.

"One, we tell them the news report was false and their husbands are alive and well. But then we would be forced to keep secret the fact they are on another mission, one just as deadly. Two, we tell them nothing at all. On the one hand we let them continue in their misery; on the other we give them hope then may have to tell them they died later."

He thought for a moment. "Security prevents us from telling them they're on mission, to reveal that information could be bad for your career." Another beat passed. "I could tell them without your knowledge—"

"Forget that. If anyone risks a career, it will be me."

"In that case, I advise you to tell them nothing."

Mac nodded slowly. "That's what I came up with, but it seems cruel."

"It is cruel, sir, and there isn't anything we can do about that."

"It's times like this that make a career in real estate seem good."

The corner of Kinkaid's lip rose a notch. "With all due respect, sir, you might be good at the job. Think of the hundreds of couples you could intimidate into buying a home."

"Intimidate, eh? Dismissed, Sergeant."

Kinkaid rose and started for the door.

"Alan . . . thanks."

"You're welcome, sir."

CHAPTER 31

MORNING BECAME AFTERNOON AND afternoon was morphing into early evening. Tess did the mental calculation. It would be sunup soon where J. J. was . . . where J. J.'s body was.

Weariness engulfed her like the ocean swallowed a sinking ship. Is that what she was? A sinking ship? The rational part of her mind said, "Nonsense. Life will go on. You still have your work and your unborn children. Invest yourself in them. You'll get over this." The words were hollow, small, lacking conviction. It was the kind of thing well-meaning but insensitive people said to the grieving. "Don't cry. It's going to be all right."

Garbage.

It wasn't going to be all right. Not by a long shot. Sure, she would move on, get on with life. Who knows what the future held? She was strong, determined, self-reliant, and moved through life on an even keel.

She was also broken, her soul strewn around her like shattered glass. She was empty. Weak. Shaky. Depressed. Angry, and filled with a hunger for revenge.

The image of the burned bodies and car playing on the news shows was set in a constant loop. She saw it when she closed her eyes; saw it when she gazed into the distance. Worse, when the emotional exhaustion forced her to doze, she dreamed it. That was the worst. In her dreams she could hear J. J. screaming her name.

Over and over. Loud and clear and full of excruciating pain.

"God . . . dear, dear God . . ." Her prayer had dissolved to just two words. She would have to trust that God got the idea.

A knock at the door.

She didn't want visitors. *Ignore it. Turn your back. Hide in the bedroom.*

All good advice. All the desire of her heart. Instead, she went to the door and opened it.

"Lucy?" The woman's Hispanic skin looked two shades paler, her eyes were swollen, puffy, and red.

Tess steeled herself for an onslaught of anger, maybe even a slap across the face. After all, just this morning she told Lucy their husbands were safe on a military base showing off the new surveillance drones and meeting their two new team members.

"Tess—" Lucy's lips quivered until she pressed them into an angry frown.

Wordless, motionless seconds passed, then Lucy covered her face with her hands. "Oh, Tess . . ." Sobs rolled from the woman.

Tess led Lucy into the apartment and closed the door.

Then she took the woman in her arms.

Sob joined sob.

TRANSPORTATION HAD IMPROVED. INSTEAD of broken-down delivery vans, the embassy had a pair of black Range Rovers. Again, J. J. split the team, dividing human assets in order to increase the odds of success. Both vehicles came with GPS units, making finding the building easy, despite the lack of streetlights.

A strip of salmon-colored light stretched across what horizon he could see, which wasn't much. The Stygian black of night had turned a shade grayer. Sunrise was not welcome. Already, J. J. noticed more cars on the road. Not many, but the number was sure to increase as dawn approached. More vehicles meant more civilians and more eyes on them.

Nagano was the designated driver for J. J.'s Range Rover. Crispin sat in the back working on his toys.

By J. J.'s estimation, they were five minutes out. His mind vibrated with thoughts. One stream of thought was a recent memory:

"I'm going with you." Amelia made the statement sound like a fact, taking J. J. by surprise.

"No, you're not." He tried to sound authoritative. "You've seen enough action for one evening."

"I'll decide that."

"Yes, ma'am. I have no doubts about that, but I'll decide who goes with the team."

She crossed her arms. "I may be a Foreign Affairs Officer now, but I still hold the rank of Captain. Last I looked, my bars outweigh your stripes."

"That they do, ma'am, but I have a bird colonel back home who would gut me like a fish, tan my hide, and hang it in the sun as an example to all the other spec ops leaders." He drew a deep breath. "I can't tell you how much you've impressed me and my team. Truth is, most of them are afraid of you. That being said, you're not going."

"You need a translator. Do you speak Kyrgyz or Russian?"

"No, ma'am, and that is a very persuasive argument."

"I'm glad you agree."

"You're not going."

J. J. pushed the memory to the back of his brain. She might make trouble for him but he doubted she would. "Weps, when we're one block out, pull to the side."

"Roger that."

"Hawkeye, you about ready?"

"Sure am, Boss. I'm going to use the Binkster. She has more flexibility and is easier to control. The camera can also aim horizontally not just down."

"You're the expert."

"Yes, yes I am."

A voice came over J. J.'s earpiece. "Boss, Joker. We're in position."

"Standby."

Nagano pulled the Range Rover over, killed the headlights, but left the engine on.

"Foot off the brake, Weps. Those taillights can be seen from a long way off."

"Yes, Boss." He put the car in park and released the brake pedal.

"Work your magic, Hawkeye. Make your momma proud."

"Momma is already proud of me. Who wouldn't be?" Hawkeye lowered the rear side window, then handed the sphere of black plastic ribs to J. J. "Hold this out the window, Boss. It's light. Just set it on your palm."

"And if I drop it?"

"I'll fire you."

"Excuse me?"

"I said, I'll still admire you."

"Yeah, that's what I thought I heard." J. J. lowered his window then extended his arm. The flying ball felt too light to be real.

A second later the propeller began to spin, sending a column of air rushing through the rib structure and over J. J.'s hand.

"Did I ever tell you the first model of this was invented by a Japanese engineer who wanted it to search for injured people who might be trapped in a building?"

"Just five or six times. Less talk, more flying."

"Understood, Boss."

From the corner of his eye, J. J. caught Crispin extend the antenna of the control out his window. "Up, up, and away. Go get 'em, Binkster."

The device rose almost noiselessly.

"Coming around," J. J. said. He opened the door. The dome light didn't come on. They thought to turn that off before pulling from the embassy compound. J. J. slipped into the backseat. Crispin held the controller so J. J. could see the tiny video screen.

"We're straight up. You can see our car." Crispin's tone was changed. He was often glib and a tad too talkative except when working, then he had the focus of a rattlesnake staring down his next meal. "Advancing."

J. J. watched the camera switch to a forty-five-degree angle, allowing Crispin to see down and forward. The target building was a three-story, Soviet-era structure heavy on naked concrete and draped windows. To J. J.'s eye, there was very little design, it was a tall box with windows on four sides. It looked like an old office building waiting to be replaced by something newer.

Crispin kept the remote-control vehicle high and did a quick circle around the building. His comments were radioed to the others. "Three stories, bars over the first-floor windows. All windows obscured, probably by drapes. I don't have enough light to be positive." He kept his eyes fixed on the display. "I see dim light in the building, so I assume they have an emergency generator."

Crispin continued. "Windows are fixed, no sliders that I can see." The device rose and hovered over the roof. "Flat roof, gravel and tar covering. Looks fairly new. Elevator overrun. Just one elevator. Antennas. Junior might be able to identify them. Best guess is standard radio and shortwave. Maybe something more. I count six skylights. Translucent covering and I see light, so someone is on the top floor."

He sent the RPV higher and directed it over the street, then slowly descended. "Time for the money shots. Front door is solid and looks to be metal." He zoomed the camera. "Looks like heavy-duty hardware, and . . . wait. I've got a guard now. Single male packing a machine pistol."

J. J. leaned closer. "West German HK MP5 variant."

Crispin repeated the designation. "Man looks to be six foot one, maybe six foot two, late twenties."

The RPV made another circuit until it hovered over the street at the rear of the building. Unlike the part of the city they were in earlier, this section had no alleys. J. J. couldn't decide if that was good or bad. Either way, it was what the situation dealt him.

"Rear door is similar to the front. One guard, maybe midthirties, five ten or so. Packin' a . . ." He looked to J. J.

"T91, Chinese. Similar to M-16."

"Hardware is the same as the front door. Wait . . . keypad entrance. Front door probably has the same . . . hold . . . just caught a glimpse of two men patrolling the perimeter. They're moving counterclockwise. Just disappeared around the northeast corner. They're walking shoulder to shoulder."

"Bring it home, Hawkeye." J. J. leaned against the door and pondered the information, running scenarios through his head.

Option one: a straightforward street approach. That would require taking out the guards without drawing attention.

Option two: go in through the skylights. Problem: how to get on the roof without being seen. A one-story structure might be possible but still risky; three stories was impossible with guards walking around.

Option one and two together: neutralize the guards, make entrance. He paused in his thoughts. There were bound to be more guys inside. J. J. gently tapped his teeth together as he thought. An urban operation like this one was best carried out after weeks of planning, intel, and dry-run scenarios. In a perfect world that was how UOs worked. This wasn't a perfect world. They had almost no time. J. J. was making this up on the fly. Lousy way to run a mission.

"Listen up, team. All visible combatants have radios. You know what that means. We have to assume there are more hostiles inside. Be prepared for CQC." His men were trained for Close Quarters

Combat, and that went for Aliki and Nagano. J. J. wouldn't have accepted them had they no experience in dynamic entry and continuous flow. "Here's how this is going to go down . . ."

MIKE NAGANO, WITH THE help of Aliki, found his way to the roof of a one-story building across the street from the front entrance of the target building. He pushed the legs of the Harris bipod forward and rested the long-barreled M110 sniper rifle on the lip that ran the edges of the building. The suppressor was in place. Next he flicked up the covers of the AN/PVS night sight, then settled the crosshairs on the smoking man at the front door.

He lay prone, still, willing his heart to slow, his breathing to calm, and his mind to expel every thought but one.

"Weps ready."

ALIKI ROUNDED THE CORNER, jogging at a fast pace, but not so fast as to leave him too winded to do what came next.

His ears rang louder than ever before, made worse by the report of weapons fired in the close confines of the truck trailer. If communications was coming over an earbud crammed deep into his ear canal, he doubted he would hear much of anything.

You should have fessed up. Should have told, J. J. But no, you didn't. If someone dies because . . .

He flushed the thought and focused on the next thing he had to do. He moved to the Range Rover where the rest of the team waited. He never had much use for God, but now that he might be a liability to this new team, he was considering starting a prayer life.

J. J. LOVED THE Army. He loved the action. Loved the adventure. It was good to him; made him a man. It also fed his need for guns and other weapons. It was an odd thing, he knew: devoted Christian; former sniper; present team leader about to invade a building. He held the belief that what he did saved lives even if it required the taking of a life. J. J. knew men who could kill without remorse. He wasn't one of them. War was war and there were plenty of examples in the Bible. He reminded himself the New Testament taught that Jesus would come back again, not to die this time, but to put an end to evil. Good rationalizations. Biblically based. Still, he never felt comfortable with killing.

He did it when necessary.

And it was necessary. That didn't mean he had to like it.

They watched and took note of the time it took for the two roving guards to complete a circuit around the building. Unless they had changed their pace or direction, they should be rounding the corner at the front of the building.

"Boss, Weps. Go."

Nagano was in a position to see when the "walkers" were in the front of the building so J. J. gave the command decision to the team sniper.

J. J. walked up the back street toward the rear guard. The man snapped his head around, no doubt stunned by the sudden appearance of a man in a black uniform, a black balaclava, and a helmet. The man raised his T91 and managed to get the muzzle up several inches before J. J. put a round in the man's chest and one in his head. The suppressor kept the gunfire to a whisper.

Turning, J. J. started for the front of the building. He stopped at the front corner and peeked around. Three bodies lay on the sidewalk. "Perimeter secure. Time to rock." J. J. moved forward in a crouch, doing his best to keep his head and back below the first-floor windowsill. He reached the front door and a second later so did the rest of the team. All except Nagano, who was still on the roof. By that time Aliki had placed a small piece of ECT—explosive cutting tape—in the center of the large door. Aliki then duct-taped a large I.V. bladder he "borrowed" from Doc to the outside of the ECT. Nagano slowed, moving with a slight limp. He flashed a thumbs-up. J. J. answered with a nod.

Crispin was right, the door was metal. There was no way to cut through or kick through it. More force was needed. The fluid in the I.V. bag would direct the force of the explosive tape into the door. Aliki worked from experience. Explosives were J. J.'s responsibility before becoming team leader and he had to fight the urge to do the work himself. Aliki proved to be adept. He motioned for the team to move back and stand clear, then slipped around to the tight line they formed along the wall.

J. J. held out his hand so Aliki and the others could see it. He showed three fingers, then two, lowered his head, then—

Aliki pushed the button on the remote detonator.

The windows shook. Dust flew to the street.

J. J. started for the door, which folded in on itself like a taco shell from the charge. He kicked it the rest of the way open and sprinted through, the tac-light mounted below the barrel of his M4 scanning the lobby on the other side. A man appeared holding a handgun. He hit the floor before his gun.

The line of men parted as they crossed the threshold, spreading out so each could train his weapon on the field before them.

The lobby contained no chairs, just an empty area with a tile floor that emptied into a space where J. J. saw elevator doors. He had no interest in the elevator unless the doors suddenly opened. He doubted they would. He didn't think the generator could provide enough electricity to run the hefty motors necessary to lift the thing. Based on the weapons he saw, they were dealing with trained gunmen, no one with experience would enter a metal box with no place to take cover.

A wide hall at the end of the lobby ran north and south, bisecting the building. J. J. sent Aliki and half the team to the south while he led Jose and Hawkeye north. On either side of the hallway were a series of small offices, all looked empty and abandoned long ago. Dust covered the floor and he saw no footprints.

"Next floor," J. J. said into the radio.

This part of the plan had been worked out before. Crispin's RPV revealed a vertical space on each end of the building that reached from ground to roof. There was a door with no handle at the base. J. J. took this to mean each extreme of the building had a stairway.

J. J. pushed the door open and held it in place as Crispin plunged into the stairwell, his weapon pointed up the steps. Jose followed on his heels. The men left room for J. J. to enter.

This time Crispin led the way, the muzzle of his weapon pointing ahead of him. J. J. and Jose followed behind, their weapons ready. At the door to the second floor, Crispin paused, made eye contact with J. J., who nodded. He snapped the door open and now Jose was in front, J. J. one step removed from being in the medic's back pocket.

The floor was dark. No overhead lights. No lights from the offices.

Another empty floor?

"Up." J. J. transmitted.

NASIRDIN TANAYEV AND RASUL Djaparov readied themselves for what Nasirdin knew was inevitable.

"What are you doing?" Rasul asked.

"Buying a few moments for us." He finished tying twine around one of the canisters of bioagent, creating a loop. He hung it around Rasul's neck.

"Wait. I am no suicide bomber. I did not agree to this. We were just supposed to take canisters to the crowds and throw them—"

"Shut up. This is for your protection. If the attackers see this hanging on you they will hesitate to fire, giving us time to make our shot. Besides, the canister is empty. They won't know that."

"You have been good to me, Nasirdin. I am grateful, so I hope you won't be offended when I tell you I don't believe you."

"Suspicion has kept us alive longer than most, Rasul. It is part of our makeup."

"What if they don't hesitate?"

"We will be dead anyway." Nasirdin tied a strand of twine around another canister and hung it over his own neck. "Remember. Head shots. They will be wearing body armor. Aim for their heads, necks, legs if necessary."

"The other men?"

"In place. The Americans will have to get through eight of our best men." Nasirdin didn't say it, but he had a sick feeling that might happen.

Nasirdin didn't wonder when his plans went wrong. It was that woman. If he ever had opportunity he would end her life with his hands around her throat. At the moment, he had two worries. Surviving the attack, then surviving Dootkasy's wrath should he fail.

COLONEL MAC SAT IN the spec ops sit room in the Concrete Palace. The monitors on the wall showed only the black and gold spearhead emblem of Special Operations Command, nothing more. He sat in the isolation waiting. He watched real-time missions in this room; held conferences with generals and admirals, even the president. At the moment he had nothing but a dark room, glowing monitors, and his aide Alan Kinkaid sitting at the control bench.

Minutes flowed at glacial speeds churning the concerns living in Mac. He gave no outward sign of worry. He just waited.

And waited.

And thought of his men brought back to life and now risking them once again on the behalf of citizens of another country who would never know the truth of the matter.

"You prayin' over there, Master Sergeant?"

"Yes, sir, I am."

"Good. Keep it up."

"Yes, sir."

Colonel Mac, decorated combat veteran, leader of men, consultant to presidents, picked at his fingernails and wondered if he was getting too old for all this.

J. J. LED HIS team up the last flight of stairs, slowing as he approached. He lessened his pace to give himself time to force the distracting thoughts from his mind. He already struggled with being a soldier with an expectant wife, but now he kept imagining her face when she learned of his "death." The news media did them no favors and a part of him wished Colonel Weidman had kept that part of the story to himself.

The thoughts passed in milliseconds and J. J. refocused on the mission. There was no time to think of anything but what lay beyond the stairway door. How many men? How well armed? Were they lying in wait, weapons trained on the door? He had to assume that was the case.

What J. J. wished he could do was use one of Crispin's smaller toys to survey what awaited them, but just opening the door would give away their presence. This was the last floor and, therefore, had to be the one holding the biotoxin.

Biotoxins. Why did it have to be biotoxins? It limited their options. No air strike, no mortar, limited use of explosives. "We have to know where every bullet goes," J. J. told the team shortly before they left. The fear was releasing the biotoxin into the building and into the environment. The mission was easy to state: secure the building and the biotoxin. Except they knew very little about the building, who was in it, or where and how the airborne poison was kept. In many ways, this was a true suicide mission.

And he pictured Tess again, this time putting the twins to bed without him.

"Joker, Boss."

"Go, Boss." The voice was weak and awash in static. No surprise. He was in a stairwell made of concrete block as was the other half of the team. That Aliki heard him at all was a miracle.

"We go in five. Start on my mark."

"Roger . . . oss . . . ive . . . your . . . ark."

That sounded close enough. "Three, two, one, mark." J. J. took a deep breath and started counting to five. Crispin crowded his shoulder.

At five, he pulled the stairwell door open and tossed in an M84 flash-bang grenade. Crispin rolled a smoke grenade at the same time. J. J. pushed the door shut.

He heard the M84 go off and felt glad he was on this side of the door. He heard a similar but more distant sound. Aliki's M84 went off. J. J. gave the smoke device a few moments to fill the hall, then said, "Go."

He yanked the door open and plunged into the smoke-filled corridor, Crispin and Jose behind him. Every man on the team wore tactical goggles to keep the smoke from their eyes, hopefully an advantage.

They called it dynamic entry, ever-forward flow until the mission is accomplished. J. J. led the flow from the north side of the corridor, Aliki from the south. This meant they were charging toward each other in a smoke-filled hall. An inaccurate shot meant one team member could down another.

Overhead lights battled the smoke, giving the space a house-of-horrors feel. An apt feeling.

J. J. pressed forward, hunched, knees bent, M4 leveled so the barrel was chest high for any man standing in his way. One appeared like a ship coming out of a fog. He held a machine pistol. J. J. spit one round through the suppressor into the man's forehead and continued forward.

A broad swath of light waited in the middle of the corridor. The light came from J. J.'s right.

He moved forward slowly, but always forward.

He neared the light. While he couldn't make out details, he got the impression a wide, open space had replaced a series of offices. *Target area.*

Step. Step. Another step closer. The only sound was the fizzle of the smoke canister behind them.

J. J.'s gun moved down and to the side. Something hard rammed his forehead, just below the front rim of his helmet, pushing his head back. Pain raced from his head and down his spine. Tilting his eyes up he saw a skinny, Asian man, his eyes wide, his jaw clenched. The man held a sidearm to J. J.'s head. J. J. saw the man's trigger finger tighten before the man fell away, a round each from Crispin and Doc in his head. Something damp and sticky splattered J. J.'s goggles.

"You okay, Boss?" Crispin asked.

"Don't know. Too startled to tell." J. J. pushed forward. He heard other sounds now. The spitting sound of suppressed gunfire. He heard a man screaming but didn't recognize the voice. That was good.

A brief burst of gunfire erupted behind J. J. He snapped his head around in time to see two men clutching at their chests and backpedaling. Behind them, an office door hung open. They had been laying in wait in a dark, locked office off the hall. He had no idea how Jose knew they were coming, but Doc had just saved their lives—for the moment.

"Watch your back," J. J. said into the radio.

"Roger that," Aliki said. "We count three down our side."

"Four here."

The smoke thinned and J. J. could see the light from the center right side of the building. What he could not do was see around the corner.

The lights went out, leaving only the tactical lights on their weapons to show the way. J. J. pulled another M84 from his vest. He radioed his intention then pulled the metal pin, when a hand seized his wrist, twisted, and pulled. More pain, this time radiating up his arm. Another pain scorched his thigh.

The M84 went off, sending 180 decibels of explosive sound and nearly eight million candela—the equivalent of eight million candles shining in a single burst—around J. J. and the others. The M84 flash-bang grenade did what it was created to do, stun and blind anyone in the vicinity. His ears hurt and rang as if his head was a bell; his eyes teared, blurring what little vision he had left; the force of the nonlethal grenade shook his marrow, making it difficult to keep control of bladder and bowel.

The hand on his wrist disappeared and J. J. reached forward with his left hand, searching, grabbing, finally seizing a shirt—not a military-issue combat vest—a shirt. He pulled hard and then snapped his head forward, praying for a bit of Providence. His helmet hit something hard and there was a crunching sound. A muted bellow followed.

Bringing his M4 back around, J. J. placed the barrel to the blurry man in front of him. J. J. blinked, then blinked again.

A hand shot out and caught J. J. in the throat.

J. J. pulled the trigger. The ill-formed shape fell to the floor.

"Boss!" Jose's voice.

"Can't see."

"I got point."

J. J. assumed Jose and Crispin had been able to prepare for the flash-bang. "Go."

Two forms brushed by him. "Joker, Doc. I have lead here."

"Boss?"

"M84 got him."

TESS MADE TEA. BOTH cups cooled on the dining room table. Tess took Lucy's hand. "I need to pray."

Lucy nodded, crossed herself with her free hand.

Both women bowed their heads.

ALIKI EASED FORWARD. WITH all the lights off, the M84 would have been especially bright. He had no idea why J. J. hadn't prepared himself for the bang and flash, but it had to be a good reason. He would ask later. If there was a later.

He, Nagano, and Pete moved closer to the area that moments ago was bathed in light. It was like approaching a cave known to be filled with angry bears. Aliki turned off his tac-light. If the baddies liked it dark, then so be it. He could work in the black as well as anyone.

When his light went, those of Pete and Nagano went out, as did those on the other end of the hall. Once, as a kid, his parents took the family to Carlsbad Caverns and paid for one of the tours. They reached a side cavern and the guide told everyone to be still; to be silent.

The lights went off. Dark was dark, black was black, but this was different. Separated from sunlight by over 700 feet of stone overhead, this black was palpable. Even breathing seemed more difficult. His heart skipped beats. Everything seemed amplified. He could hear the breathing of the other tourists. A moment later the guide turned the lights back on and Aliki saw relief on the faces of his family. Everyone beamed a smile.

He doubted he would see smiles if the lights came on again. He had no idea what he would see but it made him nervous. As in the caverns, his heart skipped beats. He strained his ears to hear the sounds of movement or breathing or the slide of a weapon being moved. All he could hear was the ringing in his ears that had been dogging him for the last month.

He stripped off his protective goggles and snapped his NGV to the front of his helmet. Black turned green as the light amplification electronics tried to arrange what little light there was into something useful.

He inched forward.

J. J. SHOOK HIS head, trying to clear it of the buzzing. His vision was coming back faster than he expected, most likely because he slammed his eyelids shut once the M84 slipped from his hand. It didn't help his ears, but it reduced the shock of the brilliant magnesium/ammonia sulfate light burst.

His head hurt, his legs felt rubbery, and his internal organs felt like they were on the verge of liquefying. It took a moment for him to realize the darkness around him was on the outside of his eyeballs. The lights were out. He reached for his night vision goggles.

He wobbled forward, still shaky from the flash-bang. It did to him what he wanted it to do to the hostiles. Maybe someday he would feel sorry for them, but not now. He had a team to lead.

He felt someone—Hawkeye?—switch off his tactical light. Fine with him. He had enough of bright lights for awhile.

Through the NVGs he saw Jose and Crispin ahead of him, moving along the hall as he had been doing. They stepped over the body of the man who tried to spread J. J.'s brains on the wall. He caught up to them in several short, but quick steps. His addled mind wandered for a moment.

Focus.

Tess. The twins—

He bit his tongue. The pain brought him back to the moment.

J. J. could see where the hall gave way to an open work area on the east side of the building. He hated this. Offices had too many doors, every one could conceal a heavily armed man. That was the thing about spec ops, they seldom got to choose the field of play; it was chosen for them.

Straightening, J. J. could see the other side of the hall. Aliki, Pete, and Nagano were moving into the area, guns pointed in the direction most likely to harbor killers.

WHAT WAS IT J. J. called this? A true suicide mission? Aliki thought he was being overly dramatic. Maybe not.

He could see J. J.'s unit on the other side of the hall. He did a finger countdown. When he retracted the last finger, he stepped into the open area and knew the others were with him. Two men stood at the far wall, next to a set of windows.

Aliki raised his weapon—

Everything went from green to yellow as the lights in the area came on suddenly. The NVG which amplified low light did the same with bright light. Aliki couldn't see.

Gunfire, loud, shots made by the two men.

Gunfire, muted, shots made by the team.

Aliki pulled the trigger and felt the M4 in his hand vibrate.

J. J. WAS THE last into the room, one second after the lights came on, giving him that one second to snap up the NVG. He saw Aliki drop to his fanny, his weapon blazing. Nagano spun and let out a howl. All continued to return fire. J. J. entered the fray with hesitation. He flicked the trigger, aiming at the men who had the advantage of knowing the room—and better sight.

The room was filled with laboratory-style work tables that reminded J. J. of his days in high school chemistry. To the right was a wall of glass, or most likely, a wall of plastic. He didn't have time to take in the details, just the impression of a storage area with a single door—a door standing open.

Rounds fired by his men shattered windows and punched holes in the ceiling. One of the shooters popped up from behind a lab table. He looked comfortable with a weapon, he looked angry, he looked like a man ready to die of a cause. He also saw something hanging from the man's neck.

It took a second to process: the man was wearing a cylinder. A bomb? No—a canister, like the one described to him by Colonel Weidman.

"They're wired," J. J. shouted into the radio. "Fall back—"

Something small, but felt like a sledgehammer, hit his protective vest at the shoulder, spinning him. The round skipped past his ear. He snapped his gaze back to the gunmen. One rose again and found a bullet waiting for him. It caught him in the hollow of the throat. He stumbled back into the wall behind him. Several rounds hit the second man and he tumbled over.

"Cease fire. Cease fire." J. J. scooted forward, his weapon aimed at one man's head. Jose moved to the other. J. J. thought he was hearing something; something too indistinct to cut through the buzzing in his head.

Then he heard Jose swear. A glance showed Jose draw his Nimravus knife and cut the canister from the corpse of the attacker. "Out! Out! Move!"

J. J. stepped back as Jose sprinted past him and through the door to what J. J. earlier assumed was a storage area. Jose moved through the open door and slammed it shut.

CHAPTER 32

J. J. REACHED FOR the door, and the motion sent ripples through his shoulder where the bullet had glanced off the body armor. There was no penetration but the impact made his arm feel as if it were hanging by a thread.

"No!" Jose still held the canister, his hand over the nick caused by one of the scores of bullets flying through the lab area. "Get the men out of here, Boss. I don't know how much of this junk leaked out."

"I'm not leaving you." J. J. pressed his hand to the plastic wall separating the storage area from the room in which the battle took place. Behind Jose, J. J. could see tables, two large, aquarium-like boxes with manipulator arms no doubt used to handle the really dangerous material—like the material seeping into Jose's body.

"Yes, you are. You need to evac now."

"We don't leave men behind, Doc. You know that."

Aliki stepped close. "All combatants confirmed dead, Boss."

"Joker, get Boss and the others out of here. Do it now." The medic's voice was muted by the transparent security wall. Aliki cocked his head to the side. "What?"

"Boss, we got company." Pete stood by the window looking at the street three stories below. "Got a mob moving in."

"Armed?"

"Roger that."

J. J. took two seconds to think. "Secure the stairwells. No one gets through the door. Clear?"

"Yes, Boss." Pete and Crispin headed down one end of the hall; Nagano, after giving Aliki a slap on the shoulder, started down the other.

This mission started with all the elements necessary for complete failure. The conditions were still in place.

Jose pressed himself to the door. For a moment J. J. thought he was moving closer to be better heard, then he realized the obvious: Jose was blocking the door. "Boss, I appreciate what you're doing, but if this stuff is as bad as I think it is, then I'm dead already. I died the moment I grabbed the canister. I-I . . ." He coughed. "I don't know how much got out. I got to it right away, but . . . I just don't know." He grimaced as he removed his helmet and black balaclava.

"Doc, what is it?"

"Please. Leave. You gotta get the team out. Please, Boss. Don't make me beg."

For the first time since meeting Jose in Basic Training, he saw tears in the man's eyes—eyes redder than tears could make them.

His eyes were hemorrhaging. J. J. radioed Pete. "Junior, I need the SAT phone. Now."

Pete emerged from the hall in dead run. "Here, Boss."

"Get Colonel Weidman on the horn."

A few moments later, Pete handed the phone to J. J. "Colonel, I need an evac team asap. I need a rescue team with chem suits. I have a man who's been exposed."

"Give me a sit rep."

J. J. did, fighting back tears and anger.

"Expect a Chinook in ten, get your men to the roof. You'll be making a SPIES evac." The Special Purpose Infiltration and Exfiltration System sounded flashy but mostly it meant J. J. and team would soon be dangling beneath a massive helicopter. A definite thrill ride.

"Understood, sir." He switched off the phone and handed it back to Pete.

"What did he say, Boss?"

"He was very specific. He said you and the others are to go to the roof. A helo is inbound."

"Did the locals lift the no-overfly ban?"

"I don't know. I didn't ask. Tell Joker to prepare the team for a SPIES lift."

"Yes, Boss. Let's go."

"I'm staying here."

Pete petrified in place. "Excuse me, Boss?"

"You heard me. Get out of here."

"Not without you, Boss." Pete set his jaw as if his words were the final comment on the matter.

"Junior . . . Pete, I've never known you to disobey an order. This is an order. Get your butt in gear."

Pete hesitated. Started to turn. Stopped. Turned back to J. J. and opened his mouth, then shut it again. He keyed his radio. "Joker, Junior. Boss has ordered us to the roof for exfil."

"Roger that."

Pete walked away from J. J. looking as if his boots had turned to concrete.

"Please, Boss, please go. The longer you stay in this room the greater the danger to you."

"Yeah, I figured that." J. J. looked into his friend's face and saw the faces of Jose's wife, Lucy, and the faces of each of his four children.

He touched the wall then leaned his head against it. "I'm so sorry, Jose. I'm so, so, sorry. This isn't right. You sacrificed yourself for the team, for me."

Jose chuckled weakly. "I always wanted to go out by falling on a hand grenade. I guess this is close enough."

When J. J. looked up, he saw blood running from Jose's eyes and nose. He also saw blisters the size of dimes forming on his face and growing as J. J. watched. "There's got to be something in your med kit."

Jose shook his head. Coughed. Leaned against the door, this time for support. "Not . . . for this. I didn't . . . pack for chem warfare, just for your usual . . . gun battle and bombs." He slid down the wall until he was seated.

"Stay with me, Jose. Do you hear me? I'm giving you a direct order. You will stay alive."

"Yes, Boss. Whatever you . . . say."

The canister slipped from Jose's hand and rolled on the smooth floor. J. J. could see a stream of white liquid pour from the nick in the metal container. "Please God, please, please, please . . ."

Jose stopped responding. Blood mixed with a clear fluid oozed from his ears and mouth, drying slowly on the skin.

J. J. removed his helmet and balaclava. "I let you down, Buddy. I blew it. You were my responsibility. I should have planned better; should have anticipated better; shoulda . . ."

The words and thoughts were ridiculous. Soldiers lost buddies. It had always been that way. It would never change. Neither would the temptation for team leaders to second-guess themselves. They came to rescue an American woman, a female soldier, a diplomat, and it cost them another life—the life of a friend.

An unwanted image floated to the churning surface of his mind: the photos they left behind at Manas. "For them and for those like them, we do this."

The windows of the building began to shake, then the sound of two powerful rotors pressed through concrete and glass. The helo was here.

"Boss, Joker. Our ride is here."

J. J. didn't move.

"Boss, Joker. Do you read?"

"Yeah, I got ya."

"The pilots brought a few Rangers with them. They just fast-roped on the roof and set up a perimeter. The crowd got sight of the helo and the fresh troops and are dispersing."

"Understood, Joker. Is there a bio-chem team?"

"Yeah, Boss, some men in funny suits are headed your way."

"Understood."

After a long pause. "You coming up? There's another helo inbound."

"I'll take the next ride."

"Boss, you need to be up here."

"I'm staying with Doc." He spoke the words with finality.

The radio stayed quiet and J. J. used the time to clear his eyes of tears. A few moments later four men in full body suits and face masks appeared like aliens out of a sci-fi movie. Four other men followed: Pete, Crispin, Nagano, and Aliki.

"I ordered you men to the roof," J. J. snapped.

"Yes, yes you did," Pete said, "and you did it with flair."

"Then get back up on the roof."

"Yes, Boss. Will do." They continued into the room. "Just as soon as the team is assembled. The *whole* team, I mean."

"You are defying a direct order." J. J. tried to sound furious but the fire in his belly had turned to ashes.

Crispin looked at Pete then the others. "Yeah, that's pretty much what we're doing. At least, I think that's what we're doing."

"Yep," Joker said. "I've defied orders before and it felt just like this."

J. J. wanted to be angry, to fly off the handle, to apply his boot to four butts, but he couldn't raise the rage. Instead, he felt admiration.

"Back away," one of the men in suits said, then entered the secure room. They had to lean into the door hard enough to move Jose's body. It seemed the final indignity.

The men carried a stretcher which they left outside. They moved with purpose and with obvious practice. Then they began to rush. It took several minutes to lift Jose's body into a protective suit and another minute to carry him to the stretcher. J. J. was surprised to see their haste. Surprised until he heard, "He's still alive."

When they reached the roof, a metal rescue litter was on its way down from the helo. Jose was transferred to it and slowly raised to the helicopter, where another man dressed in a safety suit guided the device into the open, side door of the Chinook. A moment later a harness on a line descended to the rooftop. J. J. donned his helmet and started for it, but one of the men who took Jose's body held up a hand.

"Sorry, but you'll have to take the next one. This bird was considered contaminated the moment your man was loaded onboard."

One of the other men slipped into the harness and was lifted skyward. In turn, each suited man ascended to the helo which peeled away.

The next Chinook hovered over the building, its two rotors pounding the roof and the men on it. A rope with a series of harnesses tumbled out the side, and J. J. did something he hadn't done since Ranger training: Hooked himself to the rope, as did each of the men in his unit. The half dozen Rangers on the roof did the same with a second rope.

Once certain his men were properly secured, he nodded to one of the Rangers who radioed the helo.

J. J. and the others were lifted from the roof and left dangling in the prop wash as the helo rose and started for Manas Air Base. Below, he saw a caravan of military vehicles he assumed belonged to the Kyrgyzstan military. What was in the building—bodies and biochem—was now their problem. As the helicopter moved north, J. J. saw rioters, protesters, and looters. Buildings and cars burned. The further north they went, the more carnage he saw. The city had lost its mind.

Not one of the people below could know how close they came to being exposed to a substance that would leave them dead in the streets. J. J. prayed there were no other canisters out there.

TO J. J., LUCY looked as if she hadn't slept in weeks. Her normal makeup and perfectly styled hair was absent. The fact he was seeing her over a video conference system bridging half the world didn't help.

"He's better, Lucy. The doctors think he'll pull through just fine, although they don't know if there will be long-lasting effects." He hated being that honest. What he wanted to say was Jose was outside playing basketball, but that would be a lie.

"Is he conscious?"

He rubbed the skin of his hands which felt slightly oily from the decontamination cleaning he endured. "Yes. He does nothing but criticize me and talk about you and the kids."

"Pain. Is he in much pain?"

For a brief second, J. J. thought about lying, but he had moral objections to doing so—that, and he was a lousy liar. He was never able to tell a fib and be believed. "Some, but not as much as I would expect. The doctors have him on morphine and other things I don't understand. He sleeps a lot."

Lucy wiped at her eyes. "Where is he now?"

"He's being airlifted to Germany for more advanced treatment. My brother will be calling you soon. He's arranging for a flight so you can visit him. Can you get someone to watch the kids?"

"Can I bring the children?"

"No, I'm sorry . . . It would be best they not see him. His skin is still recovering from the blisters. I'm told those are minor things."

"I see. Yes, my mother will take care of the children. Do you think he'll come home with me?"

J. J. shrugged. "I really don't know, Lucy. That's up to the doctors. My guess is, he'll be in the hospital for several weeks, but then I'm just a soldier, my medical knowledge ends with Band-Aids." He leaned closer to the camera as if he could whisper in Lucy's ear. "I want you to know he saved not only the lives of the team members but probably thousands of lives of others. He is a true example of what Jesus said, 'Greater love has no man than to lay down his life for his friends.' He was willing to do that without hesitation."

"He has always been my hero." More tears in Lucy's eyes.

"Mine too, Lucy. Mine too."

J. J. TURNED THE video conference center over to the rest of team to call family and assure them that, like Mark Twain, their deaths had been exaggerated. He was certain no one would tell how close they came to fulfilling the news media prophecy. He was the last to make a call.

Tess looked more beautiful than he had ever seen her. "You're looking good, kid."

"You too. Especially now that I know you're alive."

"I heard about the misinformation. I'm sorry."

"Why? Planning your funeral was fun. I got a pink coffin for you."

"I always did look good in pink."

"Of course, now I have to cancel all those dates I made with other men."

J. J. chuckled. So did Tess.

Then she dissolved into tears.

J. J. AND THE team moved to the official telecommunications site on the base and stared at a very weary-looking Colonel Mac.

"Glad to see you guys are alive. You gave me quite the scare."

"Joker is a drama queen," J. J. said.

"I've heard that."

Aliki didn't respond. J. J.'s next conversation with the big man would involve questions about his now-obvious hearing problem and a lecture about endangering the team, a lecture sure to scorch the skin from his face. At the moment, he didn't see any need to mention the problem to Colonel Mac. Not yet anyway.

"Jose on his way to Germany?" the colonel asked.

"Yes, sir. Left twenty minutes ago. He said to give you his regards. Sir, I plan on putting his name in for a medal, blue one with five stars on it."

"And I plan on approving it." He cleared his throat. "I know I asked a lot of you, but I'm afraid I had no other choice. Time was working against us."

"No problem, sir. This is what we do. No complaints here, just questions."

"Such as?"

"I was given the impression all American flights over Kyrgyzstan were banned. Did you or Colonel Weidman just order the flights anyway?"

"Wanna take that, Colonel?" Mac said.

"Sure." Weidman sat at the back of the small theater-style room. "We had the blessing of President Oskonbaeva. He also ordered the military to the building with the bio-chem lab. It seems saving his daughter put him in a better mood."

"Do we know who was behind the attack?" Pete asked.

"Our president has been in contact with his Kyrgyzstan counterpart. The dust has settled, but he's starting to think his prime minister was behind everything. He was staging a coup without it looking that way. The riots, the protests were orchestrated to focus on key areas. The bio-chem attack would be blamed on the United States, forcing us to close the base. At this point we're guessing, but our intel guys think he was after the three billion the Chinese offered the country if we got the boot, and he was going to get a hefty pile of cash for himself. That's still speculation."

"Where is he now?" A female voice said.

J. J. turned to see Amelia Lennon enter.

"Sorry to be late. Jildiz is quite the talker—when she can breathe. Oh, and she's doing fine. Still confined to bed, but she's getting the care she needs at the Embassy. Her parents are there keeping her company."

"Any word on where the prime minister is now?" J. J. asked.

Colonel Mac said, "He took a helicopter from Ala-Too Square just like the president did, except this time the chopper went all the way out of the country: to China."

"So he's going to get away with it?" Amelia said.

Mac shook his head. "Word has it the Chinese will return the helo. They might return the prime minister with it."

"Does that mean the base is safe?" Crispin asked.

"I doubt it," Amelia said. "This country needs cash and lots of it. Three billion is serious money. Besides, those riots could have only been arranged if the locals really do want us gone. An influx of money from China and Russia and the removal of a sore spot from their land will probably prove too much for the president to resist."

"But we saved his daughter." Nagano seemed put out.

"True," Amelia said, "but you didn't save the daughters of every member of parliament. The president will have to rescue himself."

"We saved his daughter," J. J. said, "but if you hadn't been there in the first place she probably would have been dead long ago."

"Thanks," Amelia said.

"You know," Nagano quipped, "I'm not married."

J. J. turned to see the sniper aiming his eyes at Amelia. "You know you're talking to an officer, don't you?"

"I'm just thinking out loud, Boss. Nothing more."

"One last thing," Colonel Mac said. "Sergeant Kinkaid and I paid a little visit to the president. Don't ask, I'll explain later. Anyway, Kinkaid asked President Huffington if he would be kind enough to have the FBI look at the video that made us all think you were dead. It turns out those burned bodies aren't yours."

J. J. cocked an eyebrow. "That's good to hear. I'd hate to wake up and find out I was dead. How could the FBI tell?"

"Footwear, Sergeant Major. Footwear. The corpses weren't wearing military boots."

"It always comes down to shoes," Amelia said.

AS THE TELECONFERENCE WAS breaking up, J. J. asked Colonel Weidman if he might have the room for a few moments. The colonel consented.

"Aliki, Mike, hang back a sec."

The two exchanged glances, then in near unison: "Sure, Boss."

When the room emptied, Nagano asked if they should sit.

"Nah, this won't take long." J. J. looked up and into Aliki's eyes and spoke louder than he would normally. "I need some advice and I think you're the best guy to ask."

The big man shifted his weight. "Glad to help, Boss. What can I do?"

"I'm not sure how to handle a problem. Let's play 'Just Suppose,' shall we? Just suppose you were leading a team and one of your soldiers had a physical problem. Let's pretend it's something with, oh I don't know, his hearing. You know what happens to guys like us from time to time: too much noise, and explosions, the kind of stuff that can damage an eardrum. Those things happen on mission."

"I've heard of that, Boss." Aliki chewed his lip.

"Now just suppose that soldier didn't tell anyone, or maybe just confided in, say, a friend." He faced Nagano for a moment then returned his attention to Aliki. "Such a thing could be a problem in the field, or am I exaggerating?"

"I agree, such a condition might be a problem in the field. In fact, I believe that more now than ever."

"Do you? Good to hear. So the question is this: How should a guy like me handle such a thing?"

"Well, um . . ." Aliki looked at the floor. "I suppose, if the soldier were a man of honor with a stellar service record, I might drop a hint and let him get checked out by a civilian doc."

J. J. nodded. "That's a good idea. It would keep someone like me from having to make a note of it in the mission report. Do you think the soldier's friend would make sure his buddy got checked out?"

"I think you could bet on it, Boss." Nagano seemed to be standing straighter.

"Well, if I ever come across such a situation I'll follow your suggestions." He moved to the doors. "I wonder if the mess serves barbecue."

EPILOGUE

J. J. WAS THE last off the commercial aircraft that delivered him to Columbia Municipal Airport a short distance from Fort Jackson, South Carolina. The rest of the team arrived two days earlier, but J. J. requested and received permission to stay with Jose at the U.S. Army Hospital, Heidelberg. He spent his days sitting with Jose, who showed remarkable progress. They talked of old times, tried to make sense of European soccer, and read.

He also made certain Jose had plenty of private time with Lucy. Jose couldn't leave his bed, but he could hold his wife's hand for hours.

J. J. allowed himself to believe Jose would live long enough to give him a bad time in the years ahead. The thought gave him great joy.

"Why didn't you leave when I told you to?" Jose asked the first evening.

"Because I'm team leader and, well, you're not. That means I get to order you around. The reverse isn't true. Besides, you saved my life once."

"True, but that was just business."

"Just business, eh? I'll remember that the next time you're dying before my eyes."

Jose gave a crooked smile, it was all he could manage. "Well, I'm going to give you another order, J. J."

"I plan to ignore it."

"I doubt it. Go home. Go give Tess a big hug for me."

"I can hang another day or two."

"No, you can't. Get out of here, or I'll crawl out of this bed and make you leave."

"I don't think you can manage it, but I think you'd try, then I'd have your wife to deal with. Of the two of you, she's the one who scares me." J. J. stood.

"Thanks for everything, J. J."

"You're a hero, Jose. A red, white, and blue hero, and I am a better man for knowing you."

"Whatever. Get out of here. I'm going back to sleep and dreaming of the Mexican Riviera."

That evening, J. J. caught a commercial flight out of Heidelberg Airport. The trip was long, and recent events quickly put him into a sleep coma, something he wished would last for a week. His desire for sleep faded when the Lufthansa A380 touched down in South Carolina. He waited until the plane was nearly empty before disembarking. He walked through the terminal, past security, and into the area of the airport where family waited for arrivals.

Standing in the middle of a crowd was the only person he could see. Tess was beautiful in every way. A few moments later, J. J. took his wife in his arms and embraced her deeply, longingly, thankfully.

Then he pulled away, dropped to one knee and placed his mouth near her belly. "Hey kids, Daddy is home."